STEAMPUNK WRITERS AROUND THE WORLD

VOL I

A Bilingual Anthology

Cover © jay johnstone 2017
illustrations © jay johnstone 2017
Alex Davis (English Editing) & Steph P Bianchini (Spanish editing)
stories © is with each individual author 2017

the story of your heart & La Historia de tu corazón by Josué Ramos
[first published in Galician "A historia do teu corazón", Contos Estraños. Volume 8 (Urco Editora, 2015)]
El Alférez de Hierro by Fábio Fernandes
heirs by Marcus R. Gilman
Pólvora y Vapor by Aníbal J. Rosario Planas
Providence in the Pacific by Ray Dean
Las cadenas infinitas by César Santivañez
The Swarm By Milton Davis
Unmade by Suna Dasi
The Golden Apple By Petra Slováková
La maldición de la espina By Elaine Vilar Madruga
Cuauhtlipoca, el águila humeante By Paulo César Ramírez Villaseñor

First published by Luna Press Publishing 2017

steampunk writers around the world © 2017. All rights reserved. No part of this publication may be reproduced, stored in a retrieval system, or transmitted in any form or by any means, electronic, mechanical, photocopy, recording or otherwise, without prior written permission of the copyright owners. Nor can it be circulated in any form of binding or cover other than that in which it is published and without similar condition including this condition being imposed on a subsequent purchaser.

www.lunapresspublishing.com

ISBN-13: 978-1-911143-20-8

CONTENTS

FOREWORD

There are those times in our lives when we plan a trip and have all the specifics worked out, only to find that there are all kinds of other unexpected destinations along the way. Quite unintentionally, our little trip becomes an ongoing journey.

Steampunk is just like that, too. Our first step may be a story to read, or a song to dance to, or an outfit that makes us look and feel like we are walking down a fashion show runway. But there is always something else out there in the community to encourage us forward. There are so many possibilities to explore that it can become an expectation that there is still something more to see around every corner.

Steampunk is a global aesthetic, interest, and community. In every country, there are people expressing their view and vision of what steampunk is for them, combining culture, history, personal choices, and a healthy dose of asking 'What if'.

Though physical distance may separate people, technology and information can bring us all closer together than ever before. While our individual travels may keep us relatively local, our steampunk spirits can soar around the world thanks to social media and Internet search engines. Invitations, pictures, and updates of events anywhere in the world are just a click away.

It is so easy to get caught up in the amazing creativity and the diversity of expressions. Culture and history can be seen in play as people bring some of their heritage into their visions of steampunk. With every new image, blog post, or forum discussion, our journey becomes a bit more intriguing. Falling into that rabbit-hole of endless steampunk items to explore, myself, it was easy to find new friends along the way, each one following their own leads and interests.

With friends spanning so many countries and still so much to see and learn about, it occurred to me that every steampunk should know about these great things, and be able to make connections and friendships like I did.

That simple desire to share and make new friends, to showcase the endless steampunk journey, led to creating the annual global blogathon, Steampunk Hands Around the World. It was conceived as a way of bringing together content creators from around the globe to highlight and emphasise the best and most interesting examples of what steampunk, and steampunks, can be. Together we showed that steampunks are not alone, and our community is not limited by distance or language.

This anthology, *Steampunk Writers Around the World*, is one of those new, unexpected journeys born from the original short trip, and it exemplifies the core idea of bringing people together from around the world to share their creativity and passions, despite any distance and differences. It is an inclusive, bilingual publication representing different countries, cultures, and perspectives, with each author sharing their unique, alternate nineteenth-century world.

However you live your own steampunk life, as you settle in to read these stories, remember that the whole of the steampunk community and all of the treasures it holds are at your fingertips. Distance and language cannot hold you back, and new friends are waiting to greet you.

Kevin Steil
Airship Ambassador

STEAM PUNK

THE STORY OF YOUR HEART

Spain

THE STORY OF YOUR HEART

By Josué Ramos

He could see him inside the casket, defenceless and dead, and couldn't force himself to stand closer. He wanted to touch him. But he kept his hands in his pocket, ashamed.

"We're going to incinerate him in an hour," the employee mumbled without looking up, his eyes hidden by his hat.

"Can you give me a few minutes alone with him, please?"

"Sure, of course. All the time you need. Are you family?"

"I'm his father."

*

Daniel Beltran felt dizzy to be surrounded by so many people, so much excitement and so much joy. He hadn't known his class would be so big. Slouched in a corner, keeping the still-shut door in sight, he couldn't stop his legs from trembling.

The courtyard was divided into circles of chatting friends – they all seemed to know each other – and only a few, like him, waited alone.

The groups that were the biggest, noisiest and most sure of themselves belonged to the sons of noble families. Daniel recognized at least one royal Borbon among them. Those families dominated Spain's colonies across the galaxy, maintained contact with the Empire and made sure everyone paid their taxes to the metropoli and kept quiet. Less conspicuous were the nouveau riche: young men from families made wealthy by business. Finally, more discreet but much more numerous, other young students: middle class or working class, the ones who yearned to find their way into important circles one way or another.

But Daniel didn't feel like he belonged anywhere. He came alone, he sat alone and he stayed alone. He told himself he must do what his father wanted for his career and attend every class during the seven years that the studies would last until he earned a medical degree, but he felt he would never fit into the system.

And although he hoped no one would notice him during those seven years, peace only lasted seven weeks. The other students spotted him soon enough. He was too evidently different to avoid indiscreet questions. It didn't take long before everyone was watching him. And he didn't have to wait for jokes to be told behind his back.

But it was in one of Dr. Mendoza's classes, Non-invasive Transplant Surgery, when things really got difficult.

Dr. Mendoza was recounting the history of modern transplants one more time while Daniel pretended to be interested and tried to hide the fact that everything he heard made him sick. Mendoza began by talking about the scientific advances and surgical techniques developed in England and France at the end of the nineteenth century. Later, thanks to everything that had been learned about medicine toward the world wars, he said, transplant applications led to cosmetic surgery in peacetime and, by the mid-twentieth century, everyone could get transplants for anything.

Mendoza himself had gotten his teaching post thanks to his eyes, extracted from a black slave with exceptional vision. Now he had eyes that let him observe every detail during class – and during exams – although he had needed to pay a little bit more since that man was said to see better than anyone when he was working in the mines in almost complete darkness. And Mendoza had no regrets. Besides, while he'd had to tighten his belt a bit, he'd taken advantage of the chance to recover twenty percent of the expense by selling his original eyes in an auction house. He never failed to repeat that story again and again.

"Why don't you ask us this on the exam, eagle eyes?" a boy shouted from the back of the hall. "We'd all pass with flying colours since we've heard it so many times."

"Silence please," was all the doctor said, raising his perfect writer's hands.

Daniel wondered if they were original. The professor had never talked about them, only about his eyes.

"If it wasn't for scientific advances, you wouldn't be here. Your father would never have amassed the fortune that lets you study medicine."

"My father never worked in transplants. He had a mining business."

"I'm afraid you're wrong, Mr. Martinez. The human body tends to deteriorate and is always subject to some sort of failure. Always.

We may be nobles or plebeians, rich or poor, Spaniards or slaves, but we all live subject to that. We overcome it thanks to transplants. Your father benefitted from them by selling the most healthy slaves that worked in his mines as if they were gold. And the income from those sales allowed him to increase his profits every year, right? All due to transplant science. To the production and sale of material for transplants."

"You're really lucky, Martinez," a Borbon said, laughing. "If it wasn't for decolouration techniques so the donor skin adapts to the buyer skin, no one would ever buy anything from your old man."

"Now you see how important these scientific advances are in your lives, gentlemen," the professor continued as everyone laughed. "They do more than you think. And, thanks to them, we can correct our defects or change whatever we need to be more happy with ourselves."

"Not always, from what I can see." Another boy laughed, looking at Daniel. "Mr. Chocolate there seems to be completely original."

Daniel shrank in his seat, flushed, his head about to explode.

"What are you talking about, son?" the professor asked, surprised. "What do you mean?"

"I mean that Mr. Beltran has been healthy and happy with himself since the day he was born. At least it looks that way."

"And from what it looks like, he must've been born in the jungle..."

The whole class laughed, egged on by those two perfect boys. They looked a lot alike even though they weren't related: blond, blue eyes, implanted chins because theirs had been too weak, the same nose, eyes, skin, eyebrows, hands... And the most perfect bodies ever seen. Daniel had wondered more than once if anything was still theirs within the artificial shells formed around their tiny brains.

Dr. Mendoza raised both hands again, trying to calm everyone down as he walked toward Daniel's desk.

"Is that true, Beltran? You've never had an operation?"

"Never, Doctor," he murmured, wishing the earth would swallow him up.

"Never? Problems with money, perhaps?"

"No, Doctor," was all he said.

"Mr. Beltran, pay no attention to them. They're just talking foolishly. But I would appreciate it if you came to my office after classes are over, please, if you don't mind."

Daniel nodded and couldn't pay attention for the rest of the day.

He was lost in thought until he heard the siren that marked the end of classes, when he headed toward Dr. Mendoza's office.

*

"So... you've never been operated on."

"No, Doctor. My father has been. But I..."

"And this colour? I really don't want to be impolite, but I think this tan..."

"It's not a tan, Dr. Mendoza. It's my natural colour, inherited from my mother. Should I be ashamed of her?"

"No, of course not. Please forgive me," the professor murmured paternally. "I like you. You're a fine young man and you learn fast. You'll be a good doctor. That's why I'd like to help you." As he spoke, he took a form from a box and began to fill it in.

"If I write you a letter of recommendation, you could enter a special transplant program for model students. I'd have to oversee each one of your requests, but I think the state would allow a minimum of perhaps... Ten operations? We could implant specially trained eyes, surgeon's hands... I don't think there would be any problem getting you all the physical improvements you'd need to exercise the profession. And you wouldn't have to worry about the expenses. We'd only have to adjust the credits that..."

"No, please, Doctor. No."

"Is there perhaps some physical improvement that's more important to you? Some defect you haven't been able to correct? Because we could also..."

"No," Daniel repeated, nervously but firmly. "Please say no more. I don't want to be operated on."

"Mr. Beltran, don't be ashamed. This aid program was created for diligent students like you. If the problem is that you don't have money..."

"That's not it, Doctor. I don't need anything."

"But isn't there something you'd like to improve?"

Daniel kept thinking about his heart problem. His chest was drumming furiously. With every beat, his heart seemed to want to shout its origin... But his mind reacted in time.

"No, Doctor. I'm fine the way I am. I'm comfortable with myself."

"Please think about it carefully, my boy. I'm offering you the hands and eyes of a surgeon. The next time a professional dies in this field, the state will have them removed and set aside for you."

"They wouldn't be my eyes or my hands."

"But they would be a guarantee that you can't refuse. Imagine what it would be like: when you finish your studies, your resume could include that you were trained at the university with them already implanted. You could go on to work in the best hospitals in Hesperides, in any of the colonies, even on Earth. Wherever you wanted to go."

"What would be the difference between that and cheating on exams?"

Dr. Mendoza set the form aside, sighing.

"Mr. Beltran, why did you choose this line of studies? Don't you plan to practice when you graduate?"

"Yes, Doctor," he answered, not very sure of himself. "I want to do that."

"And do you think anyone would trust a doctor who's never been operated on? By God, Beltran, if it doesn't seem fair to receive organs from a surgeon, at least accept some other improvement, anything. If you never get an operation, if you're healthy and happy with your body, you're breaking one of the basic rules of your future profession. It's an offence to medicine, the economy, the entire system. And if you don't have a single operation listed on your curriculum, believe me, no matter how good your grades are, you'll never get a job equal to your skills."

Daniel didn't reply.

"Think about it a couple of days, won't you?"

"May I go now?"

"Yes, you can go," Mendoza said, tearing up the form and throwing it in the garbage. "Go."

Daniel arrived home that night in silence, and he went to bed without eating dinner, saying he had a lot of homework. Instead, he only thought about his future. If he only got a heart operation... After all, it was no indulgence. It was necessary. A transplant would correct his congenital heart defect. But how could he close his eyes to the origin of what doctors themselves called "prime material"? How could he ignore the story his heart told him with every beat?

A little before he was born on Earth, the capital of Spanish Guinea had been renamed Santa Isabel, although it had been founded as Port Clarence by the English. Several years earlier Spain had succeeded in expelling the British, taking definitive control of the colony, and its old businesses flourished. The colony's population increased, and Spanish corporations held greater presence in the area again. His father had been sent there as a foreman by a Madrid diamond mining company. He had a good salary, a good job and respect from all the other colonists until he met the Guinea woman who became Daniel's mother.

Secretly, and against the business's rules, Beltran paid enough bribes to pull enough strings to rescue her from the slave trade and marry her.

But everything got more complicated when Daniel arrived. His mother had been willing to die in order to give birth to him, and she did, although she knew he would be born with a congenital illness and dark skin as an inheritance. Didn't he owe her something in exchange? His life, his freedom, his integrity… Didn't he owe her everything?

The rich and noble set the price for new flesh according to the latest fashion and sold the old flesh as if it were used clothing. Little by little, black slaves had been sent from hard labour to farms to form flocks like sheep to meet the demands of commerce. And the middle class and the working class, following the lead of the grandees of Spain, turned to barter like the most natural thing in the world.

Daniel still recalled the day when his father had exchanged hands with the neighbour who lived in the apartment upstairs; though he had hardly been three years old, he remembered it as if it were yesterday. Back then, he was still afraid to go down the building's steep stairway alone. But when he walked hand in hand with his father, he wasn't afraid at all.

That day, his father let him go for just a second to greet the neighbour coming up the stairs.

"That's Manuel. Do you know him?" he said as he took Daniel's hand again. "He lives here on the fourth floor and he's a jeweller."

The man looked down, smiled and patted him on the head without speaking, but he was so strong and rough that he couldn't help hurting the boy.

"It looks like he has hands for hard work," Daniel murmured, gazing at the neighbour's big hands. "They're not like yours."

"He's right." The jeweller laughed. "It's getting harder and harder to handle tiny jewels with these hands. I'm afraid I'm going to lose my job any day now."

And so, in such an innocent way, his father's hand suddenly let go of Daniel's. He couldn't remember anything more. He only knew that the next time he saw his father, he seemed different. He was smiling. He had needed a working man's hands, big and strong, and thanks to Daniel he had gotten them. But starting then, the hands that had always helped him walk down the stairs fearlessly were in the apartment upstairs or setting jewels in the store around the corner.

What would his mother say if she knew everyone wanted him to throw away the heart she had given her life for, the heart she had created inside herself for him? What sense did it make to tear the heart out of another Guinean and keep it for himself? No. He would do what his mother did. And if he had to die so his hands would not be stained with blood, so be it.

*

After his first year of studying medicine, Beltran thought summer vacation would be a relief: freedom. But with what he had learned in class, when he walked down the street he couldn't help analysing everyone's transplants and implants. Bulging eyes, a snub nose, blonde hair, athletic legs, a pianist's hands... And although it seemed strange, people with mechanical implants wandering through the streets or begging on the sidewalk looked more like real people to him than all the rest.

He always saw a man at the same corner who played works by Dionisio Aguado y Garcia adapted to the violin. In spite of a metal hand, he handled the instrument like a master. His pants were threadbare, and one leg had been removed at the groin so the joint mechanisms of his artificial leg would fit better, but he moved the leg hardly any more than necessary. With each tiny movement, the hydraulic system discharged steam that in midsummer roasted the man until he sweated as if he'd just come out of an oven. In winter, alley cats huddled up to him until he kicked them away, but in summer no one wanted to get near him. And when he had to walk back home, he carried his mechanical arm on his back so the steam wouldn't smother him. In spite of all that, he seemed more human than anyone with a transplant. Not even Daniel's father seemed like his father anymore.

Suddenly, squealing brakes and a sharp steam whistle shook Daniel out of his reverie. From out of nowhere, a delivery truck loaded with fruit and vegetables was coming right at him. The steam boiler and the violin shrieked in terror. A sharp pain in his leg and pressure on his chest blinded him. The world became black. The lights went out.

*

When he recovered consciousness, he was in an enormous hall filled with beds on both sides of a narrow passage. Only a few nurses were caring for patients. The curtains were so thin and worn they no longer served any purpose. The bedclothes were stained by blood and spit, and here and there on the floor were pools of sawdust. The intense pain in his chest kept him from sitting up.

"Oh, you're awake, son." His father smiled. "Relax, try not to move. Should I call the nurse?"

"No..." He coughed. "You don't need to."

"Should I ask for a painkiller?"

"No. I just want to know what happened."

"A truck turned over just as it was passing and crashed into you. You have a contusion in your chest and a broken leg. But don't worry, when you finish filling out this form, everything will be taken care of."

The pen in his father's fingers looked like a giant needle dripping venom.

"What's it for?" Daniel managed to ask in spite of the pain.

"To get you a new leg, of course. What else? They found one almost identical to yours at a farm nearby. They'll amputate it and bring it when you sign. And by the way, they're going to extract a chest so you aren't in pain anymore and we can finally solve that problem with your heart. It's expensive, but we can pay for it. The only problem according to what they've told me is that the donor is much darker than you, black as coal." He laughed. "The decolouration is going to be expensive. But if we save for a few months..."

"No, Papa! I don't want it!" Frightened, he struggled with all his strength to sit up. "My heart isn't the one that's bad. Yours is."

"It's all right, Daniel. We have enough money. We only need to save a little for the decolouration. They've given us a financing plan that..."

"Are you crazy? How can you say this? I don't care about the decolouration!"

"But your leg..."

"It's my leg! And I'm not going to let anyone take it from me!"

The neighbour's rough, strong hands gripped Daniel's shoulders and pushed him down against the bed. The intense pressure in his chest made it hard to breathe.

"Calm down, Daniel! Calm down. I'm going to call the nurse to sedate you, okay?"

"No, please."

"It's for the best. You can't get anywhere with that broken leg."

Terrified, he watched through the holes in the curtain as his father walked away. His heart beat so hard it seemed to be trying to escape its death. And the fear hurt more than the pain. Slowly, he sat up. He swallowed a cough so he wouldn't make noise and, biting his tongue, he stood up. He could see the bone poking out from the ripped pants. He could hardly place the leg on the ground. But he wasn't going to spend another second lying in that bed.

The open window led to a dark alley. Although it was on the ground floor, climbing through the window and jumping out would be torture, but it was his only chance. With all his strength he leaped toward the street. The pain in his chest almost made him lose consciousness. But it was his chest. He breathed deeply and got up as best he could, dragging the leg. But the pain was from his leg. And he would drag it with him for as long as he had to.

He didn't know where to go. He didn't know what to do. He only understood that he could never go back home. He couldn't keep pretending to be part of the system and continue his studies. If he couldn't even go to a clinic without fear, how could he ever stand to work in one? There was nothing left for him.

After walking for half an hour, almost senseless, half-conscious and delirious from the pain tearing through his body, he could not go on any farther and fell amid garbage and boxes, suffering some kind of attack that seemed to tie him to a cot. Dr. Mendoza appeared out of nowhere in a Spanish foreign legion uniform stained by mud, sweat and battle, but with an impeccable diamond necklace hanging around his neck. He smiled maliciously, waving a scalpel as if he were directing an orchestra. Daniel looked at him speechlessly, only able to express his terror through his eyes, begging for his life.

Suddenly awake, he pushed aside the imaginary surgeon's hands that held him here and there, cutting, tearing, pulling off skin...

"Don't worry, young man," a friendly voice murmured, holding his arms. "It's all right. You're safe."

Daniel looked around. He was in a room he didn't recognise. The woman wasn't a nurse, and it wasn't a hospital.

"Where am I?" he said, touching the bandages on his chest. "What have they done to me?"

"Don't worry," she said. "Everything's fine. You're safe."

He shivered and tried to sit up.

"Wait, I'll help you." She adjusted the pillow.

When he was sitting up, Daniel felt pain in his leg. If they had exchanged it, he wouldn't feel anything. It was still there. In fact, it was in a splint. The pain from the fracture was still there. He smiled.

"They haven't given me a transplant."

A child laughed next to him. There were two boys and the woman. One boy was barely five years old, and he got a smack on the head for laughing. The other boy was a little younger than Daniel.

"We don't have money for that here, young man. I'm very sorry," the woman said, adjusting the worn bedsheets. "We can take care of you while you heal the traditional way, but if you want expensive operations, you have to pay for them yourself."

"Thank you," Daniel said with tears in his eyes. "Thank you very much."

*

Since he had nowhere else to go, Daniel lived with that family while he healed. He spent his time looking out the window at the people in the neighbourhood, one of the poorest and humblest to be found in Spanish society on Hesperide, and he learned more from them than in all his years of study.

Late one day, almost at nightfall, Luis, the oldest son, dashed into the room with a crutch in his hand.

"Let's go, Daniel," he said, waving it in the air. "Tonight we're going out."

"Where did you get that?"

"I bought this from an old man when I got out of work with some of what they paid me today," Luis said with a smile. "It was his late wife's; he's been saving it for me for days."

"And the price?" Daniel said, watching him dislodge a brick from the wall with a sharp knife.

"Don't tell my mother, but today was payday." The young man took a metal box from the hollow brick and opened it to count the cash inside. "I've been saving for a long time without telling her. Besides, when my father died and we had to sell him for pieces, she gave me some of the profit. But she thinks I spent it all."

"Your father?"

"Yes. He wanted to leave me his arms. He was really strong, you know? But I was too little and they didn't fit me. And arms for my age were too expensive. So my mother decided to give me what we made from them. And now, with inflation, I can't even afford adult arms. But with this," he said, shifting the money from one hand to the other, "with this we can go get something great. Get up. You've been there almost a month and you need to get out."

And without another word, he put the box for his life savings back into the wall and took Daniel out onto the street.

*

"The next item was acquired in the liquidation of goods from a business that went bankrupt only a few days ago. It's just like new," the auctioneer said. "The opening price is a thousand pesetas."

"A thousand pesetas!" Luis whispered, trying to hide his excitement. "It's a bargain!"

"I thought we were going to exchange your arms..."

"But what a great price, Daniel!"

"I don't need it. My leg is already almost healed. You didn't even have to buy the crutch."

"One thousand five hundred!" Luis shouted. "Don't be silly, Daniel. Without the crutch, we couldn't have left the house. Besides, now you're like my brother. Let me do this for you, please."

"Two thousand!"

"No, look around. Do you see how many hands are raised? A lot of people are interested in this item and the auction house knows it. The opening price is low so that more people bid it up. Don't be fooled."

"Three thousand! That's why we have to act fast. You can't go back now. Look at the leg. Look at it there on the table. It can be yours."

"Five thousand!"

"The only thing they're doing is raising the price," Daniel answered, growing more upset.

"Five thousand two hundred fifty!"

"Six thousand!" Luis said. "Daniel, be more optimistic. We can get it."

"Six thousand seven hundred!"

"No, please, I'm not interested." Daniel felt faint. "Stop it, please, don't do this." His heart suddenly jumped, making him drop back in his seat.

"Seven thousand!"

"What happened, Daniel? Are you all right?"

"Yes, yes, I'm fine. It's just that I haven't been out for a long time, and I'm tired. I'm going to go out and get some air."

"All right. Eight thousand! I'll stay here."

"Nine thousand!"

"No. Come with me please. Help me."

"Ten thousand! Are you crazy? We're about to get it. Go on outside. I'll come get you to sign the papers."

When he stood up, Daniel felt faint. He walked down the aisle, looking at the greedy eyes of poor people spending their savings to look better, at the eyes of the lame, full of pain and suffering, who needed that leg to keep their jobs, and at indifferent faces of those who didn't care who brought it home. Eleven thousand... Twelve thousand... Thirteen thousand... The price kept rising. Voices faltered. Fifteen thousand... Luis's voice couldn't be heard.

"Twenty thousand!" an old man shouted, almost begging. "Twenty thousand!"

When Daniel got to the back of the hall where people stood crowded together, he felt metal brush against his leg. A young man stumbled and tripped him and, although he seemed embarrassed, he reacted fast enough to help Daniel keep his balance.

"I'm really sorry," the young man said. "Are you all right? Sometimes I can't control this..." Ashamed, he lowered his head like a broken doll.

Daniel was petrified to see the freakish thing he had for a leg, worn out and without a foot, a rusted mass of bent metal shorter than the other leg. It looked like it had stopped working years ago. Compared to that, even the old violinist's leg worked better.

"Don't worry. It's all right."

"Twenty-five thousand!"

"Going once... Going twice... Sold to the gentleman for twenty-five thousand!"

At the murmur of disappointment filling the hall, Daniel turned to look at the auctioneer. He was smiling. The old man who had only twenty thousand began to weep disconsolately.

In front of Daniel, the young man collapsed.

"You... are you all right?"

"Yes. Don't worry. I don't have the money to buy it either." He smiled nervously, trying to pretend it didn't bother him, even though his face was redder than the old violinist on a long summer hike. "I was left behind after your brother offered three thousand, so..."

"Oh, he's not my brother. He's... Listen, I'm going to go out and get some air. I can't take it in here anymore."

"Yes, I think it would be good for me to go out for a while, too."

"Do you need help?"

"No, I'm all right," the young man murmured, lowering his head and shrugging off Daniel's arm. "I can still walk alone."

As Daniel walked behind him, he was about to give him a hand a couple of times. The young man seemed nervous, and he limped so badly he kept losing his balance, his leg catching and tripping people at almost every step.

"How long ago...?" Daniel asked when they were outside, gesturing at the leg.

The night was reflected in the young man's eyes. A darkness from deep inside seemed to shine through them. "It was always like that," he answered, looking away and leaning against a wall covered with countless posters, one over the other, calling for revolutions that never came. "I was born without it and I lost track of how many times we changed it."

"You never had one of flesh and blood?"

"We never had enough money. The metal ones don't grow with you the way real ones do. They're much cheaper, but you have to keep getting bigger ones. Before, we could barely afford it, but now, since my father died, it's harder every time. My mother hardly earns enough to feed us and I can't keep a job." He nervously drummed the metal with his knuckles. "We bought this one years ago from the mother of a friend who..."

The wind was cold and sharp. Daniel pulled up the collar of his coat. The entire colony was so frozen that everyone was numb.

"And, well, it was used, worn out when I got it."

Pain. Remorse. Fear... Who would want to feel anything in a world so corrupt? The dusty, raw breeze made Daniel's eyes water. He tried to hide the tear falling down his cheek. "How old are you?" He took a step closer.

"Nineteen... I just had my birthday."

Daniel stood at his side, the wood of his splint next to the metal of the young man's artificial leg.

"What are you doing?" the young man asked.

"It will work... I think it will be right for you. It would reach your height quickly. And in a few months it would adapt to your growth rate."

"What are you talking about?"

"Donating my leg. You need it more than I do."

"You should wait to see if your brother gets you a new one... Besides, your broken leg is the right one, not the left one."

"I don't want a new one. I never did. And I don't care what happens to me. I only want to give you my leg, my healthy leg, my left leg."

Daniel didn't hear much after that. He couldn't take in anything the young man was saying. Only a few words ricocheted through his sluggish mind, making him smile:

"I wish I had the same colour skin as you. That way your leg would match me better."

*

A few months later, a revolution against the metropoli broke out among the lower classes on several planets. Daniel felt something like hope in his sickly chest, a feeling so unfamiliar that he couldn't remember how to keep it alive. Spain didn't hesitate to launch an attack against a distant planet invaded by England, whose name no one knew how to pronounce, in the hope of diverting attention. All the colonies united with the metropoli in the uniform patriotic fervour the press created for them. Rich people read it out loud in the cafés. Poor people felt its warmth in the newspapers they used as blankets at night. And that was when Daniel's ears closed to the world and his eyes to reality.

He crossed the street with a weeping, trembling young man whose broken arm had healed so poorly that he couldn't enlist. Daniel looked at the back and front of his own hand and smiled. He didn't even bother to remove the ring with the family seal when he had the entire arm taken off.

Months later, when everyone was proud of the Spanish victories against England and the revolutions had been put down and forgotten, he rescued another young man from beneath a car using his only remaining arm. The young man had no parents. He had to work for a living and had no one to help him. Daniel accompanied him to the hospital, limping on his crutch.

The doctor said the young man would lose a leg and never walk again. After that, Daniel couldn't leave the house. A single crutch was not enough for a man without any legs.

But the neighbours never forgot about him or his generosity.

They never forgot him.

*

Gabriel Beltran reached a trembling arm toward the coffin. He felt ashamed he couldn't use his own hand to touch his son one last time. Filled with doubt, he lay that hand from another man on his son's chest, which still held his failed heart. The contrast between the white, clumsy hand from the neighbour upstairs on that dark mulatto chest was even greater than the contrast between life and silent death.

He wept, sobbing because he couldn't look him in the eyes or see his face ever again. The only thing left as testimony to his short life was that heart and its story there in the casket, like the one his mother had lain in when she left them so long ago. A heart so big no one wanted it, so grand the world could not understand its worth, but true to its ideals to the end.

STEAM PUNK

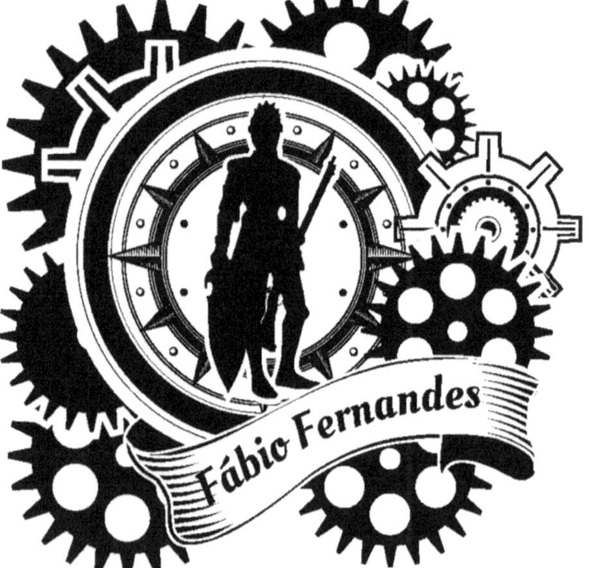

EL ALFÉREZ DE HIERRO

Brazil

EL ALFÉREZ DE HIERRO

By Fábio Fernandes

Para Paulo Leminski, que nem desconfiava.

Luto para viver, vivo para morrer
Enquanto minha morte não vem
Eu vivo de brigar contra o rei
Milton Nascimento, *Caxangá.*

Sentado frente a la larga mesa de escritorio, el hombre lee. Es tarde y solo la luz de la lámpara le hace compañía. No tiene esposa y los pocos esclavos que posee ya se han ido a dormir.

Mantener la atención en la lectura es difícil. Los pensamientos vuelan lejos. "Cuando la cabeza no obedece, el cuerpo padece," acostumbraba a decir su padre, ya fallecido. Él piensa en su padre. Y eso fortalece su volunta. Su concentración aumenta.

*

Su padre le llamaba Quim. En aquel tiempo él apenas era un niño que soñaba con ser soldado.

'Vas a ser doctor,' le decía su padre. 'Para eso trabajo.'

Y cuánto trabajó. Tenía tierras para cultivar, otras para arrendar, unas cabezas de ganado … y así lo iba llevando. Le daba para vivir.

Y habría hecho más, pero no todo sale como lo deseamos. A los nueve años de edad, la madre de Quim murió. Su padre decidió trasladarse con armas y bagajes a Vila de Santo Antônio, a leguas de la hacienda de Pombal, y dejar las cosas en manos de un agregado.

Não podía dar certo. Por aquel entonces Quim era apenas un niño, y sus hermanos eran aún más pequeños. Nadie sabía lo que había sido de la hacienda. Solo dos años después, cuando el padre se unió a su madre en la tumba, los parientes se dieron cuenta del pésimo negocio que su padre había hecho: la hacienda se había hundida bajo tantas deudas.

'Vas a trabajar,' le dijo el primo que acabó por quedarse con su tutela. 'Aquí todos trabajan, quien no trabaja no come.'

*

Su primo le llamaba Joaquim. No era mala persona, pero tampoco era un hombre rico. Trabajaba como dentista cirujano en Santo Antônio y ponía a su mujer y a sus seis hijos a trabajar para ganar más dinero.

Joaquim comenzó a trabajar a los once años, primero como vendedor ambulante, ayudando a una esclava *de ganho da família a vender quitutes*, y, tras ganas confianza, pidió ser arriero. Quería ganar *chão, viajar para ver esse mundo de meu deus*.

Y cuánto vio. Recorrió todas las Minas Gerais, montañas, colinas y valles que no parecían acabar nunca, a lomos de mula, del sudeste, lindando con el estado de Rio al sur, hasta cerca del páramo baiano en el extremo norte. Incluso años después, ya hecho un hombre, trabajando para el gobierno en el reconocimiento de terrenos y explotación de recursos de aquella misma región, nunca había dejado de sentirse impresionado con la miseria de la gente y de la tierra.

Decidió que no quería una vida semejante para sí ni para los suyos, si un día llegase a tenerlos.

*

El hombre continúa leyendo bien entrada la noche. Lo necesita y lo sabe. Después de los acontecimientos recientes, necesita una luz más fuerte que la de los candelabros para mantener alejados a los demonios de la noche — y también los fantasmas que aparecen tan reales.

Además de los tratados de metalurgia, tiene delante un libro que no conocía y que había recibido como herencia. *L'Homme Machine*, de La Mettrie. *El hombre máquina*. Su francés está un poco oxidado, pero le sirve.

El libro es realmente interesante. Su autor, amigo de Diderot y D'Alembert, compara el funcionamiento del cuerpo humano al de una máquina. Se acuerda de la primera vez que lo hojeó, cuando lo encontró, ya hacía tiempo, pero no había tenido tiempo de examinarlo más detenidamente hasta ahora. Y si no era ahora, no sería nunca.

*

A los veinte años, se hizo socio de una botica de asistencia a los pobres en un pueblo de Rosário, en Vila Rica. A esta altura, ya había aprendido un poco de práctico de Farmacia, aún sin tener estudios formales. Con su padre había aprendido a leer y escribir; con su primo, entre un viaje y otro, los elementos básicos del oficio de dentista, lo que le valió el apodo con el que pasaría a ser conocido en adelante.

El pueblo de Vila Rica lo llamaba *Tiradentes*.

*

Corrían los tiempos del Rey. El rey Juan de Portugal, que tenía como Primer Ministro al marqués de Pombal, quien técnicamente era quien mandaba aquí y allá, aunque era más bien acá (y más fuerte representado) a través del vizconde de Barbacena.

Antes de llegar Barbacena a Brasil, la vida era buena — por lo menos para los de buena familia. Quien fuese noble o rico vivía cómodo con el gobierno de Lisboa. Al final, quien no debe no teme, y nadie debía nada: la producción de oro había dado de sobra durante décadas para saciar el hambre metalista de la metrópoli de más allá del mar. Y cuando sobra en las minas, no hay necesidad de rascarse los bolsillos, pues cada cual se lleva lo suyo y todos quedan satisfechos.

Pero todo llega a su fin algún día, y el oro de Minas Gerais también.

No era exactamente el oro del interior de las minas, sino el oro aluvial, aquel que se recogía al batear en los innumerables riachos, ríos y *boqueirões* en las inmediaciones de las Gerais. Los yacimientos que proporcionaban ese oro tenían los días contados.

Era agotamiento puro y duro; pero no era así como don Luís da Cunha Meneses, el gobernador de la Capitanía de Comercio durante la década de 1780, veía la situación. En sus cartas a la Corona, don Luís dejaba claro que se trataba de "descaminho" — un nombre elegante para referirse al contrabando. Esclavos y hasta blancos que trabajaban para los dueños de minas se llevaban pepitas y polvo de oro en las dobleces de la ropa, en los cabellos (y los cabellos *pixaim* de los negros se prestaban muy bien a esta actividad, resaltó el gobernador en una de sus cartas) e incluso, ¡blasfemia de blasfemias!, dentro de santos de madera huecos, que algunos habían tenido la desfachatez de cargar por las calles de Vila Rica durante las procesiones. Por tanto, siempre finalizaba don Luís en sus cartas, que la Corona mantuviese la calma, que las medidas debidas estaban siendo tomadas, aunque el oro no fuese siempre fácil de recuperar.

Lo que el gobernador de la Capitanía olvidaba de aclarar en sus cartas a Portugal era, a pesar de que buena parte de lo que decía era cierto, que también había un tipo de *descaminho* extraoficial cobrado como propina por parte de la propia Capitanía. Y que esto provocaba un agujero mucho mayor en las arcas de la Corona que el tal contrabando de negros y blancos pobres.

Pero de esto se encargó otra carta.

*

Era verano, pero la noche del 8 de Septiembre de 1787 estaba fresca, casi fría. Un sábado ideal para uno de las famosas veladas de Alvarenga Peixoto en São João do Rei.

Estaban todos, además de los anfitriones, Peixoto y su esposa, doña Bárbara Heliodora: sus amigos abogados, Cláudio Manoel da Costa, Tomaz Antônio Gonzaga; el padre Rolim; el canónigo Luís Vieira da Silva; y algunos amigos militares: el adjudicador Domingos de Abreu Vieira, el capitán José de Resende Costa, el coronel Francisco Antônio de Oliveira Lopes. Y el alférez Joaquim José da Silva Xavier.

Tras la cena, entre copas de coñac francés y vino de Porto, mientras los poetas más jóvenes pedían licencia para versear a las mozas y los invitados se acercaban a escucharles, los más viejos formaban otros círculos más discretos.

Domingos se acercó a Gonzaga y le preguntó: '¿Envió usted la carta?'

Cláudio asintió con la cabeza.

'Salió esta mañana temprano. Debería salir para Lisboa en una semana.'

Domingos asintió.

'Y hasta final de año estaremos libres de esta bestia humana.' Cerca de ellos, Joaquim escuchaba en silencio, saboreando con moderación su copa de Porto. Estaba de acuerdo, pero rezaba para que la bestia humana del gobernador de la Capitanía de Minas Gerais no fuese sustituida por una peor.

*

La respuesta tardó, pero no falló.

La noticia del nombramiento del vizconde de Barbacena como gobernador y capitán general de Minas Gerais, el 11 de Julio de 1788, fue muy bien recibida por los descontentos que habían firmado la carta exigiendo medidas de Lisboa contra los desmanes y la corrupción del gobernador de la Capitanía. Antônio Gonzaga era uno de los que apoyaban la decisión de la Corona:

'El vizconde me conoce,' dijo todo orgulloso a sus amigos en su casa, en una discreta recepción con el único propósito de celebrar la llegada del sustituto. 'Y escribí unos sonetos para celebrar el nacimiento de su hijo, hace unos años.'

'¿*Unos* sonetos?' dijo Cláudio, en tono jocoso.

'Dos o tres, no me acuerdo,' respondió Gonzaga, con visible falta de modestia.

Los brindis se sucedieron y la bebida era abundante. Todos estaban felices.

Joaquim también. Por ahora.

Para él, acostumbrado a los rigores del ejército — tanto de delegaciones como de contingentes militares — un superior era casi siempre igual a otro. Solo cambiaban los nombres.

Mientras tanto, tiene otras cosas de las que ocuparse.

Desde que volvió a Vila Rica, Joaquim pasó años trabajando para recuperar la hacienda de su padre. También él había sido tentado a participar en los *descaminhos* tan populares; no aceptó. Aunque no concordase con el destino final del oro — y siguiendo el refrán, quien roba a un ladrón tiene cien años de perdón, estaría más que perdonado hasta por Dios Nuestro Señor — sabía lo que pasaba con aquellos que eran pillados robando oro. Como boticario y como alférez, no era nadie, ¿y quién cuida de los que no son nadie en este mundo?

*

'La cuestión de la jerarquía siempre era de las de más profunda importancia en tiempo de guerra, no solo por la disciplina militar, sino también en el momento de la derrota,' piensa el hombre cerrando el libro. 'Alguien tiene que sufrir la caída.'

Entre coroneles, capitanes y sargentos mayores, o, como dice el refrán, entre muertos y heridos, todos se salvan.

A excepción, ocasionalmente, de algún que otro soldado.

O de un alférez.

'Como saben poco de mí,' piensa Joaquim mientras recorre los túneles bajo Pico do Itabirito. En las entrañas pequeñas y estrechas como los intestinos de una serpiente, desciende hasta la forja donde su esclavo, Sebastião, ya lo espera.

Si el calor no se vuelve insoportable solo es porque ya está acostumbrado. Sería absurdo quejarse. Joaquim sabe que Sebastião, hijo de africana, por ejemplo, sufrió mucho más en su vida entera que él, hijo de portugués, y que no tiene motivos para enfadarse por un simple calorcillo de nada. (Y no obstante sabe que sufriría intensos picores si la Conjuración, o Inconfidencia, como ya la estaban llamando las bestias en tono despectivo — ¡como si el movimiento revolucionario que intentaban crear fuese cosa de comadres! —, cayese como un castillo de naipes y todos fuesen apresados.)

'¡Sebastião!' exclama, mientras se sacaba la casaca y la camisa. '¿Está todo listo?'

'Está,' responde el negro sin apartar la vista de lo que está haciendo. Suelta el martillo sobre una placa de hierro que la otra mano asegura con fuerza con un par de alicates cuya única diferencia con la que el boticario usa para sacar los dientes está apenas en el tamaño. El hierro está rojo, incandescente.

Bajo la luz brillante de las lámparas de sebo, él se pone a trabajar al lado de Sebastião. El tiempo les muerde los tobillos como una manada de perros rabiosos. Y el *Tiradentes* no va a dejar que pase.

*

La verdad era que Joaquim era un hombre insatisfecho. Y ese descontento que cargaba en su vida no era cosa nueva.

Cuando había dejado de ser arriero, tanto para dejar de lado los desmanes de su primo, que, aun siendo su tutor, le quitaba el cuero quedándose así con la mayor parte de lo muy poco que ganaba con las ventas, tanto para ganar independencia financiera y — sueño de su juventud — para recuperar la hacienda de su padre y tener una vida digna, Joaquim trató de arreglárselas como pudo; además de la botica que había abierto en Vila Rica, comenzó a trabajar como minero, lo que le valió la contratación por parte del gobierno para volver a trabajar en la frontera con Bahia.

Fueron años trabajando bajo la tutela del viejo ingeniero de minas Antônio Eustáquio, un hombre bueno pero severo, y taciturno, aunque siempre tenía la palabra exacta para el momento adecuado, para sus empleados y para sus amigos. Con el paso del tiempo Joaquim se transformaría de uno en otro.

Pero ni siquiera la amistad con Antônio Eustáquio, que quería que Joaquim continuase trabajando en las minas, fue suficiente para impedir que se alistase en el ejército de la Capitanía de Minas Gerais; era 1870, contaban con treinta y cuatro años y aún no tenía posesiones. Por más que le gustase aquel viejo ingeniero, sabía que como militar ganaría más, y además, contaría con la posibilidad de ir ascendiendo, sumando con ello más posibilidades de mejorar su situación.

Al principio, las cosas se sucedieron como lo había imaginado. Un año después, Joaquim fue nombrado Comandante de Destacamento de los Dragones en la patrulla de Caminho Novo, la línea ferroviaria que servía como ruta de enlace de la producción minera desde la Capitanía hasta el puerto de Rio de Janeiro.

Fue un período difícil. El destacamento de Joaquim era poco numeroso y mal abastecido. No fueron pocos los avisos que el comandante tuvo que enviar a la capital solicitando más soldados, armamento, munición y hasta alimentos.

Y por si la falta de soldados fuese poco, Joaquim aún tenía que lidiar con las deserciones. Los desertores normalmente eran castigados con la muerte, pero como no estaban en guerra Joaquim simplemente mandaba un grupo — los cuatro gatos de que podía disponer para capturar a los huidos y ponerlos en grilletes. Las condiciones de los presos no diferían mucho de la de los escuálidos y malnutridos soldados de Joaquim.

Fue entonces cuando se dio cuenta de que no era el único que encontraba injusta la miseria del interior de Brasil. Estaba muy lejos de ser el único, en realidad. De Ilha do Governador a Vila Rica, pasando por el puerto de Pilar do Iguaçu, la ciudad de Xérem, la concejalía de Conceição do Alferes y otros curatos y pueblajos, Joaquim siempre encontraba hombres dispuestos a intercambiar unas palabras sobre cómo debería Brasil separarse de la metrópoli, o al menos conquistar una cierta independencia financiera, teniendo en cuenta cuánta riqueza era llevada a Portugal e lo poco que sobraba para los propios brasileños, que no salían de la condición de miserables. Joaquim, como militar, no podía opinar, al contrario; si le pedían que hablase, se sentía en la obligación moral de defender al Rey, pero como ciudadano, no tenía evitar concordar con los que se quejaban. También él y su bolsa sentían el peso de la mano gananciosa de Portugal.

Su único confesor durante ese tiempo fue el viejo Antônio Eustáquio, a quien hacía breves comentarios sobre el estado de las cosas a lo largo de Caminho Novo y dentro del destacamento (siempre sin entrar en muchos detalles, que el comandante era discreto) y daba a entender que un día las cosas tendrían que ir a mejor, porque a peor ya no podían ir.

*

Empeoraron.

Durante años de servicio en el ejército, años de mucho servir y poco recibir, habiendo llegado a duras penas a alférez, mero trámite previo a la oficialidad, y viendo a otros de su mismo rango y menos preparados ascender en la carrera militar (pero de padres nobles, portugueses o ambas cosas), Joaquim dejó pasar el nombramiento de mariscal de patrulla de Caminho Novo, que se le debía hacía por lo menos dos años. Fue directo al cuartel general de Rio para darse de baja de la caballería en 1787, tras casi siete años de fiel servicio.

"Siete años de pastor Jacob servía", escribió en seguida para Antônio Eustáquio, comenzando la carta con el célebre soneto de Camões. "al padre de Raquel, serrana bella; mas no servía a él, servía a ella, que a ella sólo por premio pretendía."

Era demasiado orgulloso para decir que se había arrepentido de su proyecto militar, pero los versos del poeta portugués eran suficientes para el viejo maestro. Recibió de él una respuesta corta y simple, "No seguirá estando triste el pastor al que con engaños le fuera así negada su pastora, como si no la hubiese merecido. Venga acá a verme y recibirá a Raquel, en lugar de a Lea.

Sin entender la respuesta aún más críptica del ingeniero, Joaquim volvió a las Minas.

*

La casa de la hacienda de Antônio Eustáquio quedaba a cerca de cuatro leguas de Vila Rica, cerca de Pico do Itabirito. Para cuando se bajó del caballo, el sol ya se estaba poniendo. Todo era silencio. Lo recibió a la entrada un esclavo, que tomó las riendas de su caballo.

'*Seu* Antônio está encamado,' dijo el hombre, un negro alto y fuerte, cuya camisa parecía a punto de reventar de tan pequeña para su cuerpo o de tan grandes sus músculos. 'El señor puede entrar, que él está en su aposento. Cualquier cosa, mi nombre es Sebastião.'

Joaquim asintió con la cabeza y entró en la casa. Estaba oscuro y el olor era desagradable. Era un olor entre dulzón y podre. El alférez ya lo había olido más de una vez en su vida.

Al entrar en el aposento, le llevó un tiempo acostumbrarse a la poca luz que apenas se colaba por los postigos abiertos de las ventanas. Por los vidrios casi no pasaba más claridad. El cuerpo gordo del viejo ingeniero sobre la cama asemejaba un anticipo de cadáver. Si no era peor era porque el viejo aun daba señales de vida; hablaba en bajo y gesticulaba a una criada que sostenía una bacinilla en las manos a los pies de la cama. Al acercarse, sin hacer ruido, Joaquim vio la ropa de cama levantada a la altura de las piernas del viejo; la pierna derecha estaba cubierta por una gasa de algodón, parecida a un pañuelo, pero con manchas parduzcas. De allí provenía el olor.

Gangrena.

Al percibir su presencia, Antônio Eustáquio estiró las manos ya curvadas en forma de garras. 'Dios mío, qué viejo está,' pensó el alférez, sin darse cuenta de la cantidad de años que llevaba sin ver al viejo maestro y tiró de Joaquim por las solapas del abrigo: 'Me caí en la mina,' dijo, con la voz baja y ronca. 'Tenga cuidado cuando baje.'

'¿Qué mina, doctor Eustáquio?'

A pesar de su amistad, nunca había dejado de llamar al ingeniero respetuosamente por su título. El viejo tosió con esa tos fina de quien está perdiendo el aliento. 'Y el alma,' pensó Joaquim sin querer. Pero prosiguió después de un tiempo: 'Sebastião se lo mostrará. Conceição, lleve a Joaquim allá al terreno y diga a Sebastião que ya es la hora.'

La criada, que solo ahora Joaquim vio que ya había salido y vuelto a entrar del cuarto, respondió apenas con un gesto de cabeza y salió de nuevo.

'Vaya con ella,' dijo el viejo. 'No se preocupe que aún no es mi hora. Usted tiene una cosa muy importante que hacer. Sebastião le llevará allá. Su Raquel — añadió.'

*

Viajaron montados en dos mulas del propio Antônio Eustáquio. Según el propio ingeniero, la entrada a la mina quedaba a menos de dos leguas de distancia, pero para evitar ojos curiosos, él y Sebastião iban siempre por un camino más retorcido, que daba la vuelta a un morrete rodeado de arbustos y matojos, para finalmente, tras veinte minutos — con la noche ya oscureciéndolo todo y solo la luna llena impidiendo que todo se tornase en brea — llegaron a su destino.

La entrada estaba bien cubierta por piedras, pero cuando terminaron de apartarlas del camino, Joaquim percibió que aun así la abertura apenas le llegaba a la cintura. Tuvo que encorvarse para seguir a Sebastião al interior.

Era un túnel largo y oscuro, más aun de aquellos a los que se había acostumbrado a recorrer en exploraciones pasadas. Había sido excavado por una o dos personas como mucho. Y debió de llevar mucho tiempo. Con mucho esfuerzo.

'¿Su pierna…?' comenzó Joaquim.

Sebastião soltou um muxoxo.

'Viejo tozudo,' dijo. 'Le dije que se quedara en casa, pero él insistió en trabajar. Cuando la piedra cayó sobre él, yo estaba en otra cámara. Me costó levantar la maldita.'

Joaquim miró hacia abajo, pero no vio ninguna señal de desprendimiento. O el túnel al que Sebastião se refería estaba en otra parte de la mina o el trabajo de limpieza había sido impecable. Pero Antônio Eustáquio no exigía menos de sus hombres.

De repente, un brillo cegó la vista de Joaquim por un segundo. Tuvo que llevarse la mano a la cara.

A la luz del candil, la cámara brillaba a su alrededor. Como un cielo estrellado en el interior, o por lo menos era lo que él pensaba cuando había empezado a trabajar de minero años atrás.

Pero, fijándose bien en la piedra negra rallada de rojo oscuro, la imagen que le venía a la cabeza ahora era más bien otro.

Entrañas de un animal ensangrentado.

'Hematita,' dijo, en voz baja.

*

'¿Entonces?' preguntó el viejo, con una sonrisa deformándole el rostro de tal modo que le hacía parecer una calavera. Una calavera mejor preparada, pero que aun así servía de recordatorio de que la muerte se acercaba. '¿Le gustó lo que vio?'

'Mucho, doctor Eustáquio.'

'Esta veta de hematita tiene una peculiaridad,' dijo el viejo con dificultad. 'Contiene un porcentaje de ilmenita mayor de lo normal.'

Ilmenita. Joaquim había leído recientemente al respecto en un *periódico* inglés. También era conocida como titanio.

'Los papeles ya han sido enviados a la comarca. Mipropiedad es ahora suya. No diga nada. No tuve hijos y usted fue mi mejor alumno.'

Joaquim no supo qué decir. No entendía que había hecho para merecerlo. Pero lo peor de todo no era eso: era la pregunta que quería salir de su garganta y que no tenía valor para hacer.

Antônio Eustáquio tosió y agarró febrilmente la manga de su abrigo. Como si supiese lo que Joaquim iba a preguntarle, dijo, con voz ronca y casi sin energía: 'No es oro, lo sé. Pero no le engaño; no es Lea en lugar de Raquel. Ese metal es más precioso que el oro que los imbéciles de la metrópoli tanto desean.'

Y Joaquim preguntó: '¿Por qué?'

'Porque con oro no se hacen cañones,' respondió.

*

Antônio Eustáquio murió al amanecer.

Joaquim y Sebastião lo enterraron en el pato trasero, a la sombra del almendro cuya sombra el viejo tanto apreciaba. Ahora, junto con la casa, el terreno de la haciendo y los dos esclavos, era de Joaquim

No era la hacienda de su infancia, pero por ahora serviría.

*

Joaquim sabía bien que la producción de minería de hierro de Minas Gerais era mucho mayor que la de oro. El oro se acabaría un día; el hierro, solo cuando todas las colinas fuesen niveladas a ras de suelo y transformadas en inmensos cráteres. Solo si toda la Capitanía dejase de existir.

Otra cosa que el alférez también sabía muy bien — o, mejor, exalférez, aunque ahora la gente aún lo tratase por su título de Vila Rica, cosa que Joaquim nunca sabía decir si le enorgullecía o le irritaba — era que las minas de hierro no escaseaban en la región. Uno de los mayores mineros era conocido suyo desde hacía años, Inácio José de Alvarenga Peixoto, que había comenzado con hierro pero que ahora estaba metido en una locura de proyecto en São Gonçalo do Sapucaí:

abrir un canal para mejorar el flujo de la producción de las minas de oro del pueblo y al mismo tiempo lavar las tierras. Era un proyecto ambicioso, pero decían las malas lenguas que con él, además de con las veladas poéticas que celebraba cada semana en su casa, estaba agotando todo su dinero.

Aquellos con los que se juntaba, tanto en la botica como en las veladas, estaban pasando por la misma situación desesperada: falta de fondos. Las conversaciones asumían un tono aún más sombrío y amenazador que aquellas que había tenido durante su período en Caminho Novo: en aquellas aldehuelas las personas poco sabían más allá de la pobreza de sus propios bolsillos. En São João do Rei y Vila Rica, también hablaban mucho de la independencia de las colonias norteamericanas y de la formación de un nuevo país, los Estados Unidos. La cuestión de la separación de la metrópoli comenzaba a ser cada vez más abordada en las conversaciones entre los círculos del clero y la élite minera.

'Si Bahia y Pernambuco ya la han conseguido, ¿por qué no nosotros?' preguntaba uno en la botica.

'Un momento, que ellos no la han conseguido,' decía otro.

'Pero ¿cómo que no, hombre? ¡Si hasta tienen un gobierno y una bandera!'

'Pero luchan contra los portugueses desde hace décadas.'

'No se olviden,' interrumpía un tercero que también esperaba al boticario, 'de que son holandeses, y no brasileños, los que están detrás de esa independencia.'

Entonces todos callaban. Porque era verdad.

'Sin contar a aquellos soldados,' rompió el silencio el primero, 'en bajo.'

'¿Los *cartésios*?' preguntó, casi como quien sintiese vergüenza de pronunciar tal nombre.

El tercero se santiguó.

'¡Virgen Santísima, no digan ese nombre!'

Porque si había algo de extraño y terrible en aquella tierra dividida eran los *cartésios*. Un arriero paulista con quien Joaquim cabalgó por los caminos de las Gerais los vio una sola vez y nunca más los olvidó.

'*¿Cómo havera de?*' dijo, encendiendo su cigarrillo de paja junto a la lumbre tras acabar su comida de harina y cecina. 'Era algo terrible de ver. Parecían un grupo de saúva. Señor, ¿las ha visto usted alguna vez, *Seu* Joaquim?'

Joaquim movió la cabeza. Conocía a la hormiga negra, pequeña, común, de esas que se ven por todas partes, en las ranuras de las paredes, en el suelo, siempre en fila. Pero la saúva, solo la conocía de nombre.

'Si la saúva pasa por encima de un bicho, el bicho está perdido,' continuó el arriero. 'Lo cubren por completo, le entran por todos los agujeros, se lo comen por dentro y por fuera. Y se lo comen rápido pero no lo suficiente, porque el bicho sufre de dolor. *Se der pra, se mexer, ele ainda tenta dar no pitote*, pero conseguirá nada, porque a esas alturas el bicho ya se ha ido al encuentro de su creador, eso si es que tiene alma, el Señor me perdone por hablar así.'

Joaquim no podía estar menos preocupado en saber si el bicho tendría alma. Le preocupaban más las almas de sus compañeros.

*

Los *cartésios* existían desde hacía casi un siglo. Habían surgido de una lógica disciplinar creada por un militar francés al servicio del príncipe Maurício de Nassau. Durante el largo período de tiempo que Nassau pasó en Brasil, una pequeña guarnición fue entrenada según sus rígidos principios para que todos funcionasen como uno solo; según decía quien los había visto, aunque casi nunca se dejaban ver. Unos decían que sus uniformes eran del más puro blanco; otros, que naranja, de la casa de Orange; y aun otros, que eran negros como la noche, y que incluso había africanos entre ellos, reclutados bajo la promesa de ser liberados si aceptaban entrar en la orden de los *cartésios*. Pues los *cartésios* (apodados despectivamente por los baianos como *castésios*, porque no se acostaban con mujeres ni bebían alcohol ni jugaban) eran prácticamente una orden religiosa. Solo les faltaba el reconocimiento del Vaticano. Pero decían que Renatus Cartesius, su creador, era un hombre sin fe, y que la forma de pensar de aquellos soldados, llamados *cartesianos*, de religión nada tenía. Se regían por la lógica.

'¿Y la lógica cartesiana les ordena no dejar nunca supervivientes allá donde van?'

'Parece que no, *seo* Joaquim.'

'Como las *saúvas*.'

'Pues sí.'

*

Fuera como fuese, los tales *cartésios* no eran lo que más preocupaba a Joaquim. Primero, que hasta donde él sabía eran pocos, no llegaba a formar un ejército; segundo, según se decía popularmente — hasta algunos periódicos viejos de la capitán que su primo había guardado en una canasta y que él había leído y releído con avidez cuando era joven — bastaría un pelotón de cincuenta hombres para derrotar a la tropa del gobernador general Antônio Teles da Silva y ganar el control de Salvador para evitar la insurrección contra los holandeses. Con Bahia ganada, el resto del nordeste se abriría al control de Nassau. Cuando partió en 1648, tras la ejecución de los traidores André Vidal de Negreiros, Filipe Camarão y Henrique Dias, la Nueva Holanda, compuesta por las antiguas capitanías de Pernambuco, Sergipe, Bahia, Ceará, Maranhão y Grão-Pará, estaba definitivamente consolidada como nación. Portugal, por tanto, tendría que poner mayor atención en el resto de Brasil.

*

Joaquim, entretanto, no podía estar menos preocupado con la historia del país vecino. Todo lo que le interesaba en aquel momento, golpeando hierro caliente, moldeando con lentitud y mucho sudor el metal que poco a poco iba tomando la forma tan deseada en los planos y proyectos iniciales de Antônio Eustáquio, era defender su ida. Pues sabía que todos sus colegas conspiradores en aquel momento estaban siendo apresados, y si a él también lo pillaban todo estaría terminado, pues no tenía una posición acomodada y nadie que lo defendiese.

Todo lo que tenía era su nombre.

Joaquim José da Silva Xavier.

Quim.

Tiradentes.

Alférez.

Hombre.

*

Durante los más de cien años de dominio holandés en el nordeste, la sede del gobierno brasileño se desplazó primero a Rio de Janeiro y después a Minas Gerais, donde sería más fácil defender el oro de Brasil. Oro que no hacía cañones, pero que pagaba muy bien a los portugueses que aún tenían como colonos; según los documentos de 1750.

Según el archivo real, la capitanía de Minas Gerais debería enviar a la metrópoli cien arrobas de oro al año: mil quinientos kilos de material. La pena porque la cota no se cumpliese era la tasa de la Derrama: la población de hombres de buena posición era obligada a poner lo que faltase de sus propios bolsillos.

Por muchos años, los ricos — es decir, los nobles, terratenientes, asesores y auditores, hombres de dinero — no se habían tenido que preocupar, pues el oro brotaba de sobra del suelo.

Cuando don Luís empezó a escribir cartas al Rey dando parte de la escasez aurífera, la ley de la Derrama aún no había sido abolida — en esto hay que ser justos con el antiguo gobernador de Capitanía. Era corrupto, pero tenía claro cuál era su lugar. El vizconde de Barbacena, desgraciadamente, no estaba nada preocupado con la solvencia de los hombres de bien.

Y ya había anunciado un cobro de Demanda para Febrero de 1789.

*

Joaquim pasó el año 1788 enterrado dentro de la mina del viejo Antônio Eustáquio. Le costaba considerarla suya, pero los papeles que había ido a buscar a la auditoría de la comarca no tenía dudas: la minera era suya. Y eso incluía a Sebastião, y su esposa y a la criada Conceição, los únicos esclavos del viejo ingeniero, que lo acompañaban desde había años. Ellos vivían en una cabaña tras la hacienda, con su propia huerta y hasta unas gallinas; debían de ser felices, pues no habían huido. Joaquim tampoco les había ofrecido la libertad. Necesitaba que alguien cuidase de la propiedad mientras él trabajaba en la ciudad y cuidaba de la mina. Aquella hacienda solo lo era de nombre; no pasaba de un *sitiozinho reles*, menor que la propiedad en la que se había criado — y que todavía quería recuperar.

¿Pero cómo? El dinero de la botica no sería suficiente y lo que se plantaba en la hacienda solo les garantizaba sustento, a veces ni eso.

Antônio Eustáquio no había explorado la mina para fines comerciales, pero había dejado planos para algo más ambicioso. En las pocas horas de madrugada que habían tenido para conversar, el viejo ingeniero le había indicado un cajón de la cómoda junto a la cama, en el que Joaquim encontró un montón de papeles, todos llenos de anotaciones y diseños. Y algunos libros, la mayoría de metalurgia y uno de filosofía. *L'Homme Machine.*

Fue el principio de una obsesión para el exalférez.

La hematita fundida se convertía en un metal al mismo tiempo duro y maleable, y los grandes depósitos de titanio acumulados convertían la aleación resultante en un metal algo más leve que el hierro convencional. La idea de aquellos proyectos del viejo ingeniero consistían en volver a las armaduras clásicas de los tiempos de los conquistadores españoles, pero dando mayor movilidad a los soldados.

Durante meses fabricó y probó diferentes versiones de armadura. Las placas que cubrían el pecho, la espalda, los antebrazos y parte de las piernas no eran suficientes para proteger de un ataque de cara o de espalda — al final, en una escaramuza, con un golpe bien dado en el cuello o en las juntas el metal de nada serviría — pero sí para repeler la mayor parte de los disparos de los mosquetes; era en eso en lo que Antônio Eustáquio pensaba al diseñar los primeros esbozos.

Joaquim había experimentado con abrazaderas y espinilleras y no las encontraba ni muy cómodas ni muy leves. Era necesario hacer las placas más finas.

No consiguió avanzar nada con relación a los pies, pero Sebastião tuvo la idea de cortar herraduras para pegarlas como una especie de punteras en la punta de las botas. Añadiría un peso extra al caminar, pero lo compensaría proporcionando una protección adicional y tal vez una forma excepcional de ataque, ya que una patada con tal puntera bien podría romper una canilla desprotegida. Sebastião sugirió además reforzar con ellas las articulaciones de los tobillos para que sirviesen de contrapeso, lo que a Joaquim no le pareció mala idea.

Poco a poco, la armadura iba siendo montada. Todas las noches, al volver de Vila Rica, Joaquim se unía a Sebastião en el trabajo de forja y cada dos noches probaba las placas. A finales de 1788, ya tenía suficiente material para tres armaduras completas. Una para sí; otra de reserva, aunque a petición de Sebastião y por sus servicios, se la había dejado probar, y que le dejara experimentar no le había venido mal (aunque Joaquim las guardaba consigo, en un baúl de la casa de la hacienda). Y una tercera, que pretendía mostrar a las fuerzas armadas en Rio de Janeiro.

El trabajo había llevado tanto tiempo porque Joaquim intentaba hacer las cosas con la mayor calma, rigor y capricho posibles. Tarea difícil para un hombre de cuarenta y un años, casi sin posesiones, sin mujer y sin hijos. «Ya es hora de asentarse de una vez», pensaba mientras martillaba el hierro en la mina o arrancaba los dientes de los pacientes como boticario; y había unas mozas de buena familia y en edad casadera en los saraos de Alvarenga. Quizá la próxima vez.

*

Entró con ánimos en el salón de Alvarenga y Bárbara Heliodora en la noche de Año Nuevo. Los negocios iban bien, en la medida de lo posible, y ahora podía tomar a una muchacha como esposa y crear una familia. Y si la venta de la armadura al Ejército iba bien, entonces, ¿quién pondría límites a sus sueños?

'¡Llegó nuestro alférez!' exclamó Tomás Antônio Gonzaga, taza de vino en mano, con aspecto de haber bebido ya unas cuantas.

'Aquí estoy,' dijo Joaquim, estrechado la mano de su amigo.

'¿Cómo que alférez?' le corrigió Alvarenga, acercándose de brazo de su esposa, Bárbara Heliodora, que añadió: '¡Joaquim José es ahora dueño de una mina!'

Joaquim se quedó un poco avergonzado. La mina no era un secreto, pero poca gente sabía de ella, y no le gustaba hablar al respecto.

'No esperaría que yo, habiendo sido *ouvidor / auditor* de la comarca,' dijo Tomás, 'no llegaría a enterarme de algo así, Joaquim. ¡Venga, brindemos por el nuevo propietario de mina de Vila Rica!'

'*Imagine*, no hace falta ...'

'¿E por guardar luto por Eustáquio?' se enmendó Alvarenga. '¡Entonces brindemos también a su salud, hombre!'

'¡Bebamos por el difunto!' dijo Cláudio Manuel da Costa.

'¡Y bebamos también por la vida!' dijo Tomás. 'No he podido evitar fijarme en que hay aquí unas muchachas bastante hermosas ...'

'Ciertamente que las hay-' le interrumpió Alvarenga. 'Yo mismo le presentaré a los padres de algunas de ellas. Pero, de momento, vayamos a la salita, que tenemos mucho de qué hablar.'

Al entrar a la salita, Joaquim pudo ver a varias personas, la mayoría de ellas conocidos de Vila Rica, São João Del Rei y hasta de Rio de Janeiro. El adjudicador Domingos de Abreu Vieira, el padre Rolim, el canónigo Luís Vieira, el coronel Francisco Lopes, su primo, el coronel de milicias Joaquim Silvério dos Reis, el capitán José de Resende Costa, el sargento mayor Toledo Pisa y algunos otros.

A decir verdad, casi todos los que formaban aquel grupo se reunían periódicamente desde hacía algunos años, motivados no solo por los desmanes de la metrópoli y del gobernador de la Capitanía — y ahora del vizconde de Barbacena — sino también por los ideales de Ilustración franceses y de la Independencia de los Estados Unidos. Muchos, como Tomás, Cláudio, sus padres y algunos militares — y exmilitares, entre los que se contaba el propio Joaquim —, estaban en el floreciente movimiento únicamente por sus ideales. Pero los terratenientes se juntaron por motivos más prácticos: su completa bancarrota debida a la escasez de oro aluvial en la zona y la obligación de colaborar con la cota poniendo de sus propios bolsillos para llenar las arcas de Portugal.

*

'¿Cuánto tiempo tenemos?' preguntó Alvarenga.

'Poco más de un mes. El vizconde pretende hacer valer la Derrama a mediados de febrero. Aun no estipuló nada.'

'Lo cual lo hace todo aún más peligroso,' dijo el padre Rolim. 'De hombres, sin palabra, no se fía un pelo, ¿qué dirá si no hay contrato firmado?'

'Entonces está decidido,' dijo Tomás. '¡Derrocamos a Barbacena e instauramos la República!'

'De acuerdo,' dijo Cláudio. '¿Y en cuanto a los soldados?'

'¿Cuántos milicianos sería capaz de reunir, coronel Silvério?' preguntó Joaquim.

'Así, de repente, trescientos,' respondió sin vacilar.

'Son pocos.'

'Suficientes,' dijo Silvério, muy serio.

'Pero los hombres de Barbacena tienen cañones. ¿Los tiene usted?'

'Tengo dos que pertenecieron a mi abuelo. Y funcionan perfectamente.'

Joaquim pensó en hablar de las armaduras en aquel momento, pero prefirió callar. Tres armaduras no harían nada en aquel momento.

'¿Cuándo?' preguntó.

'Cuanto antes,' dijo Tomás.

'No puedo reunir a mis milicianos y entrenarlos en menos de veinte días. Si consiguiésemos reunir más de trescientos; en ese caso …'

'No podemos esperar hasta después de la declaración de la Derrama,' dijo Alvarenga.

'Que sea el día de la declaración,' dijo Silvério. 'Les tomará por sorpresa.'

El coronel Francisco asintió.

'Tiene sentido,' dijo. 'Intentaré reunir algunos hombres de confianza para enriquecer el caldo.'

Después de los acuerdos iniciales, pasaron el resto de la noche celebrando la llegada de 1789. Bebieron, comieron, versearon. Si se sentían felices, solo lo podía saber cada uno en su fuero interno. Joaquim solo sabía que no podía hacer más por ahora.

*

El día de Año Nuevo, Joaquim no salió de la hacienda. Se quedó a descansar y leer, acostado en una hamaca. Intentando no pensar en la conversación de la noche anterior.

Y fue desde la hamaca que vio a los *cartésios* acercándose.

A decir verdad, no tenía forma de saber si eran los afamados soldados holandeses o no. Pero al ver el minúsculo grupo de seis hombres, vestidos con ropas sin color, marchando como militares, en pares, uno a la retaguardia y uno a la vanguardia, se acordó de lo que el arriero le había dicho años atrás.

Saúvas.

Y venían en su dirección.

Joaquim se levantó despacio. Su mosquete estaba dentro de la casa. Llamó a Sebastião. No hubo respuesta.

Los hombres siguieron marchando hasta sobrepasar la cerca que marcaba el límite de la hacienda. Joaquim cruzó el porche en dirección a ellos.

'¿Quién va? ¿Vienen en paz?'

Los hombres siguieron marchando. Joaquim empezaba a ponerse nervioso. '¿Qué hace ese negro con mi mosquete?' pensó. '¿Qué está pasando? ¿Habrían ido a robar a la mina? ¿Por tan poco? ¿Así es como acabaría su vida?'

Entonces el hombre que llevaba la delantera hizo una señal y se paró. El resto del grupo obedeció.

'¿Joaquim José da Silva Xavier?' preguntó el hombre, con un tono de voz extraño, casi metálico, el rostro sin expresión.

'Está hablando con él. ¿Cuál es el motivo de esta invasión?'

De repente el hombre tenía una carta en la mano. Joaquim no pudo ver ni de dónde se había sacado el sobre.

Aceptó. Observó el lacre de cera. No tenía marca reconocible de anillo ni el sello de Casa Real.

Lo rompió y sacó la carta.

Su contenido era simple pero no daba lugar a dudas.

'¿Para cuándo?' preguntó el hombre.

'Treinta días,' fue la respuesta.

'¿Y si me niego?'

'El contrato está firmado,' dijo el hombre, 'en la misma voz sin timbre.'

'¿Qué contrato?'

Desde la muerte de Antônio Eustáquio, Joaquim había revisado toda la documentación referente a la mina. El viejo ingeniero no había dejado nada pendiente.

'Treinta días,' repitió el hombre, levantando de nuevo la mano. Como si fuese un solo cuerpo, todos los miembros del grupo dieron media vuelta y retomaron la marcha con el mismo ritmo de antes, con la diferencia de que el hombre volvió a ocupar la delantera, cambiándose con el de la retaguardia. Joaquim se quedó allí parado, carta e mano, sin arma ni respuesta.

*

Después de que los *cartésios* desaparecieron entre el polvo de la carretera, su primera reacción fue salir corriendo hacia la cabaña de Sebastião. Se lo encontró tirado, atado de brazos y piernas con una cuerda de rafia y con la nariz y la barbilla cubiertos de sangre seca. A su alrededor, piezas del mosquete, cuidadosamente desmontadas.

'Era un grupo,' dijo Sebastião, con la voz gruesa y nasal, mientras Joaquim cortaba las cuerdas. 'Para cuando los vi, ya habían caído sobre mí.'

'Como un enjambre de saúvas,' dijo Joaquim, 'que no había oído siquiera un ruido tras la casa.'

'Como una bandada de buitres cayendo sobre la carroña,' respondió Sebastião, frotando los brazos, bastante lesionados. 'La diferencia é que no estaban vestidos de negro.'

'Lo sé. Vestían de color tierra, ¿no?'

'Color tierra y color de arbusto. Se mezclaban con los árboles *y a capoeira* de tal modo que ni los pude ver.'

Joaquim respiró hondo. La diferencia de los *cartésios* con los buitres no estaba solamente en el color de sus uniformes. Estaba en el hecho de que podrían haberlos matado a los dos si hubiesen querido.

Sacrificados, destrozados, aniquilados por completo. Su presencia allí solo había sido una pequeña demostración de poder.

Y la carta, una manifestación de su voluntad.

∗

Joaquim pasó dos semanas visitando el registro de la comarca en Vila Rica en busca de algún contrato antiguo que le pudiese dar una pista, cualquier cosa. No encontraba nada. Llegó a pensar en ir a Rio, pero todos los documentos de la mina estaban en Vila Rica, y además tenía mucho que hacer allí.

Al final de cada día, volvía a casa y de allí se dirigía a la mina. Trabajaba, ora solo, ora con Sebastião, en los bocetos dejados por Antônio Eustáquio. En nuevas placas para el pecho, la espalda, las piernas, los brazos. En algunas mejoras que el viejo ingeniero no había imaginado, pero que Joaquim consideró interesantes. En fin, nuevas armaduras para nuevos tiempos.

Y ese era el problema. El tiempo.

∗

A primeros de febrero, recibió una visita en la botica.

'Salve, señor Joaquim,' dijo el hombre, de barbilla cuadrada.

'¿Cómo le va, Coronel?' respondió Joaquim. '¿Viene a quitarse un diente?'

El otro rio y sacudió la cabeza: '¡Válgame Dios! Aun no me hace falta. Este cuerpo es fuerte y tengo todos los dientes, con la gracia de Nuestro Señor Jesucristo. Solo he venido a tener unas palabras con usted, si tiene algún tiempo.'

'Incluso me vendría bien hacer una pausa. ¿Qué ordena el señor?'

'Adivine, señor Joaquim. Este humilde siervo de Dios no manda nada, apenas pide. Es una cosa simple y que no le va a exigir demasiado. En realidad, hasta pienso lo contrario: le quitará un peso de la espalda.'

'¿Y qué peso sería ese?'

'El señor ha de saber las cosas que se van diciendo por ahí. El señor, como boticario y dentista, ha debido de oír muchas conversaciones …'

'Conversaciones al azar …'

Entonces Silvério se volvió contra él en un arrebato que le sorprendió: '¡Eso lo debe decidir la autoridad, señor Joaquim! ¿O no?'

'Por supuesto que sí,' Joaquim respondió sin miedo, pero con desconfianza. '¿Pero de qué autoridad habla el coronel?'

Entonces Silvério dos Reis sonrió de oreja a oreja. Una sonrisa perturbadora para Joaquim.

'La autoridad con la que me ha investido el vizconde de Barbacena. ¿O acaso el señor no sabe que soy el nuevo comandante de los milicianos de Vila Rica?'

Joaquim alzó las cejas.

'¿Conque el señor tiene ahora más de trescientos hombres consigo?'

'Todos los hombres que el virrey tenga a bien concederme, señor Joaquim. Hombres mejores que los nobles que andan por ahí compartiendo secretos en veladas poéticas ...'

'Entonces, ¿quiere el señor decirme qué *manda*, coronel?'

A Silvério no se le borró la sonrisa de la cara. Irritaba a Joaquim, que no conseguía ocultarlo y maldecía por su gran transparencia.

'Pues muy bien. Yo mando lo que el señor comparezca mañana en Casa dos Contos para un interrogatorio oficial.'

Joaquim se fijó bien en los ojos de Silvério.

'¿Se puede saber por qué, coronel?'

Silvério dejó caer una mano pesada llena de dedos gordos en el hombro de Joaquim.

'Recapacite, hombre. Esa revolucioncilla suya no va a servir para nada. Todo el mundo se está dando cuenta. Domingos, Francisco Lopes, Malheiro do Lago, todo el mundo ha sido puesto ya depuesto a cambio de condonar sus deudas. Si usted va mañana a hacer su denuncia formal, le garantizo personalmente que cualquier deuda que pueda tener le será perdonada.'

'Yo no tengo deuda alguna con Portugal, coronel.'

Silvério miró fijamente a Joaquim.

'Ahí se equivoca, señor Joaquim. Todo traidor tiene deudas con la Patria a la que abandona.'

*

Nada más se dijo, no hizo falta. Aquella tarde, Joaquim le encargó a su socio que cerrase la botica y partió hacia la hacienda. Escoltado por dos soldados comandados por Silvério dos Reis, que no quería arriesgarse a una posible fuga de uno de los principales conspiradores. Los soldados debían montar guardia en la hacienda durante toda la noche y conducir a Joaquim hasta Casa dos Contos la mañana siguiente.

Y sería eso mismo lo que habría pasado de no ser por una nube de langostas en el medio del camino.

Fue tan rápido que solo después Joaquim sería capaz de establecer la comparación, y aun así, cada vez que recordaba lo sucedido, metáforas diferentes tomaban el lugar de la plaga bíblica: remolino, plaga de ranas, no faltaron apariciones del otro mundo ni pesadillas del otro, él que no era de dar crédito ante ese tipo de cosas (*não faltaram nem assombrações do outro mundo nem pesadelos do outro*). Pero nadie que presenciase a los *cartésios* en acción y viviese para contarlo volvía a ser la misma persona.

Ciertamente, los dos soldados no volvieron: en pocos segundos el polvo de la carretera envolvió a Joaquim, una confusión de manos, pies y gritos ahogados, un relincho o dos de caballos que rodeaban al suyo. Nada más que eso, nada más que algunos segundos de un alboroto que ni a eso llegó, de tan extrañamente silencioso que era.

Y los dos hombres estaban caídos en el suelo, las gargantas cortadas. Sus caballos ya no estaban. Solamente Joaquim, aun montado en el suyo.

Dominó el escalofrío que le empezaba a subir por la espina y clavó las espuelas en el lomo del caballo. Ahora ya no había marcha atrás.

*

Cuando llegó a la casa de la hacienda, su objetivo era uno solo: recoger las armaduras y huir a Rio de Janeiro. Allí buscaría ayuda. Si se quedase, solo conseguiría ser acusado de asesinar a dos soldados. No habría más esperanza de perdón para él, si es que en algún momento la hubiese tenido.

Pero alguien lo esperaba junto a la entrada.

Cláudio.

Le pareció extraño ver a su amigo allí. El más callado de los colegas revolucionarios, Cláudio Manoel da Costa era uno de los más viejos del grupo. Tenía ya casi sesenta años, y era un hacendado en buena posición. Demostraba tanta insatisfacción como los demás, pero sus beneficios daban y sobraban incluso pagando su cuota de la Derrama. A Joaquim siempre le había parecido curiosa la participación de Cláudio en la tentativa de revolución.

Un pensamiento sombrío se apoderó de él al instante en el que se apeó del caballo. ¿Estaría allí a sueldo del virrey? ¿Sería Cláudio Manoel da Costa uno de los denunciantes?

Antes, sin embargo, de que pudiese expresar cualquiera de sus dudas, Cláudio levantó su mano derecha y le dijo dos simples palabras, en un tono de voz serio, casi mecánico: 'Cincuenta armaduras.'

Eran las mismas palabras que estaban escritas en la carta que el líder del grupo de los *cartésios* le había entregado semanas antes.

'¿Usted, Cláudio?' preguntó pasmado.

Su colega bajó la mano y respondió: 'Soluciones desesperadas para tiempos difíciles.'

'Pero ¿un pacto con los *cartésios*?'

Cláudio sacudió la cabeza en negativa.

'Un *contrato*, Joaquim. Un contrato firmado entre Antônio Eustáquio y la República de Nueva Holanda, y cuya recaudación le fue entregada hace tres semanas por una patrulla avanzada del Regimiento de los Cartesianos.'

'¿Y cuál es su parte en esto?'

'La misma de siempre, Joaquim. Así como usted, un hombre de buena posición, un hombre de carácter, que se revela contra el rumbo que este país ha tomado y dispuesto a hacer todo lo que esté a mi alcance para salvarlo de las manos de la metrópoli.'

'¿Incluso entregarlo en bandeja a los holandeses?'

Cláudio respondió y comenzó a cantar, casi en tono profesional: 'Considere esto una especie de gran juego, Joaquim, un ajedrez político en el que se entrega a la reina para que el rey no caiga. La metáfora monárquica resulta ruin en un momento como este, lo sé, pero el ajedrez resulta el mejor ejemplo.'

'Vila Rica es la reina, entonces.'

'Exacto.'

'¿Y el resto de Brasil?'

'Libre de Portugal. Ese es el nuevo contrato con la Nueva Holanda.'

'¿Y quién lo firma?'

'Eso, mi viejo amigo,' le explicó, en un tono más sombrío, 'no se lo puedo decir.'

'¿Y si no tuviese las cincuenta armaduras?'

'Sería lamentable, pero no constituiría una carga significativa para nuestra empresa. Usted podría compensar la falta de esas armaduras.'

'¿Cómo?'

Solo entonces Cláudio sonrió. Una sonrisa demasiado parecida a la de Silvério dos Reis. Joaquim temió lo que estaría por venir.

*

Vino de frente, por detrás y por los flancos.

La Toma de Vila Rica sucedió la noche del 13 de Febrero de 1789.

Las calles de la ciudad estaban en silencio y en silencio permanecieron durante toda la madrugada. En las sombras de los callejones y de las calles sin iluminación, las saúvas invadían la ciudad. Sus pasos no eran marciales como los del grupo con el que Joaquim se había topado semanas atrás en la entrada a la hacienda: aquello era una demostración de disciplina militar para civiles, nobles y clero.

Esto, entretanto, era lo que el Regimiento de los Cartesianos, herederos del entrenamiento militar de Renatus Cartesius, nombre latinizado del coronel francés René Descartes, sabían hacer mejor: ataques invisibles.

Unos decían que Descartes había inventado esas técnicas por sí mismo; otras fuentes, aparentemente más fiables, decían que se había servido no solo de su propio entrenamiento marcial sino que también había aprendido, durante una estancia diplomática en Japón, una metodología especial basada en el control del cuerpo y de la mente, estrategias de ocultación y uso de la fuerza del enemigo contra sí mismo. Su pequeño tratado *Discurso Sobre el Método de la Guerra*, que al principio había sido de uso exclusivo de los *cartésios*, circulaba ahora libremente por Nueva Holanda — como herramienta de reclutamiento, decían los más cínicos. Pero el hecho es que el Regimiento de los Cartesianos crecía y era respetado.

En la noche de la Toma, los pasos de los *cartésios* eran tan silenciosos que Joaquim se sentía como una campana ambulante. Por seguridad, se había apeado de su caballo a la entrada de la ciudad y lo había amarrado en una pequeña fuente de camino a la Plaza. Se había cubierta las placas del tronco con un gibón de cuero y se había quitado las espuelas de las botas. Encajó con cuidado las abrazaderas de los brazaletes, los probó para ver si no hacían ruido durante el camino, se dio por satisfecho y siguió.

No estaba solo. Cláudio lo había convencido de que sería mejor llevar por lo menos dos *cartésios* no solo como protección pero también como auxilio. En el calor de la refriega, toda ayuda era poca. Pero

Joaquim no estaba muy seguro de que estuviesen allí para protegerlo o para para ejercer la misma función que los soldados de Silvério.

Fuese como fuese, él cumpliría con su parte. Como hombre de bien.

Hombre.

Alférez.

Tiradentes.

Quim.

Joaquim José da Silva Xavier.

∗

En la entrada de la mina, Sebastião terminaba de ponerse la armadura. No se había parado a ponerse el jubón ni las espuelas —solo se había calzado las botas para no perder el equilibro con la gran cantidad de metal que llevaba. Siempre preferiría andar de pie en el suelo, o como mucho usando alpargatas en días de fiesta.

Pero aquella noche el barullo iba a ser bueno.

Había enviado a Conceição a Irmandade dos Pretos, en las afueras de la ciudad. 'En momentos como este es bueno ser invisible,' pensaba.

'El esclavo solo es bueno en el campo y en la cama,' dicen los blancos.

Todos unos buenos hijos de puta.

Joaquim no era mal señor, hasta donde se podría decir que un señor fuese bueno para su esclavo, pero Sebastião había aprendido a duras penas, tanto con sus padres como con las marcas de latigazos que tenía en su propia espalda, que no hay buen señor. Lo bueno es ser libre.

Terminó de encajar la bayoneta de *alvado* en el brazalete derecho. Sebastião tenía una última tarea que realizar para Joaquim, y la realizaría con gusto, porque así podría cobrarse su libertad.

∗

Cuando Joaquim llegó a las inmediaciones de Casa dos Contos, el *cartésio* de su izquierda le hizo un gesto para que se fijase en el tejado.

Solo con mucho esfuerzo consiguió percibir que la parte alta de Casa dos Contos estaba llena de *cartésios*, encogidos y encaramados como gárgolas de alguna catedral europea de la Edad Media.

Y abajo, en cada esquina de la casa, un soldado armado con un fusil al hombro montaba guardia, sin importarle el que estaba inmediatamente sobre su cabeza.

Joaquim asintió asombrado durante varios minutos. Como si fuesen títeres movidos por cordeles invisibles, de repente tiraron violentamente hacia arriba de los dos soldados que podía ver desde donde estaba, por el cuello. Y antes de que sus fusiles cayesen al suelo, lo mismo pasó con ellos: las armas subieron a los cielos como pájaros. Durante toda esa acción, no se oyó ni un solo ruido.

'Sin pegar un solo tiro,' pensó Joaquim, sintiéndose un peso muerto.

El *cartésio* de su derecha le hizo un gesto. El camino estaba libre. Podrían entrar en Casa dos Contos.

*

Hasta donde Sebastião podía ver, eran seis. Pero esta vez estaba preparado.

Las antorchas que había dejado encendidas a lo largo del camino empezaron a apagarse de repente, sin siquiera un soplo de viento. Desde donde estaba, escondido en la entrada de la mina también oscurecida, esperó que los *cartésios* se fuesen acercando.

Cuando había dicho a Joaquim que todo había sucedido demasiado rápido cuando los soldados holandeses lo habían atacado, no mentía; pero tampoco había contado toda la verdad. Los *cartésios* eran sorprendentemente rápidos aunque tal vez no debería ser tan sorprendente, ya que Sebastião pudo ver mulatos e indígenas en medio de tanto blanco y rubio. Durante muchos días estuvo pensando: ¿cómo habrían conseguido acercarse a él sin hacer ruido? Y concluyó que aquello había sido por la suma de dos cosas: muy buenos conocimientos de lucha y su propia distracción.

'Muy bien,' pensó Sebastião, mientras esperaba que los *cartésios* le obsequiasen con el aroma de su gracia. 'Son muchos, pero yo también sé luchar.'

Cuando la primera pareja se acercó a la entrada de la mina — otra cosa que Sebastião había observado era que siempre atacaban en parejas — o negro no dudó: disparó las dos pistolas que Joaquim le había dejado.

Oyó un grito ahogado. La hora había llegado.

Salió corriendo de la boca de la mina y se dirigió hacia su derecha. En aquel mismo momento sintió una cuerda alrededor del cuello y un golpe seco en el estómago. El *cartésio* que lo había golpeado soltó un rugido de dolor al sentir la placa de hierro en la mano desnuda, pero Sebastião no pudo aprovechar el momento para atacarle: levantó la mano derecha y, girando la bayoneta encajada en el brazalete, comenzó a cortar la cuerda al tiempo que reculaba para evitar el tirón que lo ahogaba.

Esto dio tiempo a la pareja de *cartésios* que estaba tras él para agarrarlo.

Pero no antes de que lanzase la pierna derecha hacia atrás y le soltase una patada a uno de ellos. La gravedad hizo el resto: perdiendo su punto de apoyo, el otro *cartésio* se desequilibró durante una fracción de segundo, y para un maestro de la capoeira como Sebastião eso bastaba. Extendió la pierna y le atinó al holandés en el pecho con un golpe de martillo. Pudo oír cómo se le quebraban las costillas.

Fue entonces cuando los otros doce *cartésios* lo rodearon.

Sebastião soltó una sonrisa burlona. Tenía la seguridad de que había más soldados escondido entre los matojos, esperando.

'Pueden unirse ustedes también,' los desafió. 'Aun no me han hecho sudar.'

Uno de los *cartésios* dio un paso al frente y alzó una mano, entonando en una voz de tono mecánico: 'La mina nos pertenece. Esta lucha es innecesaria.'

'Puede que la ciudad sea suya; pero no la mina.'

'¿Por qué defiende una tierra que no es suya?'

'¿Y quién le dice que esta tierra no es mía?' respondió Sebastião indignado. 'Vivo aquí desde que nací. Mi padre llegó aquí desde África siendo un niño. Este suelo y esta mina son más míos que de cualquier blanco.'

El *cartésio* se mantuvo en silencio durante varios segundos. Inclinó la cabeza, sin apartar la vista de Sebastião.

'Usted podría sernos útil.'

Sebastião rio.

'Lo que yo quiero es ser libre. En mi tierra, no en la de otros. Y sé bien lo que le pasó a mi padre cuando salió de su tierra para venir a vivir aquí.'

'Puede quedarse la mina.'

'¿Cómo?'

'Un contrato,' dijo el *cartésio*. 'Puede quedarse con la propiedad de la hacienda. La mina es suya, pero no podrá trabajar en ella solo. Alquiler.

Pagamos bien. Y usted se comprará su libertad.'

'¿Y qué pasa con el señor Joaquim?' Sebastião no se dio cuenta de que estaba preocupado por el hombre que había adquirido su posesión del viejo Antônio Eustáquio, pero cuando se dio cuenta ya las palabras habían volado de su boca.

'Tenemos otra propuesta para el señor Joaquim,' respondió el *cartésio*. 'No podrá negarse.'

*

Joaquim entró en Casa dos Contos acompañado de ocho *cartésios*: los dos de su escolta o otros seis que habían descendido sin hacer ruido por las paredes del edificio.

Luego, en el patio de entrada había casi veinte soldados armados de la guarnición del virrey. Joaquim respiró hondo.

'Deberían haber traído armas,' le dijo al *cartésio* de su derecha.

'No necesitamos armas,' respondió el otro.

Entonces comenzó la batalla.

Joaquim sintió los impactos de los tiros en el pecho. Perdió el aliento, pero no se paró para verificar si la placa del pecho había sufrido algún daño. Si estaba de pie era porque había funcionado. Corrió en dirección al soldado más próximo y alzó el brazo derecho. La pistola que a duras penas había conseguido adaptar a su brazalete pesaba más de un kilo, pero Joaquim se había entrenado mucho todos los días para aquel momento.

El tiro resultó certero en la cara del soldado.

Cuando se giró para seguir en dirección al próximo, el suelo ya estaba lleno de soldados muertos. Solo un *cartésio* yacía en el suelo, víctima de un tiro a quema ropa en la cabeza. Los demás ya estaban tomando posiciones y recorriendo el local lo más rápidamente posible. Porque la señal de alerta ya había sido dada.

'¡En nombre de Dios! ¿Qué es eso?' fue el grito que se oyó, desde el otro lado del patio.

Silvério dos Reis se aproximaba a grandes pasos, pistola en una mano, sable en la otra. Tras él, un pelotón de soldados se derramaba patio adentro. Cuando se fijó bien en él, cubierto con placas de hierro, no contuvo su furia.

'¡Usted! ¿Cómo se atreve a venir aquí armado?' le gritó Silvério. '¿Y con esos soldados holandeses?'

'Coronel Joaquim Silvério dos Reis,' dijo Joaquim, siguiendo el plan acordado la víspera con Cláudio. 'Considérese preso en nombre del Gobierno Provisional de la República de Brasil.'

'¿República de Brasil? Usted ha venido a tomar Vila Rica para los holandeses, ¡traidor cobarde!' gimió Silvério, sopesando la pistola en una mano y alzando el sable. 'Exijo un enfrentamiento hombre a hombre.'

Joaquim simplemente alzó el brazalete izquierdo. La bayoneta encajada relució a la luz de las antorchas.

Y se lanzaron uno contra otro.

Joaquim tenía la ventaja de manejar un arma corta y más sencilla de manejar. En compensación, Silvério no cargaba consigo el peso de una armadura.

La primera sangre surgió del rostro de Joaquim, que solo entonces pensó que debería haber fabricado también el yelmo y la máscara que estaban en el proyecto original de Antônio Eustáquio. Pero fue un corte superficial, y, a esos, Joaquim ya estaba acostumbrado: avanzó y cargó con la bayoneta en dirección al vientre de Silvério, que rechazó el golpe con la guarda de su sable.

Joaquim se retiró un paso y sintió la bota vacilar por la falta de espuelas. Fue entonces cuando Silvério vio su ventaja. Avanzó con todo sobre Joaquim y lo empujó.

Joaquim cayó de espaldas. El impacto fue tan fuerte que lo sacudió de dientes a costillas. Y descubrió otra cosa que percibió y no había ensayado en todo aquel tiempo: Cómo levantarse con todo ese peso tras una caída.

Silvério arremetió con el sable sobre Joaquim. Le miró al cuello. Joaquim consiguió levantar los brazaletes cruzados; aun así, el sable logró rascar una pequeña fisura entre el pequeño espacio que quedó entre los brazaletes; pero no llegó a clavarse en el cuello de Joaquim porque giró la cabeza con un gran esfuerzo en el último momento. Pero sintió la oreja derecha ardiendo.

Silvério alzó el sable para el golpe de misericordia. Joaquim reunió todas las fuerzas para un golpe que le pudiese dar un momento de descanso. El sudor le quemaba los ojos; se le hacía difícil ver algo.

Metió la bayoneta en la cintura de Silvério casi sin querer.

Silvério todavía intentó esquivarlo, pero su peso fue su ruina. Cayó sobre Joaquim y la bayoneta se enterró hasta el fondo. Silvério se estremeció. Joaquim empujó la bayoneta; cuando consiguió salir de debajo del cuerpo del coronel, estaba empapado de sangre y heces.

Se levantó a duras penas, aturdido, los oídos zumbando. Empujó el aire con dificultad y trató en vano de limpiarse con terrones de tierra. Por lo demás, no era preciso hacer nada más.

Todos los soldados del virrey estaban muertos.

El patio estaba extrañamente vacío. Algún *cartésio* que otro aun recorría la zona, pero los demás habían desaparecido. Solo una persona estaba de más en aquel sangriento escenario.

Cláudio Manoel da Costa.

Se acercó a Joaquim e puso la mano sobre su hombro.

'¿Está usted bien?'

'Lo estoy,' respondió. 'Ninguna herida grave.'

'Estupendo. Tenemos mucho que hacer.'

'¿Y Barbacena?'

'Ya nos estamos encargando de él. Lo más importante es que somos independientes. Al fin.'

'¿Todos?' Joaquim miró a su alrededor. A los *cartésios* que ya no estaban.

'No se preocupe por eso, *Comandante* Joaquim José. Usted es ahora el símbolo de una nueva Vila Rica. De un nuevo Brasil, libertado de la metrópoli portuguesa. Y esto es solo el principio.'

Joaquim se quedó en silencio. Si aquello era solo el principio, Dios le librase de ver cómo terminaría.

*

Cuando amaneció, las calles de Vila Rica seguían en silencio. Pero esta vez el silencio era diferente.

A los milicianos que se habían dedicado a amedrentar a los habitantes de la ciudad ya no se les veía en ninguna ciudad. Realmente, no quedaba soldado alguno en Vila Rica. Ninguno que la gente pudiese ver.

Los *cartésios* andaban por la ciudad, vestidos como ciudadanos comunes. Los más rubios o pelirrojos se llevaban alguna que otra mala mirada, pero la tregua entre Brasil y Nueva Holanda ya existía desde hacía años y nadie era hostilizado solo por parecer holandés. El comercio entre ambas naciones no era incentivado, pero existía; y Vila Rica era una de las capitanías brasileñas más abiertas al libre comercio.

Aquel mismo día fue publicado un aviso en la puerta de Casa dos

Contos, haciendo saber a toda la población de Vila Rica que Joaquim Silvério dos Reis había sido ejecutado por traición, así como el vizconde de Barbacena, en São João Del Rei. Y que se instauraba, a partir de aquella fecha, el Gobierno Provisional de la República de Brasil, teniendo como presidente a Alvarenga Peixoto, como vicepresidente a Tomás Antônio Gonzaga y a Cláudio Manoel da Costa como *Ouvidor-Geral*.

Pero los rumores que corrían por la ciudad no hablaban sobre los nuevos gobernantes, sino del extraño hombre cubierto por una armadura de metal, que había vengado en solitario al pueblo brasileño de Vila Rica y de Minas Gerais del yugo portugués — los detalles de cómo había sucedido exactamente, sin embargo, no eran del conocimiento del populacho, por lo que cada uno daba su versión particular de los hecho — y que había sido recomendado para el puesto de Comandante en Jefe de la Guardia Republicana. Joaquim José da Silva Xavier.

El antiguo dueño de la botica ya había recibido otro nombre de boca de la propia población, que gritaba su nuevo nombre en las calles y le daba vivas. De *Tiradentes* nunca más se oyó hablar. El protector supremo de Vila Rica era ahora el Alférez de Hierro.

STEAM PUNK

WRITERS AROUND THE WORLD

HEIRS

Germany

HEIRS

By Marcus R. Gilman

I

Admiral Von Köpitz was sitting comfortably in his armchair in Friedrichshafen Zeppelin base's officer's mess. Behind him, the panoramic window opened to a beautiful view of Lake Constance and the Zeppelins of 3rd Air Fleet. They were silver now. Silver hulls meant peace; in times of conflict, or during manoeuvres, their hull colour would change to sky-grey by the flick of a switch.

At the moment, 3rd Airfleet's duty consisted solely of patrolling and securing the French-German border with bases in Friedrichshafen, Mannheim and Metz, while the Bavarian Air Corps had a base in Strasbourg. Patrol duty was a boring assignment. Except for mutual mistrust, there was little tension between the German Empire and the Second French Empire. The German zeppelin patrols and their counterparts in French airships had developed a rather friendly understanding. It was not uncommon to exchange salutes and greetings via Morse code at Christmas time.

The afternoon sun reflected off the hulls of moored zeppelins, bathing the room in silvery-red light and giving the Admiral's chair a reddish aura. To the younger man on the other side of the desk, he looked almost like an ancient deity seated on his throne.

"So, Captain, what do you think of LZ Württemberg?" he said, referring to the craft they had toured the whole morning together with chief engineer Gruson.

"She seems to be a very fine zeppelin, the most advanced in the fleet, I presume." answered Captain Albrecht Von Kober, who had only the week before been transferred to Zeppelin Base Friedrichshafen from Berlin.

"That's correct." The admiral took a sip of his cognac. "Some of the technology the Württemberg carries has not been installed on any other zeppelin or other craft. There is more to come, Gruson told you,

I am sure."

Kapitän Von Kober nodded.

"We need a man with your track record for a craft like her." the Admiral added.

"So you are offering me the command of the Württemberg?"

"Yes, Captain, I do."

Von Kober smiled. "Just one more thing I would like to know, Admiral."

"Yes?"

"Assuming I take command, where would the first mission take me?"

"Well, it would be a very long-range mission. It would take you to the Pacific Pole of Inaccessibility. The point of the high seas furthest removed from any point of dry land, and back. I have to warn you, though. The first week or two will be aerial photography of certain important areas between here and the Bosporus. After that, however, it is India and the open Pacific."

"Count me in, Admiral."

Two cognac glasses chimed.

Kapitän Von Kober spent most of the next two weeks assembling the crew and inspecting the progress of the work on *his* zeppelin. Admiral Von Köpitz had very precise ideas how the crew was to be made up. An elite crew – no enlisted men at all would serve on LZ Württemberg, at least for now. It would consist of a technical staff, led by Gruson, one of the most gifted engineers in the Imperial Zeppelin Corps, with whom Von Kober had served before. The command crew would be led by Von Kober himself. In addition, there would be a physician, Dr. Hartmann, a Zeppelin Corps veteran, and a medic. All in all, the crew would be made up of 20 men, six commissioned and fourteen non-commissioned officers. Even the two cooks would have to have some skills in repairing and maintaining machinery. The LZ Württemberg was one valuable piece of equipment; it should not fall prey to accidents on its first cruise.

After this mission, the Württemberg would also receive its full complement of troops. There was, after all, enough space to accommodate at least 25 additional men with ease.

"Gentlemen," the admiral began. "You have all been given the details of this mission, so I can be brief." He indicated the map spread out they had all gathered around. "As you know, your first stop will be Vienna. No problem there. From Vienna, you will take the Württemberg to Istanbul, but this will take some time. We have an excellent opportunity to test our newest aerial surveillance equipment and get a more detailed map of, say, the Carpathian Mountains, in case we would one day like to build a forward supply depot there. Just in case. The more precise our maps of the area between here and Istanbul are, the better."

They all had a vague idea what the admiral was on about. Although the Ottoman Empire was on friendly terms with the German Empire, the same was not true regarding Russia and Austria-Bohemia or any of the other states in the region from Bulgaria to Serbia to Greece. If tensions would rise again, every extra bit of information could be crucial.

"From Istanbul" the admiral continued, "you will set course to our base Orientis near Basra. Orientis is a well-equipped base, so if you need any repairs, you can do it there. Also, there will be some more aerial surveillance along the way; this, however, is actually by request of the Sultan. The information we draw out of it is just a beneficent side-effect."

This was met with general agreement.

The admiral went over to the other side of the map table and continued "After the stop at Orientis you will set a course via India and the Nicobar Islands to Palau." He drew the course of the Zeppelin with a Zeiss-indicator, turning the map along the route slightly more luminous.

"At Palau, there will be another brief stop. You will then proceed towards the Pole of Inaccessibility. This will also be your longest stretch of uninterrupted flight. If our estimates are correct, you should be able to make it back to India without the need to refuel. From India you will fly to Orientis and from there directly to Friedrichshafen. Including time for possible repairs and upgrades at Orientis, we expect you back here by May 15th. The Kaiser and King Karl of Württemberg are following the progress of this expedition very closely, so turn it into a great success and do honour to your country."

The officers shared cigars and then proceeded towards the airfield, where the rest of the crew, the construction workers, engineers and a military band were already waiting.

"Kapitän Von Kober, I shall see you again in about six weeks. Take good care of your zeppelin. It is very dear to me, too."

"I will, Admiral. *Gott mit uns*!" He saluted.

"*Furchtlos und Treu*!" answered the Admiral.

The crew filed into the zeppelin, the clamps holding it to the ground were released and, with the marching band playing the Württemberg Anthem and the soldiers on the ground shouting booming Hurrays, LZ Württemberg gained altitude and turned towards the Alps.

After a brief visit to Vienna, the Württemberg set course towards the young state of Romania. Although the zeppelin could easily cruise at around 50 knots, orders demanded a far slower pace. The primary mission now was to create a detailed map of certain very precisely defined areas. They would search out possible sites for forward supply depots and staging areas. If they were lucky, they would even find a place to build a secret Zeppelin hangar. The aerial reconnaissance and photography also needed very exact timing; all target areas had to be flown over during the hours of daylight. Every hour, Von Kober, Vogel or the navigators Richnow and Gustavson checked their position and adjusted speed and course accordingly.

At first, the Württemberg followed the Danube, then changed course towards the Carpathian Mountains. Below them, dark forests clung to mountains like a green silken sheet. Transylvania was a country of breathtaking beauty. Whenever they passed over a village, the inhabitants, especially the children, would wave and cheer. Zeppelins were signs of progress and this part of Europe surely needed some.

Since they cruised over friendly territory, duty was less regulated. In the evening, they would listen to music and news sent from Berlin, Paris and London through the æther.

Their tasks completed, they turned southwest, to the Balkans and Greece, finally arriving at Istanbul on the 8th of April.

The ancient city had seen much change during the centuries, perhaps more than any other city, and the rise and fall or decline of two empires. The Ottoman Empire had conquered and replaced the Byzantine Romans. Now the Turks were themselves besieged on all sides. After checking Austria and Russia for several centuries, much needed reforms had failed and the state was socially and militarily trapped in an earlier age.

Strangely enough, now the Ottomans were the only nation receiving support and technological aid from Britain, France and Germany. Germany and the Ottomans had been on friendly terms for a long time, mainly because of trade. France and Britain both needed an ally of sorts in case their friend Russia would ever threaten their possessions in Asia. Politics sure were complicated.

LZ Württemberg touched down on a field outside the city walls. At one end a sturdy wooden tower, topped by a Morse light, had been erected. But now, in broad daylight, a soldier was giving instructions the traditional way, using flag signals.

According to the information Kapitän Von Kober had received, Sultan Yusuf wanted to inspect the Württemberg and was also interested in ordering another squadron from the yards in Friedrichshafen.

When they arrived, however, they were informed by the German military attache to the Sultan's court, Baron Von Ledow, that Sultan Yussuf had left three days earlier for a visit to the United States of America. They had a very friendly audience with the Grand Vizier Hakan Pasha instead. He apologised for the inconvenience and had gifts sent to the German zeppelin; cigars, dried fruit and several sacks full of spices which would be available in Germany only at ridiculous prices.

The zeppelin also attracted some attention, zeppelin visits to the Ottoman Empire still being quite rare. A Yüzbası, or captain of the army, and two junior officers were given a brief tour of LZ Württemberg with the help of a local teacher who spoke fluent German.

Leaving Istanbul behind three days later, the Württemberg was now flying into territory outside easy reach of the regular air patrols of the Great Powers. There had been instances of pirates attacking and capturing air-yachts and freight airships in the past. The guns were manned around the clock.

Kapitän Von Kober was standing in the forward observation post just below the cockpit. The buttons of his uniform jacket were undone, but he was unwilling to take it off, despite the sun heating the gondola to almost uncomfortable levels. According to the instruments, outside was a dead calm, so no wind would relieve them.

"Damn, I wish we could rise higher into cooler air, but we still have some photographs to take on our way to Orientis," he complained to Lieutenant Richnow, scanning the horizon ahead through binoculars, ever vigilant of suspicious airships.

"The heat won't be a problem for very much longer, Captain," came the voice of the second navigator Gustavson from above. "Air pressure has dropped markedly in the last hour; those clouds over the horizon in the north-east are bringing a thunderstorm."

Von Kober raised his binoculars and grinned. "Very well." He climbed up the ladder into the cockpit. "Judging from the data we have so far, Ensign Gustavson, do you think we can take our beauty into the storm?"

"It could be a very intense episode, Captain. But we should still be able to climb beyond the clouds should we get tossed about too much."

"Well, who dares wins."

First the wind hit the zeppelin, slowing its progress slightly, then the rain, blurring the view in a matter of seconds. Gustavson switched on the wipers and the vision cleared and blurred in short intervals. Moments later, they saw the first forks of lightning flashing close by.

"I wish we had some Tesla converters installed," remarked Gruson "This would be an ideal environment for them."

"Yes," agreed Kaleun Vogel, "but they are still far too bulky to be installed in a flying craft."

Suddenly, everybody on board felt their stomachs lurch. Von Kober was almost swept off his feet and Gruson stumbled into a panel.

Without warning the Württemberg again lost height in another downburst. Von Kober's innards knotted up. "Richnow, report altitude."

"Approximately 120 meters above ground, Herr Kapitän. Recommend immediate steep climb."

"Yes, steep climb, full throttle." He pulled the master-tube which connected to every single room and chamber of the craft.

"Attention all stations, we are going for an extreme climb beyond the cloud level. Temperatures are likely to drop below freezing and breather-masks will be necessary. Everyone, get ready. "

Engineer Gruson pushed himself away from the panel and headed for the door."I am going to check on the engines during the climb and high altitude flight," he said. Kapitän Von Kober nodded. "Yes, good idea. Make a note of anything unusual."

He would not have had to say that. Gruson was a Prussian. He would check on the engines and make a report with Teutonic efficiency.

Gruson took a mask from the locker in the cockpit, put it on and left. Halfway to the boiler room he started to feel the upward tilt of the zeppelin climbing, which meant that he, heading towards the stern, was now walking down a steep metal walkway. He grabbed the rails and let himself be pulled down towards the boiler room. When he entered, Gruson found the mechanics Dustermann and Obermooser strapped into their chairs waiting for the zeppelin to fly level again so they could continue their work.

LZ Württemberg continued climbing and soon she broke through the clouds and once again cruised in sunlight.

III

The rough encounter with the thunderstorm remained the only exciting episode of this part of the journey. The following days became increasingly monotonous. They were passing over almost uninhabited wasteland, dotted with shrubby growth and the occasional trace of water. Where there was water, vegetation was more abundant and those places sparkled like emeralds amidst the barren landscape. They were not taking any more photographs, either. All they had to do was measure the distances between certain waypoints and note settlements that did not appear on the maps provided by the Ottoman ambassador to Berlin.

To break the monotony, Von Kober had a few drills performed. This also helped the crew stay focused; you never knew if a pirate airship might show up, even though it was unlikely this far from their usual haunts.

The only other airships the Württemberg actually encountered were two British dirigibles, probably coming out of Oman and heading home.

At about eight o'clock in the evening of April 16th the æthergraph started clicking.

"That was fast, I did not expect they were so keenly awaiting our arrival."

"It's not Orientis, Lieutenant." Kaleun Vogel was already reading the Morse code printout delivered by the machine. "It's a message from Baron Von Ledow. We are to return to Istanbul immediately."

They exchanged glances.

"Anything else?"

"No, Captain, that's it."

Von Kober reached for the master-tube. "Attention everyone, we are changing course back to Istanbul. Boiler room, full speed, keep me informed how the new equipment is doing."

IV

Marechal de Mac-Mahon, Prime Minister of the French Empire, hurried down the corridor to the Emperor's study. The captain of the Old Guard on duty saluted and quickly opened the door.

After a few minutes, the captain noticed the conversation inside becoming more and more agitated.

Sudden silence was followed by Napoleon III's cry. "He did what?"

The door flew open and the old Emperor strode out, his metal exoskeleton hissing, followed by the Marechal.

V

The sun's light was just perfect. Marcel always preferred to assemble his models at his study's window. Natural light was so much better than electric lamps. He carefully fixed the sail to the mast and held it a few seconds, so the glue would really fuse the parts.

A car stopped outside. This would be his wife's seamstress. He glanced at the clock set into his desk. She was rather early today.

Someone came rushing up the stairs and, by the sounds of it, almost stumbled several times.

Marcel quickly got up and had just enough time to open his arms and bow down slightly before his son came bursting into the room. He caught the three-year old, using Alexandre's momentum to lift the boy and circle with him through the room. His son screamed for joy.

"Pappa, Uncle Patrice is here to see you and he looks like the Emperor," he squealed excitedly when his father had stopped spinning around.

"Uncle Patrice? Mon Dieu, I wonder what he wants..." Marcel's astonishment was played for his son's benefit. This could only mean one thing: the sudden end of his holiday.

He put his son down and went over to the wardrobe. Let's get dressed for the event, he thought.

"Capitain Baquoy."

Marcel saluted. "Marechal de Mac-Mahon."

"I am sorry to bring your well-earned holiday to a sudden end."
He handed the Captain an envelope, sealed with the personal seal of
Napoleon III. Trouble.

VI

En route back to Istanbul, Kapitän Von Kober ordered a full
combat drill. The new spectral guns coupled with regular Mauser
cannons in their retractable turrets were test fired, the climbing, diving
and speeding ability tested as well as possible within the time frame they
had. The activity also kept the crew occupied; they all knew something
major must have happened for them to be recalled, so it was better to
be prepared.

Early the next morning, they reached Istanbul. Diving through thick
rainclouds towards the field below, they could see two Diesels and a
troop transport at the edge. Baron Von Ledow was already waiting, and
he was not alone.

Accompanying him were five people. One was immediately
recognisable: Prince Heinrich Von Stauffen, Count of Straubing. The
Prince was tall and handsome; he was also one of the richest men in
the German Empire and third in line to the throne of the Kingdom
of Bavaria. This made him one of the most sought-after bachelors
of the realm. Rumour had it both the Kaiser and Queen Victoria had
him marked as a possible match for a daughter, grand-daughter or
niece. The man next to him wore the uniform of an Oberleutnant of
the Bavarian Air Corps with markings identifying him as an engineer,
while others indicated a number of decorations. The other three were
civilians. Two ladies with a vague family resemblance, maybe sisters,
maybe cousins. Both were rather striking, especially the older one with
the mane of red hair. She was accompanied by a tall, burly man who
looked somewhat familiar.

Von Kober was puzzled about the civilians. He had heard rumours
about the Abwehr, the German Empire's secret service, employing
civilians with special talents. Maybe this was the case. And where did
he know the burly man from?

Greetings were exchanged and Baron Von Ledow introduced the
party; the Prince and his retinue were special envoys. Before Von Kober
could ask any questions, Prince Von Stauffen passed him a letter,
bearing the insignia of 3rd Airfleet. This was an official message from

Admiral Von Köpitz. A call to arms? But for this, a one word message via the æthergraph would have been enough. Nervously, Albrecht opened it. *My dear Albrecht.* Von Köpitz's handwriting. Albrecht read it, then read it again. He put it away and exchanged a nervous glance with the Bavarian aristocrat, who seemed just as unhappy with the situation as he now was.

"Well, your Highness, we have no time to lose."

Prince Von Stauffen and his retinue quickly boarded and LZ Württemberg set course for Anatolia.

VII

Birol drove his flock of goats over the hill. He had learned shepherding from his father, grandfather and uncles. It was a good way of life. The goats gave you milk, wool, leather, and they were fun to play with when he was a child. For the first ten years of his life, he had helped his family tend the flocks. Then the Sultan's men from the far away city had visited his village. Birol had been a strong boy, fast and nimble. He could not read but could count faster than anyone he knew. He could also find his way around the hills at night.

They had given his father more money than he had ever seen before in his life and Birol had left his village and gone to become a soldier. The first years had been harsh, then he had been send to Paris, to Berlin, to London. To learn.

Now he was back in his hills. The goats were still a little uneasy about the special animals. Clockwork in goatskins. He had reached the brow of the hill. Below, the German archeologist's camp – above, a German zeppelin. And here he stood, just a humble goat herder, and they would never know.

On a hill to the west, another flock was grazing. His friend Yasin had taken position.

Below LZ Württemberg, foothills stretched towards the horizon, slowly merging with Mount Hasan. Here, long ago, one of the greatest cities of early mankind had thrived.

Two days had passed since the Prince and his team had left the Württemberg and gone on their errand. All Von Kober and his crew could do was wait, either for a message from the ground or something else. It was the *something else* that worried him. Too many something elses.

How strangely moods transformed perception, he thought. Down there was a magnificent, exotic, almost alien landscape. He should be sitting there, drawing sketches of the volcano in his diary. Instead, he scanned the ground and the sky. Every boulder a sniper's hiding place. Every cart a mobile gun. Every speck on the horizon the scout of a fleet. Even the goat herders made him nervous.

Von Kober almost hoped for something to happen, to give him a vent for his tension. He fixed his binoculars on yet another point in the sky. After a few moments he adjusted focus and magnification.

"Richnow, possible airship north-north-west, take a look."

The second navigator swivelled the observation telescope around, taking a moment to find his mark.

"Confirmed, Herr Kapitän. Airship. French configuration. Heading our way."

Von Kober hurried up the ladder to the bridge and took the master-tube.

"Attention all stations. We have just spotted a French airship. Power up the turrets but do not extend. Boiler room, I want the Württemberg able to go to full speed, faster than ever before. Come up with something and do it fast."

"Herr Kapitän," came Richnow's voice from below. "The airship has just gone on a parallel course to ours. Ah, there's the name..." he paused.

"It's the Toulon."

The Toulon.

Every member of the Imperial Zeppelin Corps had heard of her, Captain Baquoy's vessel. Captain Baquoy, a living legend.

Captain Baquoy, the French Empire's most highly decorated captain. While on single patrol, ambushed by a pirate squadron over Siam, he came out of the engagement with six kills and not a single casualty on his side. Captain Baquoy, a personal friend of...

Oh my God! Albrecht thought. *Is that it? Is that what is going on down there?*

He went to the morse light.

On the bridge of DF Toulon, the French airmen had their binoculars fixed on the German zeppelin. They had been expecting a German craft, but not one like this. It looked almost like an oversized air yacht.

"LZ Württemberg, never heard of her. I haven't seen this shape before either. Looks rather slim," commented Lieutenant Martin.

"Yes, fragile," agreed First Officer Dequenne. "Nothing Gothic to it."

"The Germans have been working on a new class for a while. Could be the lead ship." Captain Baquoy was stuffing his pipe in the command-chair behind the officers. He did not intend to smoke, but the action alone calmed him and he needed his calm now. His orders had been vague and he was still not sure what to make of them, but they were the orders of Emperor Napoleon III himself, delivered to him by none other than the Prime Minister and Marechal of France.

"No gun turrets." Dequenne continued, listing the obvious features of the Württemberg to the captain. "At least nothing visible. Would they sent an unarmed craft? There is an unusual hatch almost at the tail. Could be an emplacement."

"We can't see its guns, I'm sure they are there."

"Merde."

"Morse signals, mon Capitain"

"What's the message?"

"Still sending... You misspelled that, boche... what?"

"What what? What's the message?"

"Mon Capitain, their captain has requested a meeting with you. He mentioned you by name, at a place of your choosing."

"It's a trap," warned Martin.

Baquoy thought for a moment. A wry grin appeared on his face. His officers had come to know and sometimes fear this grin. It heralded an unorthodox idea. "Tell them I will meet them on their zeppelin."

"Mon Capitain?"

"You heard me."

Baquoy sure is one daring bastard, Von Kober grudgingly admitted to himself when the answer came. There was no backing down now. He Morsed "Accepted" and "Please wait" then informed his crew. This caused no little commotion and direct objection from both Kaleun Vogel and Lieutenant Gruson. In the end, Von Kober had to pull rank. But they would take all precautions to give Baquoy as little a glimpse of the Württemberg as possible.

"What is taking them so long?" Martin was getting itchy.

"Martin, nothing to worry about, we just have to wait." Baquoy was standing next to him, his binoculars raised, trying to make out more details of the zeppelin. The two craft had closed in to about 300 metres of one another.

She is a beauty, he thought. He would not have expected the new class to look like this. This zeppelin was very different from the usual German designs. Not hard and edgy. Not a flying demonstration of force. He agreed with Dequenne's earlier observation. She looked fragile. Was she a pirate hunter? A frigate posing as a luxury yacht?

If this was the purpose of this new zeppelin class, then there had been a shift in the German Empire's foreign policy. Attacks on airships only happened in the Far East these days. Abyssinia had eliminated the pirate threat over Africa recently and also beaten the Royal Air Navy to it. Now the Abyssinians controlled a large swathe of Africa's airspace. The Philippine Sea and certain parts of China were the only hotbeds of pirate activity left.

Germany had interests in the Far East, then.

The Morse light of the zeppelin flashed again. Time to leave.

DF Toulon moved in closer to LZ Württemberg and extended her grapple-bridge.

Von Kober opened the hatch and stepped out. A warm wind blew between the two airships; one could almost forget it was caused by the propellors. He waved his French guest and stepped back in.

Moments later, Captain Baquoy entered.

"Capitain Baquoy, welcome on board the Württemberg. It is an honour to welcome France's most renowned airman."

Baquoy regarded the German captain. He could not say he recognised the face. Whoever he was, he was not well-known outside his own forces. Slim and of average height, short, reddish-blond hair and a typical German moustache with the ends twirled upwards. His right cheek was peppered with small scars, most likely from shrapnel. "Thank you..."

"I'm Kapitän Albecht Von Kober."

"Thank you, Kapitän Von Kober. Your French is excellent. You sound like you grew up somewhere around Paris."

The unexpected compliment made Albrecht smile. "Oh, I was actually not aware of that. My teacher always said my pronunciation was rather sloppy. I also hardly get the opportunity to speak French. I listen to Æthercast Paris a lot, though."

"I see. Now, what did I do to be invited on board this rather unusual craft you command?"

"In a moment, Capitain Baquoy, I suggest we talk in a more

comfortable place than our cargo hold."

Baquoy followed his host up a flight of stairs and down a corridor. All doors along the way, except the infirmary, were closed. No chance to get a look at anything but empty walls.

The only two other crew members they encountered were the zeppelin's physician and his orderly, both clearly recognisable by their uniforms and the fact they were standing outside the infirmary. They saluted when the two captains passed.

Finally, they entered a rather large and well-furnished room. Von Kober offered him a seat and, when Baquoy had sat down, the German captain put a cigar case in front of him.

"Please, take your pick, Capitain Baquoy, I assure you they are most excellent."

"Hmmm... I'm not much of a cigar smoker... I prefer pipe."

"Oh, in this case, if you could wait a moment?"

To Baquoy's astonishment, Von Kober got up and left. He also suddenly realised the German had not asked for his sidearm. Baquoy patted the handle of his pistol... Something strange was going on. This was far too friendly a reception. Von Kober returned with his own pipe and a silver box.

"Please, Capitain Baquoy, help yourself. I'm also a pipe smoker, but I'm afraid my tobacco is not quite as good as the cigars."

Slightly puzzled and bemused, Baquoy stuffed some of Von Kober's tobacco into his own pipe and lit it.

"Let me be blunt, Kapitän Von Kober. I've heard about your Empire building a new zeppelin class. I presume this is the first ship?"

Von Kober confirmed this.

"Now, you have invited me on board, you have not taken my gun and you are extraordinarily friendly." He took a draft at his pipe and exhaled slowly. "What the hell is going on? Do you wish to defect?"

The German's face was all the answer he needed. "That's a no, then. So, what do you want?"

"Captiain Baquoy, if you don't mind, I would like to ask you a few questions. From my questions, you will surely be able to guess what I know, presuming my guesses about your airship's being here are correct. I will also keep them vague enough so you do not have to reveal any secrets per se."

Baquoy thought for a moment, concentrating on the fleeting twirls of the tobacco smoke. "Well, Von Kober, go ahead."

"You have received your orders from someone very high up in your chain of command?"

Baquoy nodded.

"And you were the obvious choice because of certain... affiliations... and because someone involved trusts you as a friend."

Baquoy nodded again.

"My situation is mirrored, to a certain extent. I received my orders from Admiral Von Köpitz, my mentor, but the rest is probably the same. Well, I do not have a friend in a similar position."

"What do you mean when you say *mirrored*, Von Kober?"

"I think you know what I mean, Capitain Baquoy. We already have people on the ground. If you want to send some of your men, please tell me so. I wish to avert a firefight."

"Well, we intend to. But under these circumstances, perhaps I reconsider. Kapitän Von Kober, if..."

"No further questions, please, I am sorry. Our first meeting is at an end. Believe me, I would offer you a Schnapps or something but we all need to be sober now."

"I better return to my airship then."

Von Kober escorted him back to the grapple bridge; this time, they met no one on the way.

"Capitain Baquoy, it was an honour to have you on board. I hope we will meet again soon."

"The honour was all mine, Kapitän Von Kober."

Baquoy's officers exchanged nervous glances when their captain slumped down heavily in his chair on Toulon's bridge.

"Get me our embassy in Istanbul."

DF Toulon slowly widened the distance between her and the Württemberg, then her Morse light flashed: *Please remain in the area.* Württemberg answered: *We will hold this position.*

"Herr Kapitän?"

"Yes, Kaleun Vogel?"

"What was it you told Baquoy?"

"I only asked him a few questions."

"And?"

"Well, they weren't too specific, but I think he now thinks what I think."

"And this is all you will tell me?"

"Yes, Kaleun. But with any luck, you will soon find out anyway."

Towards evening, clouds started covering the sky above and light rain, accompanied by a gusty, easterly wind set in. The night was almost pitch-black and thus the night-vision equipment was of only limited use. In the distance, they saw the position lights of DF Toulon. They had switched on theirs as well, as a sign of good will. Conditions like these would have been almost ideal for sneaking up on an enemy airship. The Württemberg was the faster and more manoeuverable craft – surprise would be on their side, if they wanted. No. Such an action would start a war and whoever fired the first shot would most likely find themselves without allies.

During the night, Württemberg drew circles around a small patch of trees on one of the low hills they used as a marker. With the first light of dawn they saw Toulon had also held her position some three kilometres away.

Von Kober felt cold and stiff. He had done his best to get some sleep but had stared at the ceiling of his cabin well past midnight. Too many thoughts had conjured too many scenarios behind his eyes. They had informed their embassy in Istanbul about Toulon's presence, so maybe there were more zeppelins on the way now. But would the Sultan allow them entry into Ottoman airspace? Baquoy was surely facing the same situation. Maybe it was even worse for him. The German Empire at least had a military advisory mission at the court in Istanbul. As far as Albrecht knew, no other nation had. This could be a valuable asset now. A trump up their sleeve. Maybe.

He dressed and got himself a cup of steaming coffee. At least their supplies had been stocked up. They could hold out here for a while. Fuel consumption now was minimal. At the very least, they could out-wait the French airship.

Coffee in hand, Albrecht made his way to the bridge. Droplets of rain were clinging to the windows; every now and then one would draw in smaller ones, driven by the wind.

He sat down heavily in the command chair. No news during the night, nothing to report. Fine. No news was good news. He had not yet finished his coffee when the rear observation post reported DF Toulon closing in. Tension rose. The French dirigible made a show of her approach. Baquoy wanted to be visible. DF Toulon approached slowly, turning left and right as she went. Then she stopped, descended and lowered her shuttle-cage. Four people left. The French team Baquoy had mentioned the day before.

Time to inform the Prince and Schliemann.

VIII

Schliemann was one of Europe's greatest archeologists. His discovery of Troy had brought renown and more funds for additional expeditions than he could ever have hoped for. That was all he ever wanted. Being able to unearth the history of mankind and not worry about where the money would come from. He had never wished for becoming involved in politics. Lately he caught himself wondering if the old gods of Greece were real. The capricious Olympians. First, they blessed him with a major find, something proving a kernel of truth behind the Homeric legends, and now they made him pay for it.

He had expected the visit of his French benefactor to be a matter of his personal interest. He simply wanted to see for himself how much progress Schliemann had been making.

The very next day another party had arrived, from Germany, and things had gotten complicated. More complicated than he could have imagined. To make matters worse, two airships lurked in the skies over his dig now. Each had brought a party of special investigators. The gods must be laughing themselves silly by now.

"Dr. Schliemann?" It was that accursed Bavarian prince.

"Yes your Highness." He wearily got up from behind his foldable desk and went to the tent's door-flap. Outside, all reasons for his misery were assembled. Fittingly, the Zeppelin cast a shadow on the scene.

"Kaleun Vogel?" Von Kober was observing the scene below through the fixed telescope. He could see more details than he would have wished.

"Yes, Herr Kapitän?"

"Tell me I'm mad." He stepped aside.

Vogel's eyes had hardly touched the telescope before he used the words that had been on Albrecht's mind for quite some time.

Baquoy watched as LZ Württemberg slowly moved away. They had Morsed: *Take a look*. Marcel had a sinking feeling in his stomach and, judging from their faces, his officers shared it. Not that it helped. Misery likes company, it was said. There were exceptions to this rule.

He took a look. The feeling got worse.

Birol had carefully positioned the special goat on the brow of the hill, behind some shrubs. Now he had a little time to observe the goings-on in the camp.

Albrecht paced up and down the central walkway of the Württemberg. He had been almost right. Almost. He had underestimated the situation. What now? He had no orders and did not expect any anytime soon. Maybe Prince Von Stauffen had received new instructions he was not privy to. Not that it mattered. The door towards the bow swung open and Kaleun Vogel stepped onto walkway.

"Baquoy would be honoured if you could join him for lunch."

Well, at least there would be French cuisine today.

Baquoy insisted they would eat first and then discuss matters, so Albrecht enjoyed a very decent meal in the company of the French captain. If it had been wine instead of water, he could have forgotten the place he was, but just as with the Imperial German Zeppelin Corps, the French Armée Aeronautique did not allow alcohol on duty.

"So what do you suggest we do now, Kapitän?"

Von Kober contemplated the reflections in his glass for a moment before answering.

"I wish I knew. I think you are in a far better position. After all, he is your friend, as is well known."

"True, but I am at loss too. What am I supposed to do, talk him out of it? We have both seen them down there. They will not be separated."

"Well, if both sides agree, I am sure what Napoleon III would..."

"... wish to be the dowry?"

"Exactly."

"Kapitän Von Kober, this could actually be the solution to this situation."

"Yes, mon Capitain, but only if everybody involved is willing to play along, and maybe the diplomats down there have already come to a similar conclusion."

A brief knock on the door interrupted their conversation. Before Baquoy could reply, the door swung open and Dequenne entered.

"Mon Capitain, the Suleiman is approaching."

"I thought Sultan Yussuf was in the United States."

"Well, we have been here just long enough for him to turn back, board his flagship and come here," observed the first officer.

"Can't blame the man for wanting to know what is happening on his soil."

"True, Kapitän Von Kober. We should get ready to receive the Sultan; I suggest you return to the Württemberg and, just for show, we leave the grapple bridge out."

"An excellent Idea, Capitain. Gentlemen, I expect to see you again soon. Goodbye for now."

Von Kober was correct; about two hours later they all assembled on board the Suleiman. The massive Krupp-built Rhein-class battlecruiser had only been delivered to the fledgling Ottoman air fleet three years earlier.

Sultan Yussuf had managed to take tension out of the situation by insisting on the meeting happening in his private salon. The vast room was laid out with rugs and cushions and smelled of roses and incense.

A group of servants had prepared several low tables with food and refreshments and the Sultan had encouraged everyone to not be shy. At first no-one moved but then captains Baquoy and Von Kober both boldly went first, helping themselves to some strong black tea and Turkish biscuits. This had broken the mood, especially after Von Kober and Doktor Hartmann had sat down with the present members of the French crew and began chatting.

Despite all the friendliness between the military aviators, the two culprits responsible for their gathering still sat rather quietly by themselves. Louis Napoléon, Prince Imperial, heir to the French Empire and Princess Alexandra Stephanie of Prussia, youngest daughter of Emperor Frederick III of Germany. Earlier, the French Prince had had a brief conversation with his friend Capitain Baquoy, just after the captain had come on board.

Now, the Prince rose, letting go of Princess's hand only after it became to awkward to hold on.

"Sultan Yussuf, we thank you for your generous hospitality and apologise for the inconvenience the princess and I have brought for everyone. We understand you have postponed your visit to the Americas because of this, and we have also interrupted both my friend Marcel's leave and Kapitän Von Kober's first mission."

"My Prince," the Sultan sounded jovial, "I am sure you will go down in history as Louis the Interruptor." This earned him some nervous laughter. "There is no need to apologise. The captains," he nodded to Baquoy and Von Kober "are doing their duty as they have sworn to do, and my voyage has only been postponed by a few days. President Cody has assured me I can begin my visit any time I choose, and I intend to do this as soon as we have solved the situation at hand. Rest assured, I am in no hurry."

It was Victor de Broglie, the leader of the French delegation, who spoke next. "Your Imperial Majesty, don't you fear that either Empire could send an intervention force if this affair takes too long to resolve? After all, the future Emperor of France is involved."

"Duc de Broglie, do you think the life of the prince is in danger here?"

"Well, no."

"And do you think any civilised nation would accept matters of love involving Germany and France as a casus belli against Turkey?"

"Of course not, that would be unthinkable."

"So you see, I have no need to be concerned. I think this is a match made in heaven, fit for an epic poem. It is also a far better connection between two emperors than a surgeon."

"I beg your pardon, your Imperial Majesty?" Prince Von Stauffen's face was a mask of confusion.

"Princess Alexandra, do you know the name of the doctor who implanted your father with his artificial throat?"

"Oh..." the Princess looked slightly embarrassed. "I heard his name mentioned only once or twice... He was from New England..."

"Doctor Wilmarth!" Prince Louis Napoleon exclaimed.

"Yes, Louis, that's him."

"Mon Dieu, the same man who designed the exoskeleton for my father. I had no idea."

"You see, your families are already connected by the man who saved your fathers' lives. He also sends his regards and would also volunteer to serve as best man."

"But your Imperial Majesty, how did you know that both Imperial families were involved when not even our respective secret services were sure about the identity of the respective other? The Duc de Broglie has assured me that he, just as I, only knew the other person, so to speak, was a noble of some rank."

"Count Von Stauffen, the Ottoman Empire is not as much a backwater as is commonly believed in the west so, as a gesture of trust and good will, let me show you something. I am sure that nothing you will see now will ever leave this room." The Sultan looked around and everybody confirmed or nodded. He picked up a tiny bell and jingled it twice.

The main door opened and a young officer carrying a lifeless goat walked in; he put the goat down and saluted.

"At ease. May I introduce Mülâzım-ı Evvel, that is, First Lieutenant Tastan. He serves with the Special Division. Mülâzım-ı Evvel Tastan, please show our guests what exactly it is you brought in."

To everybody else's astonishment, the young officer drew his knife and started cutting the goat open. Some of the assembled foreigners averted their eyes but were drawn back when they heard the gasps and exclamations of the others.

Mülâzım-ı Evvel Tatsan had removed some of the goat's skin, revealing the metalwork underneath. This was no goat at all; this was a highly advanced automaton.

"You see, I have my eyes everywhere. Thank you Mülâzım-ı Evvel, that would be all."

The officer picked up the automaton and walked out.

"Now, Princess Alexandra, Prince Louis Napoleon, I offer you the hospitality of any of my palaces if you choose to stay in my realm."

"I am afraid this will not be possible, your Imperial Highness." Count Von Stauffen cleared his throat before he continued to speak. He was clearly not happy about what he had to say. "I am under strict orders by Emperor Friedrich himself to escort Princess Alexandra home. Unfortunately, she has to come alone."

"My orders concerning the Prince are similar."

"Duc de Broglie," Capitain Baquoy once more showed the wry grin which announced an unorthodox idea. "What exactly are your orders?"

Ever since they set course for central Europe, the æthergraph of the Württemberg had not been silent. Both Morse and speech messages had been coming in, Von Kober had been in constant contact with Baquoy, and both the Crown Prince and the Princess wanted to talk to each other as often as possible now that they were on different vessels.

Gruson and Baquoy's engineer, Doriot, had also rigged something up to permanently connect both the Württemberg's and the Toulon's æthergraph. They would all hear everything the other vessel received, provided it was uncoded, and be able to answer the other's call.

Both Emperors and Empresses had called in earlier, inquiring about the health and safety of their respective child. So far all was well, but this would soon change.

Just before sundown, Richnow alerted Von Kober of the presence of two airship squadrons coming their way. Albrecht grabbed the speaking tube of the aethergraph.

"Marcel, the moment of truth is upon us."

"Yes, we have seen them too, Albrecht. No heavy units in either squadron, though."

"I guess everybody wants to keep the affair as low-key as possible for as long as possible."

A warning buzz indicated another message wanting to get through.

"Oh, we are being hailed. Talk to you later."

In later years, every time the crews of the Württemberg and the Toulon would meet to celebrate this very day, what followed would always be the cause of much mirth.

Both vessels were ordered to line up so their respective squadron could form an escort. At this point, the Duc de Broglie and Count Von Stauffen both inquired with their squadron commander whether the vessel or the passenger needed an escort. Both commanders obviously confirmed it was the passenger that mattered. Württemberg changed course towards the French Squadron and Toulon towards the German.

This caused some confusion and a lot of chatter over the æther. The German commander, a Kommodore Schlegel, was the first to demand an explanation, so it was revealed the German Princess and the delegation were on board the Toulon, while the French Crown Prince and the Duc de Broglie's party were on the German zeppelin.

"After all," Capitain Baquoy pointed out over the æthergraph, "the diplomats were only instructed to bring their charge home; the type of vessel was never mentioned. No harm has come to anyone and we are simply showing good will."

For a moment, only the background static was audible in the speakers.

"My son!" came the voice of Napoleon III over the æther. "Are you completely out of your mind?"

"Pappa, I assure you, I am quite sane."

"Since this was obviously all agreed upon by everybody involved over there in Turkey," cautioned Marechal de MacMahon, "I am sure our children want to send a very clear message. Maybe we should all…"

"…better talk about this like civilised people." the brassy tone of Kaiser Friedrich III's implant-generated voice was unmistakable. "I suggest London at your earliest convenience."

There was more chatter and debate and, after a few minutes, Napoleon III and Friedrich III went off the air to discuss the matter more privately. The squadrons held position for almost an hour, then Marechal de MacMahon came back on again to order Toulon and

Württemberg to set course for Geneva.

"Well, your Highness, seems like Marcel's mad plan has paid off."

"You forgot 'again', Kapitän Von Kober. I cannot recall a single time when one of his ideas did not work as planned."

"Well, he is a living legend after all."

"True, and so are you now, I guess. Or maybe we all just became rather infamous. Well, whatever judgment history has in store for us, I cannot wait to get to Geneva."

"We should be there just before dawn, your Highness."

"Oh for God's sake, just call me Louis."

STEAM PUNK

WRITERS AROUND THE WORLD

PÓLVORA Y VAPOR

Puerto Rico

PÓLVORA Y VAPOR

By Aníbal J. Rosario Planas

Era invierno del año 1899 en Puerto Rico. El invierno en el Caribe no es nada parecido a los fríos inviernos de Inglaterra, España o Estados Unidos. La mayoría de los días de invierno en Puerto Rico se asemejan a un día de verano en esas regiones. Las noches pueden ser un poco más frescas, algo similar a un día de primavera. Al igual que todos los inviernos, los días eran templados, las noches un poco más frescas. Pero el 25 de enero de 1899, en el pueblo de Ponce, una noche fresca se transformó rápidamente en un infierno caluroso. Un acontecimiento que cambió para siempre la historia de este pueblo y de todo un país. El suceso se recuerda hoy día como "el Fuego del Polvorín". Pero antes de hablar de tan histórico acontecimiento es importante conocer un poco del trasfondo de la ciudad.

Parte I - Antecedentes

Ponce es uno de los más antiguos pueblos fundados por los conquistadores españoles que llegaron a nuestra isla. Ubicado en el lugar anteriormente conocido por los taínos nativos como el territorio de Guaynía, este pueblo, también conocido como la Ciudad Señorial, se fundó oficialmente en el sur de Puerto Rico en el año 1692. A través de los años, Ponce fue adquiriendo importancia entre los pueblos del país. Para finales del siglo XIX ya era un importante centro económico del Caribe. Impulsado por la agricultura, se había desarrollado también como un importante puerto marítimo y un pueblo de gran cultura.

En verano del 1882 se llevaría a cabo una gran feria de agricultura en este pueblo, organizada por Don Juan Mayoral Barnés. En preparación a dicho acontecimiento, se hicieron grandes construcciones en el pueblo y se trajo gran tecnología moderna para exhibir. El Parque de Bombas de Ponce fue diseñado por el Teniente Coronel Máximo de Meana y Guridi, quien para aquel entonces era el Comandante Militar de la Plaza de Ponce. Meana y Guridi era arquitecto de profesión y, por tal razón, fue seleccionado por sus superiores en Madrid para diseñar y supervisar dicha construcción. La estructura fue influenciada por el estilo Gótico Victoriano y los diseños tradicionales de los Moros. El edificio de dos plantas, mayormente de madera, se asemejaba a una mansión española o un castillo gótico, pero con grandes detalles arabescos y moriscos. La construcción fue erigida en la Plaza de Ponce, en la parte posterior de la Catedral Nuestra Señora de la Guadalupe, con una inauguración en el 1882 como Pabellón Principal de la Convención de Agricultores de Puerto Rico. El mismo, con sus intensos colores rojo y negro, fue uno de los grandes atractivos ese verano.

La feria se celebró entre el 1 y el 16 de julio de 1882. En esos días visitaron el pueblo de Ponce ingenieros, comerciantes y prominentes personalidades de todo el país y del extranjero. Aparte de una inmensa selección de frutas, verduras y otros productos de la siembra, había también una gran selección de cigarros de tabaco. Pero los productos de consumo no eran el único atractivo. También había una gran exhibición de maquinarias y moderna tecnología. Se hablaba de la misma como "el futuro de la agricultura y el progreso mundial". Fue esta tecnología del futuro la que abrió la mente de un joven adolecente que curioseaba por la Plaza. Rafael Rivera Escribi, de apenas trece años de edad, observaba con atención las maravillas en despliegue. Fue en ese momento que decidió convertirse en ingeniero. Deseaba crear una de las maravillosas máquinas del futuro. La ambición y sueño de Rivera Escribi jugaría un papel importante años más tarde en el Fuego del Polvorín.

Parte II - El Parque de Bombas

El 2 de febrero de 1883, se estableció la primera brigada oficial que operaba desde el Parque de Bombas. Esta orden había sido decretada por el Teniente Coronel Maena, en ese momento Alcalde del pueblo de Ponce. Previo a esta fecha, se habían registrado enormes y desastrosos fuegos en toda la zona sur de Puerto Rico. El clima intensamente caluroso, típico de Puerto Rico, y las grandes sequías que se experimentaban en el área sur eran factores de gran influencia para el desarrollo y expansión de estos peligrosos incendios. Desde sus comienzos como Parque de Bombas, la céntrica estructura había sido base de operación y rescate para grandes desastres naturales y los intensos fuegos en toda la zona.

El Parque de Bombas de Ponce tenía dos torres, una a cada extremo. En el tope de una de ellas se encontraban las oficinas administrativas y en el otro extremo, el área de descanso de los bomberos de turno. De estas dos plazoletas al nivel superior, salía una escalera doble de rieles de metal. Estas dos escaleras se unían al centro de la pared trasera de la estructura, para consolidarse en una sola hasta tocar el suelo del nivel principal. En este primer piso estaba todo el equipo para combatir los incendios, incluyendo los carretones de mangas, patas de cabra y hachas, vestimenta de seguridad, entre otros elementos útiles en misiones de rescate.

Al salir del Parque de Bombas, se encuentra la calle Cristina justo frente al Parque, la Catedral Nuestra Señora de la Guadalupe a las espaldas y a cada flanco, dos plazas que se unían en una sola. En las noches podías caminar por la Plaza, alumbrada por faroles de gas y con la imponente estructura como recordatorio de cierto nivel de seguridad.

Este era el refugio de héroes, que enfrentaban con valentía las intensas llamas y el horror de vidas y propiedades destruidas por los fuegos y desastres naturales. Estos hombres arriesgaban sus vidas para salvar a otros. Batallaban las intensas llamas de los fuegos, la inestabilidad de los terrenos luego de un terremoto, las peligrosas inundaciones en tormentas tropicales y los abates de fuertes vientos durante los huracanes. Cada día de labor representaba un día de riesgo. Pero ninguna de las brigadas de bomberos había experimentado un desastre como el que vivió la brigada de turno en la tan recordada noche del 25 de enero del año 1899.

Parte III - El 25 de enero

Era una noche tranquila en la Plaza de Ponce. La brisa fresca del invierno puertorriqueño hacía de esta una noche perfecta para caminar por la plaza. Los faroles encendidos proveían un ambiente romántico para los jóvenes que caminaban en la oscura noche, tratando de conquistar con la mirada a las damiselas que recorrían el centro del pueblo acompañadas de algún familiar adulto.

Hacía unos meses, los norteamericanos habían invadido la isla y la habían arrebatado del dominio del Gobierno Español. Para los civiles era difícil acostumbrarse al nuevo régimen. El alcalde actual era un militar de apellido Myer, quien mantenía presencia militar en constante vigilancia en la plaza y las calles cercanas. Los puertorriqueños hacían su mayor esfuerzo de conservar sus costumbres y evitar enfrentamientos con los oficiales del nuevo régimen.

Eran poco más de las siete de la noche (19:00, hora militar) cuando Rafael Rivera Escribi llegó a la Plaza de Ponce, lugar donde hacía 17 años, había recibido la inspiración para convertirse en ingeniero. Varios años después de la Gran Feria de Ponce, Rafael fue a estudiar al extranjero. Estudio ingeniería en el Instituto de Tecnología de Massachusetts (MIT). El mismo había abierto sus puertas apenas unas tres décadas antes de que él estudiara allí. Pero para ese entonces, era la Universidad más avanzada en ingeniería en toda América.

Rivera Escribi llegó a la Plaza para ver a su amigo, Rafael del Valle, quien era uno de los bomberos de turno la noche del 25 de enero de 1899. Rivera Escribi fue recibido no sólo por su amigo, del Valle, sino por todos los bomberos en turno, quienes quedaron anonadados por el medio de transporte en el que había llegado Rivera. Los medios de transporte terrestre comunes en la época eran caminar, montar a caballo, carreta o carruaje y, para largas distancias, la locomotora de vapor. Rivera Escribi arribó en la Plaza de Ponce esa noche en un vehículo que a simple vista parecía un carruaje. Sin embargo, el mismo no era tirado por caballos ni por ninguna otra bestia. Quienes observaban, quedaron atónitos y trataban de descifrar la fuerza que hacía avanzar a dicha maquinaria.

Alguna que otra persona supersticiosa que observaba quizás pensaba que era algún tipo de magia. Por la mente de algunos probablemente pasaron las palabras "máquina infernal". Pero aquel que tenía un poco más de conocimiento, sabía de la existencia de la locomotora y los barcos de vapor, y de seguro asoció el extraño carruaje con estas masivas maquinarias.

Cuando Rafa del Valle le preguntó a su amigo Rafa Rivera qué era ese extraño carruaje, Rivera le contestó que era un carro con motor de combustión externa. Ante la mirada extraña de su amigo, Rivera aclaró que era un carro que se movía a base de vapor, tal como una locomotora. Rivera les mostró a los bomberos el motor y todo el sistema operativo del carruaje, mientras les explicaba cómo funcionaba. Ellos no entendieron nada de la compleja explicación que ofreció el ingeniero. Su atención se enfocaba en la complejidad de lo que veían: tornillos, engranajes, conductos y válvulas en diferentes tonalidades de bronce y plata, quizás algún detalle en oro. Cada pieza parecía meramente decorativa, pero la realidad es que cada componente realizaba una función específica en el complejo sistema. Las piezas se veían muy limpias, capaces incluso de brillar bajo la luz del sol, pero en la tenue luz de los faroles de gas de la plaza, la intensidad del brillo disminuía considerablemente.

El carruaje tenía un esqueleto metálico, del cual muy poco se podía observar a simple vista. El esqueleto se elevaba del suelo y se movía por los terrenos gracias a cuatro ruedas metálicas, similares a las de un carruaje típico de la época. El esqueleto metálico servía de soporte a todo el sistema de engranajes que permitían movimiento a los diversos componentes del motor ubicado en la parte frontal, y dos filas de asientos hechos en cuero color carmesí y rellenos con paja, en el área central del carro. Los laterales estaban casi completamente abiertos. Solo tenían unos tubos metálicos que sostenían la capota que cubría a los pasajeros. La parte posterior tenía un pequeño baúl hecho en madera, adherido a un sostén metálico ubicado más atrás de las ruedas posteriores. En el lado derecho del asiento delantero había una serie de manecillas de diferentes tamaños y formas y una pequeña rueda de madera, la cual los bomberos habían visto a Rivera Escribi sujetar con sus manos y darle vueltas. El resto del vehículo estaba cubierto con metal y maderas tratadas, todo en tonalidades carmesí con detalles en bronce y oro.

Uno de los bomberos, Juan Romero, le preguntó a Rivera si él había inventado este vehículo. Rafa Rivera les explicó que muchos científicos en el mundo estaban trabajando con diferentes sistemas. Edison y Tesla habían logrado avances en la electricidad, por lo que se hablaba de utilizar estas corrientes eléctricas para diversas aplicaciones. En cuanto a transportación se refería, grandes avances se habían logrado ya con vehículos similares utilizando electricidad y medios de combustión interna. En cuanto a los vehículos de vapor, muchos se habían diseñado y remodelado en el último siglo. Pero este vehículo en particular tenía unos detalles particulares rediseñados por él. A diferencia de otros carros de vapor, el suyo utilizaba un radiador mucho más pequeño pero mucho más rápido y eficiente. El sistema de calentamiento era también mucho más avanzado a otros, por lo que en apenas unos dos minutos, se alcanzaba la temperatura óptima de operación. El vehículo podía moverse a una velocidad mayor a la de otros vehículos de su clase. Mientras la mayoría alcanzaban unas 5 a 10 millas por hora, el suyo podía alcanzar y mantener unas 15 a 17 mph.

Rafa del Valle también bromeaba con su tocayo sobre los extraños lentes que portaba. Rafa Rivera le explicó que no se trataba de unos lentes, sino de unas gafas, las cuales protegían sus ojos del polvo que podía levantar el vehículo en movimiento, afectando su visibilidad. Las extrañas gafas eran similares a unos lentes circulares hechos en bronce, pero adheridos a una extensión de cuero, que fijaba completamente al rostro, impidiendo la entrada de aire, tierra, agua o cualquier otra sustancia a los ojos.

Los dos amigos continuaron conversando con los otros bomberos en turno por un largo rato. Se intercambiaron anécdotas, chistes y carcajadas, acompañadas de varias tazas de café y un buen cigarro. Disfrutaban del ambiente placentero y refrescante de la Plaza y, cada cierto rato, retomaban el tema del carro de motor de vapor. Había sido hasta el momento una noche serena. Pero la noche tranquila se convirtió, en tan solo un momento, en una noche de terror, de lucha, de sacrificio y de honor.

Parte IV - Camino a las llamas

A sólo tres cuadras de distancia de donde estaba ubicado el Parque de Bombas, se encontraban las barracas del 5° Regimiento de Caballería y el 19° Regimiento de Infantería de la milicia de los Estados Unidos de Norteamérica. En dicha base se ubicaban también oficinas de los comandantes de área, las caballerizas y el más amplio almacén de municiones de toda la región sur de Puerto Rico. Dicho depósito de armas despachaba las municiones necesarias a diferentes puntos de la región. La ubicación céntrica facilitaba el despacho a otros ayuntamientos y proveía cierta defensa estratégica. El depósito contenía municiones para rifles y revólveres, balas de cañón, granadas, barriles de pólvora y cajas de dinamita.

Uno de los guardias de la base, que estaba en su turno de vigilancia, había tomado un receso. Luego de descargar su vejiga, se recostó sobre las pacas de heno con las que alimentaban a los caballos. Encendió un cigarro y comenzó a fumar. Pero en este estado de reposo y de seguro confortado por la fresca brisa, el soldado de quedó dormido. Aparentemente su cigarro cayó al suelo, encendiendo el heno que estaban a su lado. El calor de las llamas de fuego hizo que el hombre despertara, para descubrir que el fuego se esparcía con gran rapidez. Ya era muy tarde para apagarlo con un pisotón de su bota.

Era poco más de las nueve de la noche, cuando se escuchó la voz del centinela norteamericano gritar "fire". Inmediatamente se comenzó a alertar a todos en el pueblo. Gritos y estruendos de campanas cortaron tajantemente la tranquilidad de la noche. Quienes se habían recostado a descansar fueron arrastrados del reino de Morfeo al mundo físico, pero lleno de llamas y pánico. En unos pocos minutos, la noticia había llegado a la Plaza, donde los bomberos dejaron su conversación con Rafa Rivera para preparar su equipo y vestimenta para combatir el fuego. Comenzaron inmediatamente los preparativos a toda carrera, pues no había tiempo que perder en una emergencia. Las campanas de la Catedral Nuestra Señora de la Guadalupe comenzaron asonar, dando la alerta de desalojo a todo el pueblo. Un pequeño grupo de bomberos conocidos como la banda de cornetas salió tocando sus instrumentos para continuar alertando a quienes se encontraban en la cercanía del depósito de municiones. El gran miedo de todos en el pueblo era que las municiones y explosivos estallarían si el fuego llegaba a ellos, lo cual acrecentaría la gravedad de los daños. Sería casi imposible contener el incendio y posiblemente se perdería todo el pueblo de Ponce.

Los bomberos de la banda de cornetas comenzaron a desalojar a los habitantes de las áreas adyacentes al fuego hacia las afueras del pueblo de Ponce. Algunos fueron desalojados hacia el occidente de la ciudad; otros hacia el área del cerro del Vigía. Mientras tanto, los comandantes a cargo del almacén militar dieron las órdenes de desalojo de todo el personal y de soltar los animales de la caballeriza.

La 7ª Brigada del Cuerpo de Bomberos de Ponce, a la cual pertenecían Rafael del Valle, Juan Romero, Cayetano Casals y Besosa, Pedro Sabater, Gregorio Rivera, Pablo Ruiz y Tomás Rivera, llevaban el carro de mangas. Esta brigada era comandada por Pedro Juan Parra Capó, quien no estaba laborando esa noche. Rafa del Valle había asumido el mando de la brigada esa noche. El carro de mangas que utilizaban era nada más que una pequeña carreta de metal con dos ruedas grandes, también en metal. En un tubo de la carreta, se enroscaba la manga que se conectaría al hidrante de incendios más cercano al lugar donde se encontraba el fuego. El carro de mangas era usualmente tirado por un caballo pero, ante el disturbio, no había caballos preparados con su montura y los siete jóvenes de la brigada salieron tirando del carro ellos mismos.

Mientras Rafa Rivera preparaba su vehículo para partir, sus camaradas de la 7ª Brigada salieron por la calle Comercio, moviéndose en dirección de oeste a este para acercarse al fuego. Cuando los jóvenes llegaron a la calle Salud, fueron detenidos por uno de los soldados estadounidenses, que les ordenó retirarse. Ellos obedecieron la instrucción del soldado amenazante, pero cuando llegaron a la calle Mayor decidieron dirigirse hacia la calle Cristina para tomar dicha ruta hacia el lugar del incendio. Los bomberos de la 7ª Brigada recordaban el lema del Cuerpo de Bomberos: "Abnegación y Sacrificio". No dejarían de cumplir su misión.

Cuando llegaron a la intersección de la calle Mayor con la calle Cristina, su amigo Rafa Rivera, los esperaba con su extraño vehículo de motor de vapor. Rivera vio todo el tiempo que habían perdido sus amigos dando vueltas para evitar a los soldados estadounidenses que bloqueaban su paso. Decidió entonces ayudarlos. Los bomberos anclaron el carro de mangas a la parte posterior del vehículo de Rivera y todos comenzaron a acomodarse en el carruaje que los llevaría al lugar de la acción. Pero poco antes de poder partir, llegó hasta donde ellos estaban un mensajero de Don Juan Seix, Jefe del Cuerpo de Bomberos. El mensajero les dio la orden de regresar al Parque de Bombas. El Alcalde Militar Myer había dado instrucciones de abandonar el área y darla por perdida. Los jóvenes le insistían al mensajero que aún había tiempo, pero él les alertó de que si continuaban hacia el lugar del fuego, serían procesados por el Tribunal del Cuerpo de Bomberos por desobedecer las órdenes de Seix.

La situación era de gran gravedad. Continuar su marcha podía significar la muerte de varios o de todos miembros de la 7ª Brigada y su amigo, Rivera Escribi, un civil. De sobrevivir a tan peligrosa misión, enfrentarían cargos por los cuales podían ser expulsados del Cuerpo de Bomberos, procesados criminalmente e inclusive, ser llevados al paredón. Pero, de retroceder, ¿cuántos perecerían? ¿Cuántos perderían sus casas? ¿Sus pertenencias? El pueblo completo podría quedar en ruina y, siendo una sede económica del país, podría tener repercusiones para todos los puertorriqueños. Los jóvenes decidieron continuar con su misión, sin importar las consecuencias.

Parte V - El Fuego del Polvorín

Anclado el carro de mangas al carruaje de motor de vapor de Rafa Rivera y decididos a detener este incendio o morir en el intento, los siete bomberos se montaron en el extraño vehículo que conducía su amigo. Salieron a toda prisa, bajando dos cuadras completas por la calle Cristina, para llegar al lugar del fuego.

La base militar estaba desolada, salvo por alguna que otra bestia que corría de lado a lado, llenas de pánico por las llamas. Ninguno de los soldados estaba presente por todo aquello. Muchos habían desalojado tras recibir la instrucción de algún superior; otros no habían esperado la orden y en pánico y cobardía, habían partido mucho antes.

El fuego era intenso. A gran distancia se sentía el penetrante calor, que parecía quemar la piel incluso a lo lejos. Afortunadamente los bomberos tenían unos cascos y capuchas hechos en cuero. Estaban pintados de rojo con algún detalle en negro. Aunque su diseño no era perfecto, esto proveía algo de protección a los cuerpos de los bomberos al acercarse a las llamas. Pedro Sabater llevaba consigo un hacha y Gregorio Rivera llevaba una pata de cabra. Estos dos hombres se dirigieron inmediatamente al almacén de las municiones para poder abrirlo.

Junto al almacén de las municiones se encontraba la caballeriza. Al lado contrario del almacén, estaban ubicadas las pacas de heno, casi consumidas por el fuego. Ya la caballeriza se había incendiado y el fuego se esparcía rápidamente hacia el almacén de municiones. Mientras Sabater y Gregorio Rivera abrían las puertas de la armería y almacén de municiones, Juan Romero y Pablo Ruiz comenzaron a soltar la manga del carro en el cual era remolcada. Tomás Rivera y Rafa del Valle comenzaron a abrir la boca de incendios. Cayetano Casals y Besosa, por su parte, entró en la caballeriza para soltar algunos animales que los soldados estadounidenses habían abandonado en medio del pánico. Rafa Rivera, siendo un civil sin entrenamiento con el Cuerpo de Bomberos, no sabía cómo más asistir a sus amigos. En ese momento recordó que la razón principal por la que había pasado por el Parque de Bombas era porque llevaba para su amigo, Rafa del Valle, una invención que entendía le podía ser útil a los bomberos en caso de una emergencia como esta.

Rafa Rivera Escribi había diseñado una careta de cuero, la cual cubría el rostro de una persona desde la frente hasta la barbilla. Cercano al área de la boca había un orificio, el cual se adhería a una pequeña manga plástica. La manga se conectaba en el extremo opuesto a un pequeño tanque metálico, repleto de oxígeno. Para proveer visibilidad, el área de los ojos tenía unos cristales, que se acoplaban a la máscara de cuero con un ensamblaje circular en metal, formando una especie de gafas.

El propósito de esta invención era permitirle a un bombero poder trabajar donde hubiese mucho humo. Esta máscara le permitiría tener cierto nivel de visibilidad y, sobre todo, poder tener oxígeno fresco para respirar. Esta era la oportunidad perfecta para poner a prueba dicha invención. Ya que todos los bomberos estaban ocupados en sus respectivas tareas, Rivera Escribi se puso el equipo de respiración en sus espaldas, sujetado a sus hombros con unas correas de cuero. Se puso la mascarilla y dio vuelta a la manecilla que permitía que fluyera el oxígeno del tanque. Una vez todo el equipo estaba en su lugar y funcionando de la manera adecuada, se dirigió hacia el almacén de municiones.

Cuando llegó a la entrada del bastimento, Sabater y Gregorio Rivera ya habían abierto las puertas y habían comenzado a sacar las cajas de municiones y explosivos. Pero el almacén estaba ya repleto de humo, y se les hacía difícil respirar dentro del edificio. Ambos quedaron asombrados de ver a Rivera Escribi con esta extraña careta, pero sin mucho pensar, entendieron el propósito. Gregorio Rivera se quitó su capucha y se la puso en las espaldas a Rivera Escribi, protegiendo sus hombros, espaldas, brazos y el tanque de oxígeno que llevaba. También se quitó su casco hecho en cuero y se lo puso para que pudiese entrar en el almacén. Sabater permaneció en la puerta para recibir las cajas según Rivera Escribi las traía, para luego dárselas a Gregorio Rivera, que hacía el recorrido del relevo más distante al fuego, por no tener equipo de protección.

Mientras Rivera Escribi buscaba las cajas dentro del almacén, se las daba en la puerta a su relevo, Sabater, quien a su vez se las daba a un tercer relevo, Gregorio Rivera, para que las colocara en un lugar distante al fuego, evitando que explotaran, los otros bomberos también continuaban trabajando. Juan Romero, Pablo Ruiz, Tomás Rivera y Rafa del Valle trabajaban con la manga de incendios, tratando de apagar el fuego. Casals y Besosa aprovechó las cubetas de agua que tenían servidas para los animales en la caballeriza y las vació en varios lugares de la estructura, donde las llamas ardían. Cuando ya no pudo soportar el intenso calor y el denso humo, salió de la caballeriza, pero no sin antes haber hecho el mejor uso posible del agua acumulada, apoyando a los compañeros que trabajaban con la manga. Después de reposar unos breves segundos para recuperar su aliento, se dirigió hacia el almacén de municiones para ayudar a sus compañeros a sacar las últimas cajas.

Estas gestiones le dieron suficiente tiempo a los cuatro hombres con la manga de agua de seguir trabajando en extinguir el fuego. Rafa del Valle soltó la manga en cierto momento, ya que se había percatado de que había unos baldes repletos de arena. Los tomó uno a uno y los fue volteando sobre las áreas donde había llamas encendidas, ahogándolas.

Luego de unas horas de arduo trabajo, luego de haber expuesto sus cuerpos a la furia de las llamas, luego de haber puesto sus vidas en peligro, buscando proteger las vidas de otros, los valientes miembros de la 7ª Brigada del Cuerpo de Bomberos de la Ciudad Señorial de Ponce, asistidos por su amigo, el ingeniero e inventor Rafael Rivera Escribi, lograron contener el fuego de la Plazoleta del Polvorín. Manchas de ceniza, sudor, inclusive leves cortaduras y varias gotas de sangre cubrieron sus cuerpos, como manifestación física de su esfuerzo. A pesar del cansancio, la deshidratación y las molestias en sus cuerpos, los ocho jóvenes héroes regresaron al Parque de bombas con rostros de satisfacción y sonrisas de felicidad, tras lograr salvar el pueblo.

Pero al llegar a la estación en el vehículo de vapor de Rivera Escribi, les recibieron de manera inesperada por ellos. Había varios soldados de la milicia estadounidense junto al jefe del Cuerpo de Bomberos de Ponce, Don Juan Seix. Los ocho jóvenes que arriesgaron sus vidas y salvaron el pueblo pasarían la noche encarcelados para ser enjuiciados el próximo día.

Parte VI - Enjuiciados

El día siguiente se convocó a un tribunal de la misma institución de bomberos. Los siete jóvenes bomberos serían enjuiciados por un grupo de compañeros, que evaluarían si faltaron o no a los reglamentos y estatutos del Cuerpo de Bomberos. De ser encontrados culpables, serían expulsados inmediatamente y podrían enfrentar cargos criminales. Rivera Escribi, por no ser bombero, no estaba en juicio. Pero aguardaba la sentencia de sus amigos para saber si enfrentaría cargos criminales junto a ellos.

Don Rodolfo del Valle, padre del bombero Rafael del Valle, quien sería enjuiciado, fungiría como abogado de los siete jóvenes. Se encontraban también en la sala el Jefe del Cuerpo de Bomberos, Juan Seix; el Alcalde Militar, Myer. También el Comandante de la 7ª Brigada, Pedro Juan Parra Capó, quien no había estado presente en los acontecimientos de la noche anterior. Todos los miembros del Cuerpo de Bomberos que no estaban directamente envueltos en el juicio estaban también presentes en la sala.

Entre los presentes había división de ideas. Algunos apoyaban a los jóvenes, tomando en consideración la valentía de su riesgo y el logro de salvar vida y propiedad. Otros acusaban a los jóvenes de haber ignorado las órdenes del Alcalde, los Comandantes militares y el Jefe del Cuerpo de Bomberos.

En las afueras del tribunal, sin embargo, el pueblo clamaba a grandes voces en favor de los bomberos acusados. Para el pueblo, estos jóvenes eran héroes y merecían un gran reconocimiento, no un absurdo juicio.

Entre los reclamos contra los jóvenes bomberos, resaltaban el haber ignorado las órdenes luego de dos advertencias, una por los soldados norteamericanos y la segunda por el mensajero de Don Juan Seix. También se les acusaba de haber expuesto a un civil (Rivera Escribi) a los peligros de combatir un incendio y de haber utilizado los equipos que el civil les ofreció (el carro de vapor para transportarlos junto al carro de mangas y la máscara de oxígeno). Rivera Escribi fue llamado a ofrecer su testimonio, en el cual aclaró que la decisión de unirse al equipo de rescate fue suya y que, como adulto, estaba en todo su derecho de unirse voluntariamente a combatir el fuego, si representaba un bien para sus conciudadanos. Hizo además hincapié en que el equipo no reglamentado por el Cuerpo de Bomberos fue utilizado y manejado exclusivamente por él. Sus compañeros no podían ser enjuiciados por utilizar equipo ajeno al Cuerpo de Bomberos, ya que fue él quien lo manejó en todo momento.

A pesar de que la extraña tecnología trajo muchas dudas y preocupaciones entre los supervisores del Cuerpo de Bomberos, la atención se tuvo que fijar en la desobediencia de los bomberos, tras el testimonio de Rivera Escribi. Don Rodolfo del Valle apelaba al tribunal, poniendo en perspectiva el hecho de que la desobediencia de los bomberos resultó en evitar que las municiones explotaran, lo que hubiese agravado el fuego. No solo eso, sino que su trabajo resultó en lograr detener el fuego antes de que se esparciera a las residencias adyacentes, salvando las casas y propiedades, quizás inclusive las vidas de muchos ponceños. El tribunal, sin embargo, insistía en la importancia de respetar la cadena de mando. Todo parecía perdido para los jóvenes.

Sin embargo, cuando el tribunal recesó y el Alcalde Myer salió a la

Plaza, se tropezó con una multitud que clamaba con intensidad a favor de los bomberos. El gentío intensificaba sus reclamos cada minuto más y más. El Alcalde comenzó a temer una revuelta en la Plaza y sabía que su fuerza militar había sufrido grandes pérdidas la noche anterior. Por estas razones, decidió entrar nuevamente al tribunal y ordenar que se le concediera la libertad a los siete bomberos y a Rivera Escribi.

Parte VII - Los Héroes del Polvorín

Concederles la libertad no era suficiente para la multitud. Estos jóvenes, que arriesgaron sus vidas para salvar al pueblo, merecían un reconocimiento como héroes. Dicho reconocimiento se les dio el domingo 26 de marzo de 1899. Luego de un desfile por las calles del pueblo, en el cual los héroes iban montados en el peculiar vehículo de motor de vapor, fueron recibidos en la Plaza con vítores y aplausos. Frente al Parque de Bombas, la Banda Municipal de Bomberos de Ponce interpretó varias piezas musicales en honor a sus compañeros bomberos. Luego se les otorgaron unas medallas, condecoraciones en oro, destacando su valentía y entrega al lema del Cuerpo de Bomberos de Ponce "Abnegación y Sacrificio". Muchas actividades y honores adicionales se le concedieron a los ahora héroes nacionales. Los héroes del Fuego del Polvorín.

STEAM PUNK

PROVIDENCE IN THE PACIFIC

Kingdom of Hawaii

PROVIDENCE IN THE PACIFIC

By Ray Dean

The conceit of men in power is that they forget that it's not just the walls that have ears. Just because a man is in servitude does not mean he lacks the intelligence to understand how little he is valued… how little he is respected by those around him.

A snap brought John's attention back to the men at the table, going through their plans. They had ample need to talk among themselves, leaning over maps, poring over lists of names and numbers. They ignored the two men in the room toting pitchers of water and emptying ashtrays of cigar stubs. These servants, with no stake in the conversation, had no importance to them.

When all that was left of the meeting were a few scraps of scribbled paper, a forgotten coffee mug and scraps of food on cold plates, John Kanaka and his brother Thomas stared at each other. It was Thomas that started to collect the scraps, remembering the dismissive wave of a hand from one of the men that told them to clean up.

Thomas held out the pile of paper in his hand. "What do we do?"

John gave his brother a look as he dumped the ashes into a larger container, turning away as some of the ashes floated up toward his face. "We clean up and we go home."

"Didn't you hear what they were talking about?" Thomas struggled to put the papers in order. Some of the scraps were just that, pieces of paper ripped from the whole. Others were drafts that had been rewritten as the meeting had gone on. "They are plotting against the King!"

"The King is fine… he is touring the world! What can they do to him?" John scraped some leftover food into the trash. "These men were all talk."

Thomas heard the dismissive tone from his brother and felt an unaccustomed anger inside of his chest. "What if they meant it? Don't you care what they could do while he is gone?"

As the older brother, John was used to Thomas listening to what he had to say and following his lead. This was new for him. Confusion warred with anger, and when he looked down at the stack of papers in his brother's hand he had to resist the urge to snatch them away and burn them in the ashtray with a stub from one of the cigars. "The King has the Royal Guard to protect him and the people love him. He has been good to us for years. These men can't change that."

"But they," Thomas gestured to the double doors that led in and out of the meeting room, "want to replace him."

The clock in the hall chimed the new hour and the timely reminder seemed to shift the energy in the room.

"I," John informed his brother, "want to go home, and that is what I will do. What you do with that," he looked down at the pile of scraps with a hard set to his lips, "is up to you." He stacked the trays and set them on the sideboard. "I think you forget who you are, Thomas. You're a servant. Those men could easily cause trouble for us and our family."

The door swung closed a moment later, leaving Thomas standing alone with his thoughts.

*

Walking the length of the refinery's warehouse had always left Masanori's heart swelling with pride, but today, as he walked the length of the building for what might be the last time, he struggled to lift his chin from his chest. Beside him, his foreman and trusted friend, Tadashi, made notes in his record book as he commented on the condition of the equipment. He had nearly traversed the entire hall when he stopped. Tadashi was no longer beside him. Turning around, he saw his friend had paused a few feet behind.

Tadashi's eyes were full of concern. "You must consider–"

"*Aiyah!*" Masanori waved off his friend's dire expression. "You were always the one to worry." He tried to summon a smile. "You remind me of my mother. *Okasan* would worry over every little thing. Did I get study too hard or too little? Did I eat too much rice or too little? With you–"

"With me," Tadashi interrupted, pointing to the papers in his hands, "I worry you get too little sense... and too little money." He turned his tone and expression in a heartbeat. "I no like give you pain, but the plantation owners made you one offer. Maybe you should take it."

"The plantation owners are trying to drive me out of business and then make their own money from my refinery." Masa looked from one end of the warehouse to the other. "All this stuff... all those dreams."

Tadashi whistled through his crooked teeth. "I remember the party at the pier!" His papers forgotten for a moment, his memory full of their shared past. "The machine too heavy for them airships. Had to ship 'em in pieces on the big steamer from New York, round the Cape."

It had been the local touring airships that had spotted the cargo ship on the arrival day and dropped a message down a guideline to the stevedores. From there, the men had swarmed the piers like ants waiting for a chance to help offload the cargo.

Over two hundred boxes in nearly as many sizes found their way out of the hold and onto the pier. It had been Tadashi who had hopped up on the largest of the crates and directed the arranging of the boxes and from there onto the long train of wagons out toward the Ewa side of the island. The workers had wanted to wait until the morning when the sun would be at their backs, but even Tadashi could not have made Masanori wait. Not when the voyage time had already pushed Masa past being patient. So they drove the wagons toward the west, shielding their eyes from the brilliant afternoon sun and into the night to deliver the crates to their new home. The excitement of that day had lessened over time, and suffered from the bad luck that had followed him since.

Masa shook off the memories and used the arm of his shirt to brush away the layer of dust that had settled on the shell of the furnace. "I know you telling me the truth, Tadashi. I know my dream's nearly gone." He lifted a gaze to his friend that was full of shame and regret. "I only wish that once," he brushed the dust from his sleeve, "all of this had been useful."

"Come," Tadashi set his papers into a portfolio and held up a beckoning hand to his friend, "we go Honolulu town, have drinks, gripe some more."

When Masa nodded and moved toward the door, Tadashi's outlandish wink nearly stopped him in his tracks.

"I gonna pay."

Masa shook his head, dropping an affectionate arm over Tadashi's shoulder. "*Arigato*, Tadashi. I know I can always count on you."

"We," Tadashi reminded his old friend, "can always count on each udah."

*

Standing at the head of the pier, Eloy looked at the documents in his hands and back at the ship sailing into the harbour. The *Osprey* was expected next in port and his crew had been waiting for the steamer to pull into view.

The immense three-masted ship began to slow as it turned east through the harbour waters. There was a ghost of smoke dragging over the edge of the smokestack, the last dregs of power from the furnace. Squinting his eyes at the vessel he was able to make out most of a name – *Intrepid.*

Another stevedore, Ovidio, ran up beside him and looked over his shoulder at the papers in hand. Craning his neck, he managed to see the name of the ship before the shadow of an airship blanketed the ship in a puddle of grey. "Where's he going?" He watched as the ship dropped anchor in the last bit of deep water near *Aliʻiolani Hale*, the main building for government offices. At the edge of the water they could see people walking down Queen Street between carts and steam-powered trolleys. "That's one odd place to stop."

Eloy nodded. Both men had come to the Kingdom of Hawaii on whaling ships and had sailed these waters extensively before settling down. They were all too familiar with the shipping lanes in and around the island of Oahu. A gust of wind turned Eloy's head, catching his attention on another ship that had found its way into the placid waters of Honolulu Harbour. Again, he looked for a name. The ship sailed on toward him, but there was something about the look of it. It bore too close a resemblance to the ship anchoring oddly near the beach. "Is this one the *Osprey*?"

Ovidio shrugged and climbed up on a few boxes nearby, leaning precariously to the side to see the name on the side of the ship. "Hard... no," he shook his head, "Har-B... *Harbinger.*" Ovidio jumped back down from the crates and moved back to Eloy's side as the new ship drew even closer to the pier. With its trajectory, it was going to come to rest at the *Osprey*'s pier. "Well? What do we do?"

Sorting through the papers in his hands, Eloy shook his head. "Not on my list of ships." Shoving the papers in his friend's hands, he nodded toward the office. "Go ask the boss what we should do."

It only took a moment for Ovidio to run for the end of the pier and the manager's office. Ships in the wrong place meant delays. Delays meant money. Losing money was bad for the boss. What was bad for the boss was bad enough for the stevedores to worry about.

One of the crew of the *Harbinger* was up in the rigging, waving at Eloy with a shout.

Eloy waved back, but not in greeting – he tried to wave them off. When that didn't work he rushed to the side of the ship and waited for one of the officers to appear on deck. "This not your pier," he insisted as he called up to the deck. "You need to move the ship." He explained in rapid words that another ship was scheduled to dock and offload here.

The officer let loose a heavy sigh. "The ship stays. If you need another pier, go and find one. We'll remain here for the next few days."

A shrill whistle turned his head and Ovidio waved at him from the doorway of the pier office. Standing beside him was their boss, a shorter, thinner man than Ovidio. It was easy for him to tell the difference between the two even at that distance. His boss waved him toward the office.

The officer chuckled under his breath. "You find out what he wants and leave us alone." He didn't wait for Eloy to reply. He turned his back on the dock worker and began to issue orders to his men.

Standing outside the boss's office, Eloy and Ovidio listened to him harangue them for nothing in particular. They were too slow. They couldn't stop the ship from taking the pier. Their food, left in tin boxes on a desk in his office, stunk to high hell and made his office intolerable. When he was done, huffing and puffing with indignation, he turned to the board on the outside wall of his office and jabbed at an empty space on the chart. "Think you two can manage to get the *Osprey* to anchor here without any more problems?"

Eloy nodded and silenced Ovidio's protests with a look. "Yes, Boss." He looked down at the watch he'd pulled from his pocket. "You think, while we wait, we can have our meal?"

The older man rolled his eyes and stepped away from the door. "Fine by me, just don't bring your containers back here when they're empty. I've had enough of the smell."

Ovidio retrieved both containers and they set out to find a rowboat. They'd have to meet the *Osprey* and direct it to its new destination. As they walked down the edge of the harbour toward the little slip where they kept the rowboats, Eloy was forced to listen to his friend complain.

"Stink?" His voice growled the word out again before he continued. "My wife made fish *vin d'alhos*." He lifted the container and took in a deep breath to enjoy the scent of the marinated fish; somewhere beneath the scent were roasted potatoes.

Eloy's smile was tight. "Let's get the boat in the water and we'll eat while we're waiting."

Ovidio moved on ahead, his steps quickening. "Hurry up den!"

*

Laws in the Kingdom of Hawaii were simple to understand; even their inequality was abundantly clear. Where most could walk into a saloon and purchase alcohol with ease, Hawaiians were the exception. A law passed by their own government, interested in protecting the Hawaiians from what some would call their baser instincts, made it illegal for Hawaiians to purchase alcohol. Not every saloon followed by those edicts. The further they were from the prying eyes of 'better' society, the fewer the visits from the law, the easier it was to buy a glass of spirits. Those businesses that found themselves under scrutiny of the law could put coin in the right hands and have the law turn in other directions.

In the deep rows of Chinatown businesses, alleys led to doorways that were open to any curious enough to step inside.

Thomas, still in his working clothes, brushed aside the heavy branches of a young mango tree and slipped inside his favorite watering hole. He was in no mood for alcohol. From time to time he would have some with his brother, but today, with what he had learned, he needed a clear head to think.

The only one who looked his way was the man behind the bar. The slight figure in a dark *changshan* nodded and gestured to a chair and waited expectantly for an order.

A few words exchanged between the two and a pot of tea and ceramic cup were produced moments later. With a look to the left and then to the right, assuring him of some privacy, Thomas pulled the papers from his coat pocket and began to arrange them on the counter.

Minutes later, he was just beginning to organise them into some semblance of order when a tin box hit the counter near his elbow; the resulting puff of air shuffling some of the papers.

Thomas glared at the new arrivals, two men who were, if their smells were anything to go by, dock workers.

The taller of the two, further down the bar, offered an apology that was echoed by the troublemaker. His smile and the wink that followed it said it might not have been completely sincere.

The man behind the counter moved closer to take their orders, and offered one in return, waving at them to set their tin boxes on the floor and away from him. His turned up nose spoke volumes about his opinion regarding the remains of their homemade meal.

When the boxes were clear, a steamer basket was set in its place and the rolling cloud of steam escaped as the lid was lifted away. In his own mix of Chinese and English, the cook offered them a variety of dim sum. The man furthest from Thomas picked out a white bun with a red mark at the top and, passing it from one hand to the other, he waited while the heat of the bun dissipated.

Thomas watched the man as he bit into the plump treat. "He offered me one earlier," he explained, meeting the newcomer's eyes. "I didn't know what it was."

Eloy turned the bun toward the Hawaiian and showed him the red mix of meat inside the bun. "Taste good enough, but the bun," he chewed at the bread, "is thick."

"Not like *paodoce*," Ovidio agreed, then took mercy on the man beside him. "Sweet bread," he explained and then softy added on, "much better than Chinese bun."

The man behind the counter was busy stoking the fire of the furnace beneath the various pots of coffee and tea. He spared them a glance that spoke volumes before he went back to his work.

Eloy shook his head. "My friend should know when to be quiet."

Ovidio shrugged. He rarely worried about things like that. He did know enough to smile and nod when the Chinese man set two cups of coffee before them on the counter.

Eloy took a sip to wash down some of the *char siu bao* he'd been chewing and wisely swallowed before his friend took a drink.

The gulp of coffee that seared down Ovidio's throat had him gasping for air, just as much as the Chinese man was stifling his own laughter. Ovidio stood up from the stool he'd been sitting on, his arm reaching for the man behind the counter. It was Eloy's quick hands that put his friend in his seat and avoided an argument.

Not one to keep his hands to himself, Ovidio picked up a piece of paper to distract himself from the burning sensation on his tongue. "What are these?"

Thomas looked at the two men, wondering if they could be trusted.

"What's it look like?"

Eloy took the paper when his friend handed it over. Ovidio didn't read English very well, but there was no need to explain that when he could read the words just fine. "Notes." He turned the slip over. "Some of it is hard to read."

Thomas nodded. "My brother and I were working in the meeting room. I don't think they paid any attention to us," he shared a look with the two dock workers, "but we heard what they were talking about." Gathering the notes together he handed them over to Eloy. "They didn't mention any details, mostly scratched words down on these papers while they worked. When they left, they didn't notice they were leaving behind a lot of their notes. Our job was to pick up all the trash and throw it away."

Eloy was busy sorting through the paper. He was used to his boss's handwriting and it gave him an advantage in work like this. "But you kept these."

"I kept the papers because I heard enough of what they said. I want to stop them." He leaned closer to Eloy, putting himself even closer to Ovidio without wanting to. "They plan on taking over before King Kalakaua returns from his trip."

"Plenty time for that."

Thomas heard the new voice and felt his insides twist. Who had just walked up behind him?

Two Japanese men settled into chairs at a round table just a few feet away from the counter. The younger of the two barked out an order to the man behind the counter for some *sake* and turned his gaze back to the Hawaiian man.

"Maybe you should mind your own business." Thomas was worried; too many people could hear what they were talking about.

Tadashi shrugged. "Maybe you no talk so loud." He elbowed his sad friend. "My friend Masanori read the newspaper to me."

Thomas's curiosity was piqued against his will. "What did it say?"

It as Masanori's turn to speak up. "*The Pacific Commercial Advertiser* said he was traveling around the world for a year."

"A year?" Eloy was busy sorting through the papers. "What countries?"

Masa pondered the question for moment, struggling to remember what he had read with all the other things on his mind. "Japan, I know that is first. Egypt, India, Germany, Burma... Spain."

"Portugal," Tadashi interjected, "I remember that one."

Ovidio's attention was caught, bringing him down from the counter to the round table with the Japanese men. "England and the United States, I bet."

Nodding, Masa agreed. "There are more, but I can't remember. More than enough stops to keep him gone for a year."

"Leaving the Kingdom in danger!" Thomas was even more convinced that his worries were real. "They'll take over and he won't have a throne to return to."

Eloy rubbed the back of his hand against his temple, struggling to understand the varying handwriting styles on the papers. "What about the Royal Guard?" He and Ovidio had seen the smartly dressed soldiers patrolling the grounds of *'Iolani Palace*.

Thomas answered again, his heart sinking at the thought. "I've never seen more than fifty at a time." He gestured to the papers. "I bet they have more than fifty people helping them."

Grabbing Ovidio's sleeve, Eloy pointed at one of the papers. "Look," he told his old friend, "look what they have here."

HARBINGER – 40

Ovidio's reaction was telling. His smile fell away and between the two of them they searched the rest of the slips. He was the one to find a torn piece of paper with the letters – REPID – 40 written on it.

Masanori's concern was plain. He felt the shift of energy at the table. "What is it?"

Ovidio set the second paper beside the first. "This morning," he began, "two ships entered the harbour."

"We didn't expect them in port." Eloy looked at his friend.

"Our boss was all kinds of angry. The *Harbinger* dropped anchor at a pier that another ship was supposed to have. He let us have it."

Tadashi shrugged. "Did he think you would stop it somehow?"

Thomas jumped in before they could answer, pointing at the papers. "What do the numbers mean?"

"Cargo boxes?" Ovidio said the first thing in his head, but no one agreed.

"Forty boxes? Unless they were big wouldn't make any sense. To fit only forty boxes in the hold they'd have to be too big to carry down below."

"Then what?"

"Soldiers." Eloy looked at the group gathered around the table.

"The man that I spoke to, the one on the deck of the *Harbinger*." He looked from his friend and then around the table. "He wasn't just a sailor; we've worked on board whaling ships for years. He wasn't the same."

The rumble and hiss of the dim sum cart rolled up to their table. Hui, the son of the saloon's owner, looked around the table. "You like dumpling?" He reached forward and lifted the covers off of two steamer baskets piled in the top of his cart. "Or…" he reset the covers and opened two more, "custard?"

Eloy looked at the gathered group. "We could be a while."

Tadashi nodded. "I agree; we should get food in case one of us gets hungry."

Masanori sighed. "You always hungry."

"That is why I agreed," Tadashi picked out his food first and then surrendered the cart to his new friends.

*

Two mornings later, the group found themselves back in the saloon, trying to gauge the looks on each other's faces. Eloy was the first to break the silence and ordered coffee for the rest of the group.

Masa's nose wrinkled a little at the thought of the dark brew but he kept quiet.

Sitting down beside his friend, Ovidio pulled a piece of paper out from the cuff of his sleeve. He spread the paper out and smoothed the surface with the flat of his hand. A few strokes and the paper only curved up a little when he lifted his hand.

As Tadashi took his seat between Masa and Thomas, he kept his eyes on the paper before them. It was a crudely drawn map with few actual words or markings beyond the empty channels for streets and the boxes that denoted buildings along the way.

Eloy pointed at two Xs on the paper. "The ships."

"They're not just sailors," Ovidio reported, "we were right. They are soldiers too."

"We didn't hear much," Eloy admitted. "We had to wait until they were busy with their business before we could just 'happen' to walk past and find something to do with the rigging on the pier."

"Mostly," Ovidio chuckled, "they ignore us like the rats that run around on their ship. It is most helpful that they treat us like we are invisible to them.”

Eloy waved his friend off. “The *Harbinger* is bigger than the *Intrepid*,” he continued, “enough that they must have more cargo if each ship has 40 men aboard.”

“Something,” he friend added, “that they are waiting to offload from the ship.”

The gathered group shared looks of confusion and concern, but before anyone could ask a question, Thomas added in his news.

“My *hanai* cousin is part of the Royal Guard,” he pointed to the grounds of the Palace on the map and then moved his finger to a smaller square on the grounds, “Their barracks are on the grounds of the Palace.” He looked at the others and then back to the map. “He said almost a score of the men went with the King on his trip.”

“That doesn’t leave many of them here.” Masa shook his head. “About half, eh?”

Thomas nodded. “Even with all of them, they don’t have much experience fighting. The Kingdom pretty quiet, yeah?”

No one answered him outright as a serving cart sputtered up to the table, the over-worked gears in the motor uttering a strange squeaking song as it slowed to a stop. The young man that had piloted the contraption to the table served them their coffee with a smile and nod to each of the men at the table. “You will let me know,” he told them, “if you need help. I would be happy to help you.”

Tadashi waited for the younger man to leave before he continued. “A gift and a curse,” he sighed, “no need to fight, no experience. No experience, then lose fight.”

Thomas nodded. “If they plan to march on the palace, they will also be in front of *Ali‘iolani Hale*.”

Masa sank back into his chair. “That’s where the Legislators meet. Government offices.” He barely managed to lift his coffee cup to his lips for a sip of the bitter brew.

Thomas continued, pointing out the various buildings as he leaned across the map. “Half the guard gone… what can they do against eighty men? Two buildings to protect.”

“Then we need to give them help.” Tadashi’s fist hit the top of the table, jostling the cups enough to spill a bit of coffee over the top of the table. The young Chinese man working in the saloon was quick to come over and wipe up the spills.

“Help? How?” Thomas’s voice was near defeat. “Do you have a

gun?"

Tadashi shook his head. "No need."

"No need?" Thomas narrowed his gaze at the other man. "What are you talking about?"

He jabbed his finger at the street between the two buildings. "King Street will have eighty men… with guns… waiting to take over and what do we have?" He looked around the table and picked up the smooth wooden sticks beside his plate. "These?"

"No," Masa's voice found its way out of his throat before he even realized he was speaking. His mind was miles away, at his refinery. The last few days had been a welcome diversion from the worries of his failing business venture. "I have something."

Reaching for the map, Masa took a pencil from his pocket and quickly began to draw his own set of lines and boxes on the clean side of the paper. "I bought a machine to refine sugar," he explained. "When the Americans fought each other in their war, sugar plantations started everywhere in the kingdom. I thought it made sense, refine the sugar here, more money stays here."

Tadashi set his cup down with a heavy clunk of sound. "Not one of them plantation owners give you work. No matter how cheap you made it."

"Now I have a refinery doing nothing but rusting in our warehouse."

Eloy couldn't help but be confused. "How does that help?"

Masa turned the paper around to show the rest of the group. One by one he rearranged the pieces. The track that fed the machine took the place of wheels on a carriage. The metal that housed the machine and separated the parts of its mechanism would now be able to house people inside of it like an oddly-shaped Trojan horse, if there was a need, and the furnace would propel it forward without the need for horse or donkey. The other parts, the machinery that would have processed the sugar cane, could now serve as a deterrent should anyone try to get in the way and stop it in its path.

One by one they looked at each other around the table. Confusion to curiosity. Curiosity to hope. Hope was the feeling that brought tentative smiles to their lips and a light to their eyes.

Tadashi was already thinking ahead. "We'll need help." He nodded, his thoughts barreling on ahead. "The mechanics," he looked at Masanori. "Would they help?"

Masa took a long drink from his coffee cup. "They helped us build it; they can help us change it."

"What else needs to be done?" Eloy turned to Thomas. "Did you bring the list?"

Thomas saw the questioning looks around the table and drew out a paper from his jacket pocket. He started to explain, "I tried to remember the names of the men at the meeting. They didn't introduce themselves, but I tried to think about how they talked to each other, what they said. These are the names I could remember."

Eloy took the paper first and showed the list of names to Ovidio. Eloy, better with written language than his friend, read the names out loud. The group remained quiet until the recitation was completed.

Ovidio began to speak, his complexion a good shade paler than normal. "Some of those men own the big shipping companies."

Masanori turned his face away, leaving Tadashi to explain to the others. "The plantation owners, the ones who no do business with Masa, They on that list, too."

The news took some of the wind from their sails. Working against a nameless group of conspirators is one thing. Trying to stop some of the most important businessmen in the kingdom? That was even more dangerous.

"We can stop the soldiers–"

Tadashi interrupted, "We think."

"Yes," Eloy continued, "we think we can stop them, but I wonder why the *Intrepid* is in the centre of the harbour."

Ovidio shook his head at his friend. "You know," he scoffed, "but you no like say." He didn't wait for Eloy to speak up. "The *Intrepid* has guns aboard," he held his arms open, "big guns."

"Guns that can reach *Ali'iolani Hale* from the harbour." Eloy's words put a further damper on the group. "We need to get rid of the ship. I just don't know how."

The stutter of a metal lid against the walls of the dim sum cart silenced the group. They shared looks of warning as the cart rattled up to the side of the table. "I can help."

Eloy shook his head. "No food now."

The young man pushed the cart out of the way and pulled a chair up to the table. Sitting down he pulled the map closer, turning it so that it was orientated in the original configuration. "I can help." He pointed to the ship in the harbour and looked around the table. Each face bore a differing level of confusion and distrust.

His shoulders sinking a bit, the young Chinese man leaned further over the table, dropping his voice in tone and volume. "I can help with ship." When he was sure he had everyone's attention he clenched his fist over the ship's mark and, with a soft 'whoosh' of sound, his fingers splayed open in an explosive rush. "Gone."

"Gone?" Thomas shook his head. "How you gonna do that, eh?"

Sitting back just a bit, the slim-built man crossed his arms over his chest and smiled. "*Bienpao*," he explained, waiting for some sign of recognition.

Tadashi dropped his hands to the tabletop with a soft bang. "What you talkin' about?" He turned to Masanori for his reaction. "What he mean?"

"*Bienpao*," he repeated before pointing to his chest, "Hui make firecracker, burn ship. No problem in harbour."

Ovidio thought about the idea. "We could do that to both ships!" He elbowed Eloy in his seat. "Wouldn't that be easier?"

"And burn the other ships in the port? No." Eloy could only imagine the wildfire they would create if the fire from one ship would catch onto the others. The loss of life alone; he couldn't agree to do that. "Only the one in the harbour by itself." He levelled a look at the Chinese man. "You can do this?"

A bright smile answered back before words. "Yes, Hui can do this."

Masanori wondered aloud. "Why do you want to help us?"

Hui's smile dimmed a little as he leaned closer to the others. "The government good to Chinese people. Here, we work hard, make store, make saloon, make money. These men," he pointed to the list of businessmen organizing the takeover, "no like people like me," he pointed a work-callused finger at Masanori, "no like people like you." He held out his hand, the twinkle back in his eyes. "So we help each other."

One by one he shook the hand of each man around the table.

*

Masanori and Tadashi had the most work to do and the least amount of time to do it. The workers they needed to help them could only come after they finished their jobs for the day.

The mechanics arrived one or two at a time, on foot or horseback. They were tired and dragging their feet, carrying food pails in one hand

and tools in the other.

Greetings were exchanged and the men were quickly shown to the main work table. Lanterns held down the corners of the blueprints that Masanori had drawn out. The drawing before them was much more detailed and involved than the quickly drawn diagram from their earlier meeting at the saloon.

These men were tired, but they were eager to help. They had heard about the coming danger and found themselves happy to participate. When Masanori brought out pots of coffee, the men offered a rousing cry of thanks, which only grew stronger when he promised each man a bottle of *sake* when the job was done.

*

When morning arrived, Ovidio roused himself enough to make sure that Eloy was ready to leave. Normally, the two would head out together, but Ovidio had a few minutes more of sleep planned in reward for staying up until the wee hours of the morning patrolling the docks in search of more information.

A few minutes later, Eloy slipped into the back of the saloon, a nod to the older woman in the back kitchen. "Hello."

She turned back to her pot, stirring its contents with calm, repetitive movements.

The door at the back of the kitchen opened a crack and Hui gestured for Eloy to come outside. The package under his arm went first, finding a new home in Hui's hands before the twine was pulled free of the dull-coloured paper. Inside the shirt and pants were identical matches to Eloy's uniform. The two men shared a smile.

"You have it?" Eloy could barely keep his voice even. There were so many things that could go wrong.

Hui nodded and gestured to the small barrel on the table at his side. Prying the top free, he tilted it carefully so that Eloy might be able to see its contents. Cylinders wrapped in paper were strung together with thin filament and gathered into one larger bundle near the wall of the barrel. "Sealed with pitch." Hui traced his finger along the wall where the bundle disappeared. Just inside the wall, a small piece of flint was attached to the wood with the guidewire. "Enough to create a spark," Hui explained.

Eloy wanted to ask him if it would work, but he stopped himself.

He had to trust that Hui could do what he promised. They all had to do what they promised. Questioning one of the group now was useless. They would either save their kingdom or lose it today. It was all up to each individual piece of their puzzle falling into place. "Get changed. We need to go soon."

Hui nodded and reached for the frog-buttons on his *changshan* tunic, quickly working them loose as he mumbled a quick prayer under his breath.

*

The doors of the refinery swung open for the last time, Tadashi on one door and Masanori on the other. They put their shoulders to the inner frame and, digging their feet into the ground, they managed to get the doors moving on their hinges. The movement was slow during the entire journey; they had not used the main doors in quite some time and the hinges had rusted enough to make it a challenge.

The morning sun gave them ample reason to squint, but the fact that they had been up all night testing and refining their new creation amplified the sun into a blazing ball of light.

Tadashi held up his arm over his eyes and called a chiding greeting to his friend. "Makes you think twice about facing doorway to the East, eh, Masa?"

"Always thought it would be nice to start work with the sun, Tadashi." He crossed quickly to the *'auwai* that ran alongside the building. Bending down, he scooped up water from the irrigation ditch and splashed some of it on his face.

Tadashi washed his hands off in the water slightly upstream of his friend and nodded his approval. "After we took the rocks, I thought for sure it would be all muddy and *hamajang*. It was dark when we started and we didn't wanna bus' up the ditch."

Standing, Masa dried his hands on his pants legs. "No harm done. Besides that, we'll put the rocks to good use."

The two men turned slowly back to the hulking machine behind them. Tadashi nodded with appreciation as the morning sun gave them their first real look of its imposing visage. "It will work, Masa, you'll see."

"Come," Masanori moved forward as he gestured to his friend, "we must begin now or we will miss the fun downtown."

"And I," joked Tadashi, "no like miss this party."

*

Thomas kept quiet during the meeting. As the men chattered on, their expressions expectant and cheerful, Thomas filled cups and removed trash as he had been taught to do.

The change in his attitude had not gone unnoticed by his brother. Thomas had no words for John and would answer none of his questions. John was left to fill coffee pots and tea urns while he managed to keep an eye on his brother. Just a few days before, his younger brother had been eager to fight against these men, but now he seemed perfectly satisfied to fetch paper and ink, pour refreshments and supply them with anything they needed. It was confusing to say the least, and John was not used to his brother confusing him or remaining quiet for so long.

When the meeting was over, John blocked the door, keeping his brother in the room. "What is it?"

Thomas stood tall and stared his brother down. "I have to go now." He tried to move past John and nearly made it to the stairs when his brother grabbed the back of his coat and turned him around. "Let me go."

"Tell me what you've done," John's tone was stiff with anger.

Thomas shook off his brother's hand, shaking his head in sadness. "I've done what I felt was right. I don't need to tell you anything."

There was a look in Thomas's eyes, one that his brother had never seen before. John wanted to argue with him, wanted to make him listen the way he always had. But there was that look in his eyes that said they were done with that kind of blind obedience. As John stepped aside and watched his brother walk away he couldn't help but wonder what he could have done to stop the change from happening… or to find a way to understand the man his brother had become.

Thomas was headed down King Street toward the Palace and, as he darted in between carts and other pedestrians, John had to make a choice. Leaving his others plans behind him, he surged into the road to follow his brother. Whatever Thomas had planned, he was going to find out what it was.

*

Masa tried to keep his teeth from grinding together as another rut in the dirt road shifted the path of their gigantic steam carriage. Tadashi, sitting beside him in the operator's cabin, had to grab his seat to keep himself upright. When the machine straightened out, the two friends shared a laugh that almost sounded like a groan. "This thing," chuckled Tadashi, "gonna cause some big commotion downtown."

"This thing will," answered Masanori, "if it makes it that far."

They kept their eyes on the road, watching the tiny buildings up ahead as they drew closer.

*

"One thing I like 'bout this," Hui peered over the side of the rowboat into the harbour's dark water, "I might catch fish for mama."

Eloy turned his head over his shoulder and nodded at his companion. "If I catch something, you can have it."

The younger Chinese man smiled and turned his attention back to the fishing pole in his hands.

The two had rowed out into the harbour dressed as local fishermen and had cautiously drifted themselves closer and closer to the *Intrepid* where it was anchored.

Twice that morning they had caught sight of a sailor on the deck peering over the edge of the ship to watch them.

Each time, one of the two men had taken one hand from their fishing pole and waved it in greeting to the men aboard the ship. A few words of greeting and then the faces above would disappear.

Eloy kept his ears trained for any odd noises on the ship, and he knew when the crew began to unload their own rowboats into the waters on the other side of the ship. He turned slightly and caught the gaze of his new friend. Hui nodded in response. The men aboard the ship would now be focussed away from them. This would be their best opportunity. Quickly stripping his shirt and pants off, Hui lowered himself into the harbour in his underwear, wincing as the water sloshed up to his neck.

Scooting to the other side of the boat, Eloy held the small barrel out and waited for Hui to take it and tuck it under his arm. "You ready for this?"

Hui's grin was wide, but there was a shadow in his eyes, something that looked like fear to Eloy.

Nodding, he gave the younger man a smile. "Attach it just above the water and make sure you have enough rope."

Taking in a deep breath of air, Hui quickly disappeared beneath the surface of the water.

*

Ovidio sat outside the boss's office, a newspaper held open before his face. *The Pacific Commercial Advertiser* would make no sense to him even if he was better student. In his hurry to set up and watch the *Harbinger*, he hadn't noticed that the paper was upside down.

When the soldiers started to assemble on the pier, Ovidio felt the edge of the newspaper crease as his hands tightened around it. He kept his gaze focussed on the newspaper, even when the sudden clatter of carriage wheels could be heard.

"Just focus." He repeated the words to himself over and over again as the soldiers separated into two lines to allow the carriage to rumble up and over the top of the gangplank. The ship, larger than most that they'd seen in the harbour, had been equipped with a ramp wider than he'd seen before.

Now, as the steam-driven carriage rolled down onto the pier, the soldiers on either side of it celebrated the accomplishment. Ovidio barely resisted the urge to run away. Instead he kept himself seated, eyes trained at the centre of a page of words he'd never be able to remember.

And when the soldiers had all passed by his position he found the strength to get up on his feet. His first step had him wobbling on his feet, grabbing for the wall of the shack to keep him upright.

As he straightened himself up and began the walk down the pier, he slipped his hand into his pocket, closed it around his work knife and steeled his nerve. He was always working with Eloy, the two of them helping each other through all the facets of their jobs. Now he was going to have to do this one important assignment on his own.

Ovidio took a step up onto the ramp and paused. There were men moving around on adjacent ships, sailors and passengers alike. No one paid him any special notice; after all, they were watching the odd progression of soldiers and steam carriage down the dirt road. With a quick prayer to his maker, Ovidio made his way up the gangplank and into the ship. He had to find the anchor controls and had a short time to do it.

*

Thomas was greeted at the gate by his *hanai* cousin, Kamaehu, who took him directly inside the barracks. "Thomas, this is my sergeant. He is *He Kakiana* – the First Sergeant, the highest ranking officer of the remaining Royal Guard while the King is away."

There was no denying that the man was an officer, capable of leading men. His posture was strong and straight, giving his dark blue jacket the impression of a solid wall capped with the pristine white pith helmet that completed his uniform. Holding out his hand to Thomas, he nodded at the younger man. "Kamaehu explained what your friends are doing." His smile was a bit twisted up at the corner. "I don't know if they will be needed, but it is good to know that people are willing to help defend our kingdom."

Thomas wasn't sure that the sergeant believed their story; in fact, he was sure that the man thought he was a little touched in the head. Still, this was where he was going to make his stand. "You'll see," he told the sergeant, "they'll come and you'll see." Keeping his eyes straight on the sergeant and not on the cautious glance of his cousin's eyes, Thomas made his one request. "If you'll send someone up to the clock tower of *Ali'iolani Hale*," he explained, "he'll see the men coming from the ship in the harbour."

The sergeant did sent a man into the tower, but even the guard that took the order and started across the road did not believe they were in any danger.

They only had to wait a few minutes once the man found a good vantage point in the clock tower. Rising up on the balls of his feet and waving his bright white pith helmet in the air, the guard pointed toward the harbour and waved at the crowd beside the barracks.

Even with his training, the First Sergeant was unprepared for the sudden rush of fear and indignant anger that welled up within his middle. If what young Thomas said was true, they were about to defend the kingdom against an invasion.

Turning to his men, he quickly barked out some orders before turned back to their newest recruit. "Pick up a weapon, Thomas; you'll stand at my side."

Without waiting for an answer, the First Sergeant turned on his heel and set about organising his men in the yard of the Palace. He sent word across the street to the Legislature; they would need to lock their doors and mount some kind of defence on their own. There was no one to be spared.

*

As their hired troops passed along the waterfront, eight businessmen who represented some of the most influential and prosperous families in the kingdom stepped out from the bank building and walked down the centre of the two regimented lines. A second line was added on each side as the rowboats from the *Intrepid* reached the shore.

A sudden rush of movement from with the white wall of the palace grounds alerted the soldiers that they had lost the element of surprise. The Royal Guard filed neatly into formation, their eyes hidden by the shadows laid across their faces by the brim of their pith helmets.

When their hired soldiers were called to a halt, the businessmen stepped forward until they were just behind the first line of men. Near their centre Carson Whitley, head of a large sugar plantation, stepped even further forward and addressed the guards behind the gate. "We do not intend any loss of life today, gentlemen. We are all citizens of this great kingdom and we only strive to make it a great power in the world." He looked down one side of his committee and then down the other before turning back to address the Guardsmen. "Your King is travelling the world, enjoying the beautiful sites and exchanging luxurious gifts with other kings as he goes. When he returns in a year, what will have happened to his kingdom… to his home?"

Murmurs pulsed through the gathering crowd.

"What will be left when a kingdom suffers the loss of its leader for that length of time?"

More comments this time. Thomas could hear the disruption and felt his own stomach clench with worry as he looked to the head of the Guard. The First Sergeant made no move to speak.

Whitley's smile tightened as he continued to address the crowd. "What we propose is simple. A kingdom can only care for its people when its coffers are full. We," he held out his arms to acknowledge his compatriots, "have the skill and experience to bring the Kingdom of Hawaii great success and make our island kingdom one of the greatest governments of our age!"

*

Holding Eloy's spyglass to his eyes with as much care as he could, Masanori could see the gathering crowds on the King's road. The white points of colour, most certainly the pith helmets crowning the heads of the Royal Guard, gave him a point to focus on as they manoeuvred their machine toward town. The ground had levelled out at some point, allowing them to travel faster along the way, and as they neared the main body of Honolulu town the ground sloped toward the harbour, speeding up their travel significantly.

Shifting the speed of the tracks beneath them, the machine moved ever onward, faster and faster, belching gusts of smoke from the back end of the carriage.

*

Behind the lines of hired soldiers, from the doors of *Ali'iolani Hale*, men filed out from the Legislature with rifles in their hands. Men armed and ready to fight to keep what they had; an elected government.

Shouts of discontent arose from some of the eight surrounded by their hired men, a few wondering aloud if this was all according to plan. Whitley's close friend, Robert Cope, sized up the situation and stood beside his friend. "Blind loyalty is not in the best interests of the people," he argued on their behalf. "We understand the vast economic advances of the world and the science that makes it possible. The airships that bring us exotic produce from other countries, avoiding the long and dangerous voyages by sea, the beginnings of underwater travel that may mean great economic gain as well as a better means of protecting our lands from foreign avarice. What we offer is real experience and the determination to make it happen. Is there any man here that can say the same about the King?"

The challenge hung in the air; the crowd looked from one group to another for reassurance or inspiration. The Guard remained steadfast, staring down the greater numbers that stood in the road. Thomas felt something deep within him move. For a man who had lived the last few years of his life in menial service to others, he'd had just about enough of men like Whitley and Cope.

Stepping forward of the troops, nearly to the fence, Thomas met Cope's challenge with dark eyes and a gut full of determination. "The King will learn from other leaders and we will follow him. We elected him and he will lead us. We don't need what you offer."

Whitley's face softened a bit, with a smile that seemed more suited to address a child than a fellow man. "And how would you know? Have you been beyond the waters that surround these islands? Have you any idea what the world has to offer beyond what you know from experience, sun up to sun down?"

One of the other men that had been watching the exchange with interest finally found the thought that was buzzing through his head. Leaning closer to Whitley, he shared his revelation.

The news burst from the man's lips with a laugh. "You're the servant we hired to clean up after our meetings!" He turned to look at the men who stood with him. "I guess we'll have to be more careful when we hire busboys in the future."

The remark didn't hurt Thomas. Rather, his chest expanded with pride. "You will not succeed."

Cope angled into the conversation. "I don't know if you can fully understand the situation, sir." He held up a hand and the windows on the carriage that had accompanied them from the *Harbinger* slid down and the wide mouths of gun barrels filled the voids. A man scrambled up atop the carriage and waved a yellow flag.

Those standing on either side of *Ali'iolani* had a view of the harbour. The *Intrepid*'s cannon barrels were now visible.

Cope's smile was telling. "Perhaps a little demonstration of our... resolve."

With a whispered command, one of the barrels in the carriage window swivelled and, with a belch of fire, the wall in front of Thomas exploded into a shower of stone.

Thrown to the ground, Thomas felt an odd sensation... he was still whole. Turning onto his side he found himself staring at his brother. John's arm was twisted slightly, cradled against his middle, and both of them were covered in dust and small pieces of debris.

It was the silence following the blast that gave the crowd the most pause. For into that silence rumbled the beginnings of a new kind of fear. Rolling swiftly down the road was a behemoth of metal. The grinding crunch of the track that rushed it forward chewed up the ground like hundreds of clawed feet. The screaming steam released from the furnace stumbled onlookers away and into the relative safety of surrounding buildings.

"What the hell is that?" Whitley nearly knocked his friend Cope down as he began to move away from the path of the oncoming monstrosity.

The First Sergeant looked to Thomas for confirmation. "Is that one of your friends?"

Thomas, barely on his knees and a bit shaken, looked at the rising dust cloud and heard the excited yelling from the cabin of the machine and nodded. "That's Masanori."

Barking a loud order to his men to stand ready, the First Sergeant took a moment to stare in wonder. "I hope they can get it to stop."

*

Adjusting their direction to focus the protruding track on the carriage, Masa pushed a button on the console. Metal scraped on metal as long dormant gears ground into action. Metal tines meant to draw sugar cane into the processing machine now swung outward. As they continued forward the track picked up speed. Masa watched the pressure gauge and felt his heart speed up along with the motion of the machine.

The track rolled faster and faster until the pressure gauge rode the line into the red. Looking over his shoulder, Masa gave his friend the order, "Load!"

Pulling back a lever, Tadashi opened the gate to the reservoir. A river rock rolled down into the metal channel they'd created with an old gutter, followed by a half-dozen more stones. The next set of tines scooped up a stone and flung it from the end of the track, followed quickly by another.

The first stone landed with a loud thud at the foot of a soldier, peppering him with dirt and pebbles from the road. The second stone, fast on the heels of the first, hit the man between his chest and his shoulder, knocking him into the man behind him.

The initial shock of this new attack wore off in a heartbeat, and the lines of soldiers began to crumble with some running for cover along with onlookers in the crowd.

Whitley, sensing the disintegration of his cause, was ready to use his ace. With a command the man atop the carriage performed his last duty, raising the green flag in his hands. A moment later he hopped down, leaving the flags in the dirt as he ran for safety in the crowds.

From the clock tower at the head of *Ali'iolani Hale*, Ovidio saw the green flag and waved his own in the air, a bright red sash that he had brought from his own things at home. A sash that could be seen by a little rowboat in the harbour.

*

Hui saw the signal and, before Eloy could utter the command through his parched lips, the Chinese man pulled the rope in his hand, striking the flint within its barrel.

The device, attached to the thick wooden wall of the ship exploded, threw flames up the outer wall and curling through the belly of the vessel. Only a few cannons managed to fire on the town and only two projectiles did any damage to the Legislature building, crumbling some of the rock face, raining small pieces onto the porch and grass at the base of the building.

*

Whitley and Cope soon found themselves surrounded by less than half of their original force. The sudden explosion in the harbour that rained down pieces of the *Intrepid* had done a great deal to clear the street of curious onlookers and hired soldiers. It was the imminent danger of the machine throttling down the street that cleared the two men and the remaining guns from the street. They spilled backwards over the white picket and wire fence that ringed *Ali'iolani Hale*, giving them a clear view as the shower of rocks flung from the monstrous machine blew holes in the body of the carriage, destroying any power it had to fire at the Royal Guard. With the way cleared of the hired soldiers, the machine crawled right over the steam carriage. The brakes, aided by the challenge of grinding the armoured carriage under its tracks, finally slowed the machine down to a stop.

Thomas and his brother John, his arm tied up in a sling, brought the First Sergeant through the front gates of the Palace to greet Masanori and Tadashi, both a bit shaken but elated to make such a punctual appearance.

Making his way through the crowd on *Ali'iolani*'s lawn, Ovidio joined the group and watched as some of the Legislators marched their own captives toward the Barracks.

"I should send men to the harbour," the First Sergeant worried, "they might escape on their other ship."

Ovidio shook his head and pointed to the large three-masted ship moving slowly toward open water. "No need."

Thomas nodded. "Ovidio should know," he explained, "he's the one that cut the lines holding the ship to the pier and cut it loose from its anchor."

"They not going nowhere."

*

The back alley saloon was full that afternoon. Some of the crowd had followed the unlikely group of heroes there. Eloy and Hui, straight from the docks, had secured their table, and Hui was enjoying both a lecture and love from his mother. There was an extra chair pulled up to complete their celebration. John sat beside his brother, quiet and proud.

When Thomas handed him a cup of tea, John mumbled a thanks into his cup. He took a good look at the men around the table and asked his brother the question that had been on his mind. "How did you make this happen?"

As each man took turns explaining their roles in the grand scheme of things, curious patrons gathered up close to the table with their ears tuned for gossip and their cups emptying quickly as they enjoyed the tale.

Eloy leaned on the table and looked at Thomas. "What happened to the men... the ones that planned all this?"

Thomas let out a long satisfied sigh. "The Guard and the Legislators rounded them up and locked them in the barracks. After that, that started arguing with each other about what they were going to do with them."

Shrugging, Eloy leaned back in his chair. "We did our part. It's out of our hands."

"Just think of how many things could have gone wrong," Masa downed his cup and sighed.

"And how many things went right," Thomas grinned.

"And how lucky it was that we all ended up in the same place at the same time." Eloy filled his cup again from the pot. "And that we all survived the day." He gave it a moment of thought. "Serendipity."

"Lucky us," added Hui.

"Fortunate," it was Tadashi's turn to jump in.

John gave his brother a broad grin and lifted his cup with his odd hand. "Providence."

Thomas pursed his lips for a moment to hold back an odd sensation that reminded him of tears. He held his own cup aloft and agreed with his brother wholeheartedly. "Providence."

STEAM PUNK

WRITERS AROUND THE WORLD

LAS CADENAS INFINITAS

Peru

LAS CADENAS INFINITAS[1]

By César Santivañez

Si la esclavitud no es injusta,
entonces no hay nada injusto.
Abraham Lincoln

Las once menos cuarto y las cosas no parecían haber mejorado. La enorme barcaza de níquel decorada con grandes velas verticales bautizada como *S.S. Malinowski* aún flotaba, inerte, en las costas del Callao. Mal presagio, considerando que el armatoste debía haber abandonado la costa hacía tres horas. Si así recibían la primera noche de 1855, nadie se atrevía a suponer cómo sería el resto del año.

A un lado de la lujosa escotilla principal, con los pies firmes sobre la tierra, míster Meiggs[2] y el capitán del navío sostenían una álgida conversación:

'¡*This is it*, capitán Carmona[3]! ¡Jamás, escúchelo bien, jamás había retrasado tanto un cocktail! ¡La champaña casi se ha agotado, y aún no

---

1. Lo que aquí presento no es únicamente un relato, sino, además una teoría alrededor de las misteriosas circunstancias que rodearon a la desaparición de la embarcación bautizada como *S.S. Malinowski*, nave peruana que, de acuerdo a los registros marítimos, tuvo como fecha de botadura el 28 de diciembre de 1884. Tomo como primera fuente de información los planos del propio ingeniero creador del artefacto, archivados en la Colección X de la Biblioteca Nacional, y la bitácora del capitán Ulises Carmona, exhibida hasta el año 2008 en el Museo Naval del Perú. (N. del A.)

2. La referencia es a Conrad Meiggs hijo, el primero de su familia en llegar al Perú, incluso antes que su medio hermano norteamericano, Henry Meiggs, quien pisó por primera vez suelo peruano en 1868, para participar en la licitación del ferrocarril de Arequipa. (N. del A.)

3. De por sí, la bitácora del capitán Ulises Carmona, si bien es útil para trazar un esbozo general de los acontecimientos, no ahonda en detalles. Fue necesario acudir a diarios y demás bibliografía que me permitiera tener más luces acerca de lo ocurrido. Agradezco al Sr. Hugo Luque, presidente de la Sociedad Retrofuturista del Perú, por haber confiado en la seriedad de mi investigación y por haberme permitido el acceso a más de una hemeroteca

117

abandonamos este sucio muelle!

¡Comprenda usted que ahí dentro se encuentran las personas más influyentes de este país, y no puedo desairarlos! ¡No en Año Nuevo, *for Christ's sake!*'

'Lo siento, míster Meiggs. Sucede que los maquinistas locales no están familiarizados con este tipo de … mecanismos,' replicó el capitán, al tiempo que su voz era anulada por el rugido metálico de dos turbinas cúpricas y relucientes, de varios metros de diámetro y anexas a las aletas del *S.S. Malinowski*. Un viento recio comenzó a soplar en los alrededores, desatando verdaderas oleadas de brisa marina.

'*Finally*! *It was about time*!' refunfuñó míster Meiggs, escondiendo su amplio rostro entre las solapas de su abrigo de terciopelo y sosteniendo su sombrero de copa con una de sus manos, la que lucía menos anillos. Dándole la espalda al capitán, desapareció a través de la escotilla.

El capitán Carmona, empequeñecido tanto por el vergonzoso episodio como por el imponente navío metálico, que ya empezaba a ondular sobre la superficie marítima, se recompuso dentro de su traje de gala y se aprestó a iniciar funciones, caminando a lo largo del muelle hasta la altura de la proa, donde se encontraba su segundo al mando. Juntos esperaron el elevador de poleas, que los condujo en vertical hasta la cabina de mando. Por debajo de ellos, al nivel de suelo, no pocos curiosos se agolpaban a lo largo de los casi veinte metros de eslora del extraño artefacto, la mayoría de ellos estibadores, borrachos y mendigos, almas solitarias que no tenían mejor lugar donde pasar la noche que asomando las narices entre la pompa y boato de la aristocracia limeña.

Dentro del *S.S. Malinowski*, amplificada en su recorrido por un sistema acústico de tuberías, la voz del capitán Carmona atravesó varios ambientes de la estructura: los corredores forrados de *velours*, los jardines interiores, las puertas de plata bruñida y el salón de rapé con motivos babilónicos. Finalmente fue a parar al fastuoso recibidor, desde donde resonó, cavernosa, a través de un micrófono colocado en uno de los lamparones de cristal:

'Señor presidente, señores ministros, Sir Conrad Meiggs, distinguida concurrencia: les habla su capitán. Asumo plena responsabilidad por el retraso. Sepan, sin embargo, que el desperfecto que nos retenía en tierra ha sido solucionado. Siendo las once de la noche en punto, el *S.S. Malinowski* les da la bienvenida y les desea un feliz viaje.'

---

privada. (N. del A.)

Una miríada de manos finamente enguantadas explotaron en aplausos. Rufino Echenique, hombrecillo esmirriado y de facciones más bien genéricas, atrajo hacia sí la atención de los invitados con un ademán discreto:

'Es para mí un honor, en representación de la República del Perú, ser partícipe del primer viaje de esta embarcación, única en su género. Agradezco a Sir Conrad Meiggs por invertir en el progreso de la nación que con tanto orgullo lo ha acogido y, más aun, por haberlo hecho en estos tiempos tan aciagos, en los cuales hasta la moral de las mejores familias del país queda en entredicho. Este portento de la ingeniería es justamente el mejor ejemplo de que el intelecto y la nobleza son las mejores riendas del país ¡Que 1855 nos depare salud y bienestar!'

'Permítame felicitarlo, señor presidente. Resumió usted en pocas palabras el sentir de toda la tripulación,' intervino en voz baja Ramírez-Quesada, comerciante de mediana edad conocido por sus tortuosos manejos en el mercado del papel.

En el muelle, los advenedizos veían cómo, a medida que la embarcación niquelada se alejaba hacia el horizonte, esta se iba transformando gradualmente en una especie de monstruo marino: sendas aberturas rectangulares se formaron a babor y estribor, semejantes estas a branquias, de las cuales emergieron una serie de apéndices tubulares que se sumergieron en el agua y empezaron a succionar, haciendo las veces de cánulas gigantes. Visto desde arriba, el *S.S. Malinowski* debió parecer una especie de molusco prehistórico abriéndose paso en el mar primitivo.

Al cabo de pocos minutos de navegar mar adentro, cuando la costa se hubo perdido de vista, el capitán Carmona lanzó una mirada desafiante a los tripulantes de cabina y preguntó por la velocidad de la nave. Alguien le respondió:

'Cincuenta nudos, capitán.'

'Perfecto. Este es el momento. Cambio a segundo sistema de propulsión.'

Con claro temor, pero aun así observando cierto entusiasmo, decenas de hombres empezaron a correr dentro de la cabina de mando. Algunos levantaban palancas, otros giraban manivelas y la mayoría gritaba cifras al aire, las cuales eran luego recogidas por un oficial viejo y ceñudo, que no paraba de anotarlas en un gran registro de navegación.

En medio del calor de la noche de verano, y en medio del mar, que poco a poco se iba transformando en un horizonte panorámico, el casco del *S.S. Malinowski* lanzó un eco metálico y sostenido. El hermoso velamen se plegó automáticamente alrededor del mástil, y la superficie marina debajo de la gran estructura empezó a agitarse, poblándose de una espuma densa producida por la fuerza de succión de las costillas tubulares. Una tobera ubicada en la popa se encargaba de expulsar el agua, transformada en vapor luego de un complicado proceso de supercombustión[4]. Así, al cabo de unos instantes, la embarcación alcanzó una velocidad de casi ochenta nudos, lo cual le permitió sobrevolar ligeramente el agua de la superficie, como un guijarro lanzado a través de un charco.

Los invitados reunidos en el lujoso salón recibidor, alertados por el sonido, corrieron a toda prisa hacia cubierta, desde donde observaron anonadados el poderío de las corrientes y la columna de vapor que se elevaba hacia el cielo en una gran voluta blanquecina.

'¡Vaya potencia! ¡Vaya rapidez! Oh, *this is really one hell of a ride*,' exclamó míster Meiggs, quien, visiblemente rendido ante la excitación, cerraba fuertemente el puño sobre la baranda de metal que lo separaba de la infinidad marina.

'Ya lo creo, Conrad. Todo esto es de no creer,' suspiró el presidente Echenique. 'Aquí estamos, en medio de la nada, sin tierras ni servidumbre. A cambio, tenemos el océano entero bajo nuestros pies.'

'Definitivamente, me aseguraré de enviar al ingeniero Malinowski[5] mis más sinceras felicitaciones. Su genio es portentoso. Es una lástima que no nos haya podido acompañar esta noche,' susurró Ramírez-Quesada, secundado en silencio por Meiggs y el presidente Echenique. Los tres quedaron inmóviles, aspirando la brisa. Luego de unos minutos se sumaron a los demás, quienes, viendo saciada su curiosidad, se dispusieron a ingresar nuevamente al salón recibidor.

El Callao se perdió de vista, y la luna brilló como nunca antes.

*

Absorto en la lectura del diario de la mañana, marcado con fecha

---

4. A pesar de ser técnicamente incorrecto, este es el término con que Sir Conrad Meiggs se refería al sistema de propulsión ideado por Malinowski. La primera referencia que se hizo del mismo fue en una carta enviada a Elías Meiggs, padre de Conrad, el 30 de noviembre del 1854. (N. del A.)

5. Ernest Malinowski, ingeniero polaco, había adquirido gran fama después de haber extendido el ferrocarril Lima-Callao hasta el valle de Jauja, en 1851. (N. del A.)

1 de diciembre de 1854, Rufino Echenique refunfuñaba en medio del salón presidencial. Era de día y, sin embargo, el alto espacio de arquitectura colonial lucía sombrío y deshabitado: sendas sombras acariciaban los lomos de los libros de la estantería, las amplias baldosas italianas y las cortinas de seda. '¡Manumisión, y una mierda! ¡Esto es imposible!' estalló el presidente, visiblemente ofuscado, golpeando con ambos puños el macizo escritorio de caoba. Alguien tocó la puerta, y una voz se escuchó detrás de ella.

'Señor presidente, sir Conrad Meiggs está aquí.' 'Que pase. Que pase.'

La puerta se abrió, y un edecán prieto e impoluto dio paso a míster Meiggs, quien irrumpió en la sala como un toro salvaje, dando pasos largos y con el rostro intoxicado por la rabia. El edecán cerró la puerta tras él, dejando a los dos hombres solos en el despacho.

'*That man is absolutely out of his mind*! ¡Esta vez, Castilla ha llegado demasiado lejos!' exclamó Meiggs, dejando de lado su reputada gentileza. Luego, al percatarse de lo desatinado de su comportamiento, se recompuso, carraspeó e hizo una respetuosa reverencia. 'Ehm … debo disculparme, míster Echenique. Ha ocurrido algo: Castilla planea manumitir a los esclavos pasado mañana, a nombre del Estado.'

El presidente se acarició el rostro, en señal de nerviosismo. Llenó su pipa sin derramar una pizca de tabaco, y la encendió entrecerrando los ojos.

'Lo sé, Meiggs. Es indecible. ¡Castilla ya no es el presidente, carajo, el presidente soy yo! ¿De verdad cree que ese es el modo correcto de retomar el poder? ¿Erigiéndose como el caudillo de los animales, de los desposeídos sin voluntad ni conciencia?'

'*In fact*, míster Echenique, el plan de su adversario es bastante lúcido. Quiere ganar adeptos, formar un ejército no solo contra usted, sino contra la clase a la que representa. Está apelando a sentimientos muy peligrosos.'

'No es justo. Y la buena gente, ¿qué? ¿Y los inversionistas, y los extranjeros? ¡Ellos también son parte de este país!'

'Somos los menos, ha de reconocerlo. Y, además, seamos sinceros: hay doce millones de pesos de deudas fantasma con el Estado.' Al decir esto, quedaba claro que Conrad Meiggs era consciente de que su discurso había empezado a exasperar al presidente. Aun así, prosiguió. 'Todos saben que aquellas deudas jamás se contrajeron realmente, y que a pesar de ello están siendo cobradas *as we speak* por las mejores familias del país, y todo gracias a … la afinidad con usted y su gobierno. Es inútil que lo niegue.'

'Mire, Meiggs, si ha venido a increparme la ayuda que yo mismo le brindé en su momento …'

'Oh, *no way, Mister President.* Al contrario, vengo a devolverle ese favor.'

Súbitamente, Echenique se tranquilizó. Miro al inglés a los ojos, y reconoció en ellos la complicidad del comerciante, del amigo, del conspirador.

'Hable.'

'Recordará la embarcación cuya fabricación encargué hace algún tiempo a nuestro querido amigo, Ernest Malinowski. Ya sabe, aquella en la que planeábamos hacer aquel corto recorrido por la costa, la noche de Año Nuevo. *Well, fine then.* Propongo un ligero cambio de ruta.'

*

Encaramado en lo alto de un mástil, un grumete corpulento y algo bebido se esforzaba por no perder el equilibrio, mientras sostenía una decena de cilindros de pólvora coloreada, del tamaño de catalejos.

'¿Ya es hora?'

'No, espera.' Otro marino, firmemente apoyado en cubierta, extrajo de su bolsillo un reloj oxidado, y lo observó, inmóvil, por unos segundos. Respondió a su compañero, sin levantar la cabeza. 'Aún no.'

Mientras tanto, en el salón recibidor, un coro de voces distorsionadas por el alcohol empezó la cuenta.

¡Cinco!

Un sonido particular, como de agua en ebullición, atrajo la atención de los marinos del mástil. Antes de que tuvieran tiempo de asomar por la baranda, el mar a los flancos del *S.S. Malinowski*, de por sí convulsionado por la costillas tubulares, se agitó hasta transformarse en una espuma violenta, que refulgía en tonalidades turquesa a la luz de la luna. Nadie parecía notarlo. Todos estaban a buen recaudo en el salón principal, cobijados por la calidez de las lámparas europeas y concentrados en perderse en los efectos del champán.

¡Cuatro!

'¡Da la alarma! ¡Da la alarma!' No hubo tiempo para más. El grumete soltó los tubos de cartón, que en su caída recorrieron el mástil en toda su longitud. Al mismo tiempo, logró ver cómo diez cápsulas metálicas, totalmente selladas, emergieron de cada uno de los lados de la gran embarcación[6], tal y como podría haberlo hecho un grupo de delfines. Iban exactamente a la misma velocidad que el *S.S. Malinowski*.

¡Tres!

En el salón, alguien dejó caer una copa. El sonido del cristal roto se perdió entre el bullicio y la algarabía general. Las luces del salón, sumadas a la estrechez de las ventanas y la oscuridad de la noche, hacían imposible notar que las cápsulas metálicas habían continuado su ascenso desde las profundidades, y por un segundo se mantuvieron inmóviles al nivel de la baranda de cubierta, antes de iniciar el descenso que las sumergiría nuevamente en las profundidades oceánicas.

¡Dos!

Si acaso alguno de los invitados se hubiera percatado de los insólitos acontecimientos que se daban lugar a escasos metros de la fiesta, seguramente hubiera visto dos esferas dentadas, del diámetro de una nuez, saliendo disparadas desde una de las cápsulas, para luego atravesar el espacio nocturno y caer de lleno en las cabezas del grumete y la de su compañero, los cuales cayeron inconscientes al lado de los tubos de cartón blanco.

¡Uno!

Sendas cabezas de arpón fueron disparadas desde las cápsulas, casi con la misma fuerza y velocidad que las esferas dentadas. A estos venían atadas sogas gruesas y oscuras como serpientes. Durante aquel segundo, en que los garfios atravesaban la noche, todo volvió a ser paz y silencio en el *S.S. Malinowski*.

¡Feliz Año Nuevo!

Los arpones se incrustaron en el metal de la nave, justo cuando la algarabía alcanzó su punto máximo. Acalorados por el rapé, la efusión general y el sonido de la gran maquinaria, ninguno de los que ahí viajaban, ni siquiera el capitán Carmona y los suyos, lograron ver las doce siluetas mecanizadas escalando firmemente hacia cubierta.

Un cuarteto de cámara empezó a tocar una melodía graciosa

---

6. El 28 de agosto de 1976, se encontraron restos de cascos metálicos en el suelo marino frente al puerto de Culebras, en el departamento de Ancash (norte de Lima). Si bien su fecha de fabricación no pudo ser determinada (la confusión es ampliamente excusable, teniendo en cuenta lo avanzado del diseño), los cuadernos de Ernest Malinowski contienen planos de estructuras idénticas a las encontradas en 1976. (N. del A.)

y acompasada. Entre el fraseo de los violines se suscitaban abrazos venturosos y los mejores deseos para el 1855, la mayor parte de ellos dirigidos, como era de esperarse, al presidente Echenique. *"Que Dios lo bendiga, hoy y siempre, señor presidente"*, *"Cuando el pueblo abra los ojos, verá al gran hombre que lo dirige"*, *"Que el porvenir le sea auspicioso, señor presidente. Por cierto, quería hablarle de unos bonos que el Estado firmó a mi nombre, hace algunos meses, y que aún no he podido cobrar …"*. Ramírez-Quesada, impertinente e insidioso como de costumbre, se arrogaba el papel de hombre de confianza de Echenique y lo salvaba de esta y otras conversaciones incómodas, desviando la conversación con un mal chiste o un comentario a guisa de nada. En otra esquina del salón, míster Meiggs fumaba, solitario y oscuramente meditabundo.

Entonces, sucedió. Un fuerte golpe quebró los altos portones de vidrio del recibidor. Las esquirlas fueron a parar a los pies del cuarteto de cámara, el cual dejó de tocar en el momento exacto en que los gritos de emoción de la concurrencia dejaron paso a alaridos terroríficos, que fueron en aumento a medida que cada uno de los doce hombres altos, fornidos y brutalmente intervenidos con placas de metal irrumpieron en la reunión. Se trataba de fenómenos titánicos, de aspecto sucio y desordenado, que exhibían ya prótesis en brazos y piernas amputadas, ya varillas articuladas alrededor de la cintura, ya espinas dorsales externas engarzadas a sus cuerpos, diríase a presión. Todos, por lo demás, tenían rasgos chinos o africanos, y exhibían por debajo de los ropajes raídos varias cicatrices y laceraciones que los hacían dignos de la más visceral repulsión. El contraste que hacían con los impolutos y aristocráticos invitados de míster Conrad Meiggs, los cuales se replegaron al instante hacia la pared opuesta del salón, hacía la escena aún más impactante.

Aquel que parecía el líder del grupo, un negro calvo, fornido y de mirada estrábica, dio un paso al frente, evidenciando una ligera cojera. Su mandíbula había desaparecido, y en su lugar había una caja de metal, atornillada al resto del cráneo con toscos pernos oxidados. Por lo demás, el sudor y el agua de mar surcaban su musculatura recia y compacta, interrumpida al nivel del pecho por dos planchas de metal que se extendían al centro de su torso como las alas de una mariposa, unidas por una bisagra que subía por su cuello hasta llegar casi al mentón.

El negro empezó a hablar:

'Esta embarcación es ahora nuestra. Tienen tres minutos para abordar las chalupas de salvamento y ahorrarnos las balas. Pasado ese tiempo, los que se queden serán liquidados. No necesitamos prisioneros.'

La primera reacción fue de un pavor estático. Durante varios segundos, solo las miradas fueron el único puente entre ambos cúmulos humanos. Los invitados pudieron estudiar con detenimiento al grupo de piratas y se percataron de los rifles de avancarga, las pistolas y la gran cantidad de cartuchos y sacos de pólvora que colgaban de sus cinturones. El líder de los piratas volvió a romper el silencio:

'¿Dónde está Meiggs?'

La cabeza de míster Meiggs asomó de entre el gentío. Luego, el corpulento y acaudalado inglés avanzó hasta situarse cara a cara con aquella especie de demonio metálico. Ambos soltaron una risa quieta, mitad amarga y mitad sardónica.

'Eres tú. Lo sabía. ¿A qué has venido?' preguntó Meiggs. 'Vengo a demostrar que te equivocaste, que sí me hice a la mar, y que la libertad no me transformó en un asesino.' Guardaban el trato familiar de dos camaradas a quienes el tiempo había separado. El negro antes conocido como Sócrates[7] bajó la mirada hacia la mariposa de metal que se extendía sobre su piel oscura. Seguidamente, como quien abre una caja mecánica, maniobró una perilla y las portezuelas de su pecho se abrieron como alas. Su tórax quedó convertido en una jaula, una cavidad en donde dos adminículos parecidos a bolsas de tela color tierra se inflaban y desinflaban, manchados aquí y allá de sangre seca. El espectáculo de su anatomía contrahecha era sorprendente, a la vez que lamentable. Volvió a cerrar la caja. 'Este fue el precio que tuve que pagar por sobrevivir a la esclavitud.'

'Entonces, después de todo, lo conseguiste. *You truly are a free man*,' mientras hablaba, Meiggs lo recorrió con la mirada. 'Sigues siendo un hombre fuerte.'

'Pero ahora soy un monstruo, y actúo como tal. Toma a tus invitados, y lárguense. No queremos matar a nadie.'

Nadie se movió.

Sócrates, monstruo de ébano, extrajo de su cinto una pistola de boca ancha y finamente tallada. Con un movimiento rápido y firme apuntó a uno de los invitados al azar.

---

7. Cuando el capitán Ulises Carmona se refiere a Sócrates en su bitácora, a menudo utiliza epítetos como "piel de armadura" o "el esclavo monstruo". Ello nos puede dar una idea de la particular e intimidante impresión que este personaje ejerció en quienes allí se hallaban. (N. del A.)

'Habla.' La orden del negro fue clara y concisa, casi una semilla de amenaza. Con un quejido trémulo, que lo delataba como a un hombre al borde de la quebrazón, Ramírez-Quesada empezó a hablar hacia el cañón que lo enrostraba:

'Todo nuestro dinero está debajo de nosotros, escondido en el cuarto de máquinas de esta embarcación.'

Luego de unos instantes, el negro replicó:

'Entonces, la fiesta de Año Nuevo no es más que una excusa. Esto es una fuga. Huyen, porque saben que tarde o temprano Castilla retomará el poder, y entonces serán juzgados.'

'No estamos dispuestos a abandonar nuestra fortuna, y menos para dejarla en manos de un hatajo de delincuentes, como la gente de Castilla o, en todo caso, como ustedes.'

Dicho esto, Ramírez-Quesada falseó el talante y permaneció enhiesto, aparentemente dueño de sí mismo. Su orgullo lo hacía ver patético.

Sócrates imaginó una gran bolsa de dinero flotando en alta mar, y se preguntó hasta donde podía llegar la codicia humana. Hasta dónde podía depender el hombre del dinero, hasta el punto de arriesgar la propia vida por conservarlo:

'Hay que ver cuántos rostros tiene la esclavitud.'

*

Aire caliente. Eso, y un hedor rancio era lo que se respiraba alrededor del caldero de la fundición de míster Meiggs[8]. Algunos chispazos, como pequeñas luciérnagas ígneas, salían desde la portezuela del fogón principal e iban a morir a centímetros de Sócrates, esclavo y capataz de piel oscura y lisa, quien a pesar de sus cincuenta y tantos años aún manejaba la pala como el mejor de los hombres. Este, como todas las mañanas desde hacía quince años, alimentaba el caldero con la cantidad adecuada de carbón, canturreando y con la mirada fija en nada, en el África de sus abuelos que ni siquiera él mismo conocía, en un pasado

---

8. En el Perú, el Registro de Propiedad Inmueble se creó en el año 1888, más de treinta años después de los hechos descritos en esta historia. Por ende, es difícil rastrear el nombre y la ubicación de la fundición de Conrad Meiggs. Se cree que esta se encontraba en el distrito de Coayllo, provincia de Cañete (sur de Lima), pues ahí se han encontrado vestigios industriales de mediados del S. XIX, algunos con el rótulo «C.M. & Co.» (N. del A.)

imaginario lleno de episodios de caza y correrías a lo largo de la sabana. Porque Sócrates siempre se había considerado un hombre libre. «La libertad es un estado mental», decía, cuando alguien le preguntaba por qué soportaba los golpes y fustigaciones de Meiggs, o cuando se le increpaba su pasividad. Así era Sócrates: un negro noble y callado, pacífico como una tarde de verano.

Había, sí, un episodio que los demás esclavos recordaban bien: el día en que el capataz estuvo a punto de perder la cordura, cuando Meiggs molió a golpes a su hijo, hasta matarlo. La cordura, pero no la tranquilidad. Decían que Sócrates, aun sabiendo que el cuerpo de su negrito yacía tieso y olvidado en algún lugar del granero, ya muerto por los bastonazos del inglés, trabajó duro todo el día en la fundición, sin proferir una sola queja. Todos temieron por su salud mental, y no faltó quien creyera que aquella noche el capataz se quebraría en la soledad de su habitación. Pero no ocurrió así. Porque Sócrates era un hombre libre, y ni siquiera estuvo en su habitación, a pesar de que todos lo vieron cerrar la puerta tras de sí y no aparecer nuevamente sino hasta la mañana siguiente. «La libertad es un estado mental», y él se fue a correr con su hijo a la sabana imaginaria, a presenciar juntos por primera vez el horizonte verde, el mundo sin bastonazos.

El caldero terminó de llenarse. Sócrates se secó el sudor de la frente, y permaneció absorto un momento, escuchando los pasos que se acercaban hacia el cuarto de máquinas. Reconoció al instante las pisadas fuertes y apresuradas de míster Meiggs. Segundos después, el inglés abrió la puerta de un golpe, y se mantuvo quieto en la entrada, estudiando la gran habitación. Identificó a Sócrates a los pies del caldero, y caminó hacia él con gran autoridad. El negro agachó la cabeza, torciendo la boca en una especie de sonrisa.

'Ordene usted, míster Meiggs.'

'Vengo a darte una noticia. A ti, y a todos.' Los esclavos, un grupo de cincuenta negros que se ocupaban en engrasar y pulir la inmensa maquinaria, no dejaron de trabajar, atentos a las palabras del amo. 'Hoy es 2 de diciembre de 1854. A partir de mañana, serán hombres libres.'

El silencio fue estremecedor. Ni siquiera una noticia como esa logró que los esclavos dejaran de trabajar, impulsados por la inercia del temor al castigo, por el recuerdo del látigo en sus espaldas. Solo Sócrates se animó a decir algo, ensayando una primera conversación entre iguales.

'Lo sé, míster Meiggs. La noticia nos llegó de todos los rincones, pero no nos atrevimos a tomarla en serio. Hasta ahora. Pensamos que usted se opondría a la medida.'

'¿Yo? ¿Oponerme? *What made you think that?*' Ante el sarcasmo del inglés, Sócrates aguzó la mirada. '¿Qué es lo primero que harás, como hombre libre?'

'Nunca he navegado antes. Sin embargo, siento que debería. Me gustaría ser grumete o cocinero de una embarcación, primero de una pequeña y luego ya veré. Lo primero que haré será recorrer el muelle, en busca de alguna tripulación que necesite hombres de manos fuertes como las mías.'

'No, no lo harás. Y te diré por qué. Porque mañana, cuando despiertes, tendrás tanta libertad que no sabrás qué hacer con ella. Te darás cuenta de que tus fuertes manos son iguales a las de tantos otros que también buscan un futuro en el mar, porque sus abuelos tuvieron la mala suerte de encallar en este país, o de ser transportados desde África, como esclavos. Sonreirás al inicio, con los primeros rayos del sol, pues sabrás lo que es sentirte ya no mercancía, sino un ser humano. Luego te darás cuenta de que estás solo. Y sabrás que la libertad, en soledad, es la cosa más triste del mundo. Y buscarás a quien abrazar. Buscarás a tu hijo, y yo lo habré matado. Entonces, cobrarás conciencia del daño que te he hecho, y correrás a matarme. Eso será lo primero que harás, pero aún no lo sabes.'

'No diga esas cosas, míster Meiggs.'

'No me mientas, Sócrates. ¿Me matarás antes de recorrer el Callao y hacerte a la mar?'

'Así como lo dice, es probable.'

'Entonces, lo que hago, lo hago sin culpa. ¡Ustedes cinco, traigan esas sogas!' míster Meiggs alzó el brazo, y un grupo de esclavos corrió hasta donde él estaba. Eran negros recios, ennegrecidos aún más por el hollín y las quemaduras. Sus ojos, dos centellas blancas en medio de una porción de oscuridad, no dejaban de alternar entre el amo y el capataz. El inglés observó la puerta abierta del caldero, dentro del cual las brasas formaban ardientes montículos. Luego dijo:

'El carbón está a punto. Apresen a este hombre.'

Sócrates no se inmutó, cuando los cinco lo obligaron a hincarse y lo ataron de pies y manos. Su cuello, sostenido por cuatro manos callosas y nervudas, comenzó a palpitar. Míster Meiggs tenía razón: cada una de esas manos eran igual o más fuertes que las de él. Conseguir trabajo en el mar iba a ser duro, pero no imposible. Pero qué hermoso, pensaba, respirar cada día la brisa marina, aquel aire fresco que no se parecía en nada al infierno de la fundición, que ardía cada vez más a medida que los esclavos iban acercando su cabeza al caldero, para quemarle los ojos, el rostro, la voluntad. Pensó en su hijo, su pequeño, que seguramente seguía corriendo por la sabana imaginaria, ¿o lo esperaría quizás en algún punto del Callao? Por un momento, cuando su piel produjo las primeras ampollas y el primer puñado de cenizas ardientes inició el recorrido hasta sus pulmones, se dio cuenta de que sobreviviría. Porque sintió dos calores: el del carbón, que derretía sus entrañas, y el de la libertad, que las regeneraría a partir de la mañana siguiente. Ya pensaría en algo. Él mismo era diestro con el yunque y el martillo. Solo era cuestión de trabajo duro y paciencia, algo que él ya conocía de sobra.

Cuando el olor a carne quemada inundó el ambiente, míster Meiggs dio media vuelta sobre sus talones, y no volvió más. Las autoridades encontraron su cadáver flotando en las costas del Callao, el 5 de enero de 1855[9], junto al de Rufino Echenique, Ramírez-Quesada y el resto de los invitados a la fiesta de año nuevo que terminó con la desaparición de aquella asombrosa nave conocida como *S.S. Malinowski*, de la cual no se volvió a tener noticia[10].

---

9. Aquel mismo día, como consecuencia de la Batalla de La Palma, el ejército de Ramón Castilla triunfó sobre los remanentes del ejército oficialista. A la mañana siguiente, las casas de la aristocracia limeña fueron saqueadas por una indignada colectividad. (N. del A.)

10. Existen testimonios de avistamientos de una Malinowski de metal, navegando a lo largo de las costas nicaragüenses en setiembre de 1855. El mismo William Walker hace referencia en su bitácora a "un galeón sorprendente, con una tripulación imposible". Sin embargo, a pesar de que sus referencias puedan indicar que el *S.S. Malinowski* se mudó a aguas caribeñas, no hay mayores indicios que permitan corroborar dicha teoría. (N. del A.)

STEAM PUNK

THE SWARM

Africa

THE SWARM

By Milton Davis

I

Famara Keita shielded his eyes from the bright dry season sun, his shesh protecting his face from the stinging, windblown sand. His Sokoto stallion stirred restlessly, agitated by the scene before them. A wide stretch of barren land stretched to the horizon. It was a scene that would be normal in the Sahara, but this was the Sahel, a region that even in its driest was covered by grass and clumps of shrubs.

"By the ancestors," he said.

He nudged his horse into the emptiness. Dust whorls rose before the horse's hooves as Famara scanned the waste for some indication of life in the expanse. Though he had no clue what had occurred, it was obvious the Elders were right to send him to this place.

He was thankful for his provisions, for there was nothing as far as he could see. His horse was another matter. With no grass to graze they were forced to continue through the desolation until they found where the devastation ended. It took most of the day to the edge of night before they found the end of the barrens. The horse picked up its pace instinctively. Soon they were among the grasses, a lake shimmering in the distance. Famara reached into his bag for his binoculars; he spotted a village on the far side of the lake, fishing boats bobbing on the murky water. He would travel to the village in a few days, hoping to find someone that could describe to him what had occurred. For the moment he would set up camp then analyse the remains for clues.

He dismounted then unpacked his horse, allowing it to wander into the grasses. It took him a long while to set up camp. He travelled heavier than normal, but the extra gear was necessary. After setting up camp he walked to the lake. The water was fairly pure, good enough for drinking and perfect for his steam generator. He carried the water back to camp in the leather folding bucket he'd brought with him. It took him a moment to set up the table that would serve as lab bench.

Once the equipment was set up, he filled the steam generator with coal and water, igniting the coal with flint and grass. The generator emitted a rhythmic chugging sound; soon the table was illuminated by the soft light of his portable lamps. He lit a citronella oil lamp, driving away the insects drawn by the faint light, then walked into the sand to gather sample. Hunger interrupted his duties.

After a quick meal of sorghum, he set up his makeshift lab. He sat the microscope close to the lanterns then removed the dirt samples he'd collected earlier. Famara was a horro, a warrior for the Elders, but the ndoki trained him to run simple tests when such knowledge was required. They supplied him with different solutions which, when in contact with the proper chemicals, would change colour to indicate the presence of certain materials. He sprinkled the debris on a glass slide then placed it under the microscope. The granules enlarged under the lenses, revealing a multicoloured array of particles. This was not just sand, to Famara's displeasure. He took the first indicator solution, squeezing a drop onto the slide. The sand turned a dark green. Famara frowned; the indicator revealed pieces of human flesh among the particles. The amount present dismissed the possibility of the flesh being random. The indicator confirmed the rest of the rumour. The locusts were devouring everything, people included.

He gathered then tested more samples to confirm his findings. After the tenth sample there was no doubt with what he found. The locusts were consuming everything. He pushed back from his table, his brow furrowed in disbelief. How could these insects change their habits so drastically?

He looked toward the village on the lake again. If there were any answers, he would find them there. He unpacked his cot, then built a small fire and brewed a pot of tea. The drink relaxed him; after a few more sips he succumbed to his fatigue and slept.

Famara woke to screams. He sat upright, throwing his blanket aside then gathering his weapons. After mounting his horse, he looked in the direction from which the cries came. The village was under attack. A black cloud swirled over and through it, the people running and flailing against the unnatural onslaught. They scattered in every direction attempting to escape. When a person fell the darkness condensed around them, diminishing them into nothingness. A swirling tendril rose from the carnivorous cloud, slowly drifting in Famara's direction. Famara searched about, his eyes finally settling on the lake. It was a good distance away but it was his only chance.

There was no way he could save his horse. He jumped off the beast then slapped its rump hard, sending it galloping in the opposite direction. It had a better chance of avoiding the swarm in the open. With the horse well on its way, Famara sprinted toward the lake, shedding his items along the way. The swarm sped toward him, descending over the lake. He raised his arms, protecting his face as well as he could. If he could only reach the lake…

Locusts pelted his body as he splashed into the lake's edge. His exposed flesh stung from numerous bites, spurring his descent into the murky water. His hands bled as he completely submerged. The swarm crashed against the lake surface like lethal rain, swimming inches under the surface a few inches before falling still. Famara swam deeper, fighting to hold his breath as the swarm hovered over the surface awaiting his ascent. Reaching his limit, he swam to the surface, took a breath then descended again, managing to avoid the vicious bites. On his third ascent the swarm had dispersed. Famara trod water for a moment, then swam to shore. When he looked to the opposite bank he was astonished to see the entire village gone. He looked down; hundreds of locust bodies floated on the lake surface. He scooped up a handful then carried them to where his camp was set up. He put the locusts into his pouch then dug with his hands into the sand until he reached his equipment and provisions. He busied himself with setting up the microscope again, fighting to keep his mind off the horror that just occurred and staying focused on his mission. Once the microscope was ready he took a locust from his pouch then placed it under the lenses.

It was not an insect. It was a miniature clockwork construct, a device designed by a master of diminutive machines, most likely someone with experience in watch making. Famara increased the magnification, studying the locust's antennae. They consisted of thin copper wire, indicating the locusts were probably guided by some frequency radiated from a specific spot nearby. They probably responded to simple commands; if it was a frequency then it could be scrambled. A single passage ran from the locust's mouth to its anus. The creature was designed to work like a steam-powered saw, chewing up anything in its path then discharging it. Whomever controlled the locusts had to be within sight to control the attack, which meant he had been seen.

The artificial insect's wings were powered by a tiny spring. Famara searched for a winding mechanism and found it on the thorax between the wings. He searched his pouch and retrieved a tiny straight wrench, which he clamped over the winding key then turned as delicately as he could. No sooner did he finish winding the locust did the antennae twitch.

"It's receiving a signal," Famara said aloud. He quickly located a length of string, then tied it around the locust's thorax and around his wrist. The locust's wings fluttered and the bug flew from under the microscope lens, its escape halted by the spring.

The locust would lead him to the source, Famara thought. He would wait to see if his horse would return. If not, he would set off on foot. The horse did finally return, close to dusk, too late for him to travel. He decided to set up camp near the lake just in case the locusts returned. The night was a restless one, the locust constantly tugging for freedom while images of the village massacre repeated in his head. He'd served the elders since his manhood rites and had seen many sights, both pleasant and horrible, but never had he seen a village destroyed in such a manner. This was violence for no purpose, something that would only spark terror.

Maybe that was the reason. Someone was using the locust to frighten the villagers and force them to leave. The Elders had given him three tasks; locate the source of the threat; discover if a Book was involved and if so, obtain it; and determine if the person or persons using the technology of the Book were worth incorporating into their circle. If not, they were to be eliminated. Famara had known the moment he saw the village attacked by the swarm what his decision would be.

II

The workers trudged though the hot sun and ankle-deep sand, their umber skin glistening with sweat. The large stones bending their backs had been carved from the nearby mountains and carried the entire distance. The men staggered to the edge of the thorn bush filled moat then dropped their stones before the masons, who positioned the huge carved rocks along the moat borders, plastering them together with mortar. A thorn bush moat ringed the city's outer perimeter, a single retractable bridge leading to a towering stone gate. Wooden towers were positioned at measured distances, occupied by warriors armed with rifles. Horsemen circled the perimeter every two hours.

Famara lowered his binoculars then placed them at his side. He opened his canteen, taking another swig of water. The wind up locust tugged at his wrist, still following the signal calling it home. Over the three days he'd observed the city he'd seen swarms leave and return from every direction. He imagined the terror and destruction they left behind and anger boiled in his gut. He shuffled backwards until he was out of sight of the towers before standing on his feet and walking to his horse. The city was the origin of the swarm and, most likely, where the Book he sought was kept. Whoever controlled it was preparing for an attack. The defecses would be formidable once completed; Famara would have to make his move soon or entry would be too difficult. He would wait until dusk to implement his plan.

As the sun eased below the western horizon, Famara mounted his horse then rode up the hill, hiding his presence. As he crested the hill he raised his spyglass, studying the fortifications once more. The gate swung open and three riders emerged, galloping in his direction. He watched them for a moment then reined his horse, galloping away as if fleeing. He rode a distance, dismounted his horse then waited. The riders crested the hill and rode up to him, pistols drawn. Famara turned to face them, his hand raised. Two of the men dismounted and strode toward him; the third remained on his horse.

"Who are you?" the lead man said in Arabic.

"Just a traveller," Famara replied.

"A traveller with a spyglass?" the man replied. "I think not."

"I was looking to see if your village was a hospitable place to spend the night," Famara explained. "As I suspected, it is not."

"Kill him and be done with it," the man on the horse said.

Famara twisted out of the line of fire as he reached behind his back, throwing his knife at the mounted rider. The knife struck the man in the face and he fell from his horse. Famara dropped low, spinning with his leg extended. Both men fired their pistols as the horro swept them off their feet. He pounced on them before they could react, slicing one man's throat while clubbing the other on the head. He hurried to the man felled by his throwing knife, making sure he was dead. Famara exchanged clothes with the man, ignoring the tight fit. He dressed the man in his garments then trotted back to the clubbed man, who was regaining consciousness. Famara pulled his arms forward then tied his wrists together with a thin rope. When the man fully revived Famara squatted before him, his pistol in the man's face.

"Up," he said.

The man climbed to his feet. Famara motioned toward the man's horse and the man climbed onto the steed.

"Try to ride away and you'll get a bullet in your back," Famara warned. Famara placed the dead men on their steeds then mounted his horse. He gave the reins of the horse carrying the man in his clothes to his prisoner.

"What is your name?" Famara asked.

"Didinga," the man said.

"Who controls this city, Didinga?" Famara asked.

"Amadou Soros," the man replied.

Famara's eyes widened. "You're lying!"

He struck Didinga and he fell off his horse.

"I speak the truth!" Didinga said.

Famara sat before the man, rubbing his head.

"Amadou? It can't be…" he whispered.

After a moment he stood, lifting the man up.

"Get on."

The man clambered onto the horse and Famara gave him the reins of the dead man's horse once again.

"Ride ahead of me," Famara ordered. "We gallop through without stopping. If anyone asks why, you tell them I'm wounded. Once we're in the stables you will take me to Amadou. Understand?"

Didinga winched as he nodded.

They galloped up and over the hill, Famara following with the other dead mounted man. As they approached the gate Famara heard the familiar hiss of a steam engine and the doors creaked open. Two guards stood on either side of the entrance, rifles lowered. A third man blocked their entrance.

"Keep going," Famara said.

"But I will…"

"Keep going!" Famara shouted.

The man blocking their way tried to stop them, waving his hands and shouting. At the last minute he jumped out of the way.

Famara and Didinga rode into the stables. Famara jumped off his horse then snatched Didinga off his horse.

"Let's go now!" he said.

The guards approached. The man who attempted to block them came closer.

"Didinga! Jakada! You almost trampled me!"

The man had mistaken Famara for the dead Jakada.

"Jakada is wounded," Didinga said. "I'm taking him to the healer. Fahru and the interloper are dead."

The men changed directions, walking toward the horses. Famara nudged Didinga.

"I'll take care of it," he said. "Get back to your posts."

The men shrugged, then did as they were told.

"Which building?" Famara asked.

"That one," Didinga said, nodding toward a large stone structure in the centre of the village. From a distance it resembled a mosque, but as they drew nearer Famara could see it was designed for industrial pursuits. The structures resembling minarets were actually dormant smokestacks, the entrance wide to accommodate any large contraptions entering or leaving the structure. As they neared the building a familiar buzzing sound reached Famara's ears.

"A swarm," he said.

Didinga flinched when he heard the word.

"I hate those damned things!" he said. "I saw them chew a man to dust."

"I saw them do the same thing to an entire village," Famara said.

Didinga turned to face him, his eyes wide.

"It's those Books!" he said. "They are filled with evil."

"It's not the Books," Famara replied. "It's the man wielding them. Where did you see the Books?"

Didinga pointed to the building. Famara shoved him toward the structure. There were no guards outside; Amadou was apparently comfortable with his security. As they entered the building Famara saw a huge chamber filling the centre of the building. Mechanical locusts swirled inside, their buzzing filling the vacuous chamber.

"His laboratory is behind the chamber," Didinga said. "Come, I'll show you."

They skirted the edge, Famara remaining vigilant. They reached the opposite end of the building, standing before another door.

"Open it," Famara ordered.

Didinga grasped the latch then opened the door.

"Didinga, what are you doing here?" A familiar voice said. "What do you want?"

Famara shoved Didinga into the room then followed.

"I should ask you the same questions," Famara said.

Amadou Soros looked up from his bench, a knowing smile slowly coming to his bearded face. He stood, revealing the body of a former horro, his muscular frame clear through the single tobe he wore. He placed the tools he held on the surface, his hands going to his waist.

"Hello, Famara," he said. "I can't say seeing you here is unexpected. I hoped I would have more time."

"Your time became short when you began murdering people with your bugs," Famara replied. "How could you do this? This is not our way!"

"How could I not?" Amadou replied. "The Elders lied to us, Famara. They have no plans to use the knowledge of the Books to heal the world."

"You're wrong and you know it," Famara said. "You've been to Wagadu. You've seen the wonders there."

"Wonders that benefit no one. How long must the world wait before the Elders bestow their blessings upon us?"

"That is their decision to make," Famara said.

Amadou smiled. "Not any more."

Didinga's foot scraped the floor, warning Famara. He ducked instinctively, avoiding the man's double-hand blow. He twisted, driving his fist into the man's stomach, then rolled to avoid Amadou's throwing knife. Famara rose with pistols in both hands. Amadou dove before he fired and the bullets struck the wall behind him. Amadou pulled his own gun and the men shot as they sought cover. Didinga charged Famara again; the horro knocked him unconscious with a kick to the face. Amadou used the distraction to flee the hangar, taking the Books with him. Famara had no idea where the man fled. There was only one way to find out.

He hurried to the chamber holding the locusts. He took a throwing knife then lodged it into the seam of the chamber door. He opened the handle, slipping a stick of explosive into it. Famara raised his shesh over his mouth and nose as he walk backwards. Once he thought he was far enough away, he raised his handgun then fired. The knife exploded, blasting the chamber open. Famara was already running as the locusts poured from the chamber. With no signal to guide them, they descended on everything in sight. Didinga was consumed in unconsciousness, the tables and the hangar their next targets. Famara swatted away a few errant locusts as he made way toward the stables.

The others were still there examining the bodies on the horses. Famara shot them down before mounting his horse, reining it to full gallop toward the still open gate. Halfway to the exit the locusts burst from the hangar, attacking everything before them. Famara rode through the gate, pushing his mount relentlessly as they crossed the open grasslands. There was no lake for refuge, only the hope the locusts would wind themselves down within the village and not seek out more beyond the unfinished walls.

Two hours later his horse refused to go any farther. Famara jumped from the horse then ran a bit farther before turning to look in the city's direction. No dark cloud swirled behind him. He took out his spyglass. The walls still stood, but the wooden buildings beyond them were gone. Famara looked in every direction but saw no signs of the swarm. Logic told him the mechanical devourers had consumed everything and everyone in the camp and spent themselves, but he had to be sure. He studied the area for another hour before grabbing his horse's reins and walking back toward the city.

It was midday when he reached the outskirts. Famara released the horse then entered the city. The ground was littered with the vile locusts; human remains were scattered about. He entered the hangar to a similar scene, the only remaining object the metal chamber that held the insects. He searched every building, hoping to find some remains of the Books. As he reached the opposite side of the city he realised that would not be. The locusts had done their job.

He was leaving when he noticed something stir to his right. Locusts rose from the sand then flew to each other. Other locusts rose around him then joined the small swarm. Instead of attacking him they flew toward the east.

"Amadou," Famara said.

He ran back to his horse, mounted and galloped through the city. He found camel tracks in the sand, heading the same direction of the fading swarm.

"This is not over," Famara whispered. "But it will be."

He snapped his horse's reins and they galloped together after the swarm.

STEAM PUNK

LA HISTORIA DE TU CORAZÓN

Spain

LA HISTORIA DE TU CORAZÓN

By Josué Ramos

Podía verlo dentro de la caja, inerme, muerto, y no podía evitar mantenerse lejos. Quería tocarlo. Pero se guardaba las manos en los bolsillos, avergonzado.

'Vamos a incinerarlo dentro de una hora,' murmuró el funcionario encargado del cuerpo, sin levantar la vista de bajo su sombrero.

'¿Puede darme un momento a solas con él, por favor?' 'Sí, claro. El tiempo que haga falta. ¿Es familiar?'

'Soy su padre.'

*

Daniel Beltrán sintió mareado entre tanta gente, tanto salto y tanta algarabía; no sabía que iba a tener tantos compañeros de clase. Apoyado contra una esquina, sin perder de vista la puerta todavía cerrada, no podía evitar que le temblasen las piernas.

El patio se dividía en varios círculos de amigos que charlaban — todos parecían conocer a alguien — y sólo unos pocos, como él, que esperaban solos.

Los grupos más numerosos, ruidosos y seguros de sí mismos eran los de los jóvenes de familias nobles; Daniel reconoció a más de un Borbón entre ellos. Esos grupos eran los que dominaban las colonias que España tenía por toda la Galaxia, los que mantenían el contacto con el Imperio y se aseguraban de que todos pagasen sus impuestos a la metrópoli y guardasen silencio. Por otro lado, algo menos llamativos, los nuevos ricos; muchachos de familias que se habían enriquecido a base de negocios. Y, finalmente, algo más discretos pero mucho más numerosos, sus jóvenes vecinos: la clase media, la clase trabajadora, formada por aquellos que anhelaban colarse de algún modo u otro entre los círculos importantes.

Daniel, en cambio, sentía que no encajaba con ninguno de ellos. Entró solo, se sentó solo y siempre estuvo solo. Se dijo a sí mismo que seguiría los pasos que su padre le había marcado, acudiendo a cada clase durante los siete años que durase el curso, hasta conseguir la licenciatura en Medicina; pero sentía que jamás encajaría en el sistema.

Y a pesar de que rezaba para pasar desapercibido durante siete años, la calma no duró más de siete semanas. Pero los demás no tardaron en fijarse en él. Sus diferencias eran demasiado evidentes como para evitar preguntas indiscretas. No tardaron en convertirlo en el blanco de todas las miradas. Y los comentarios burlones a sus espaldas no se hicieron esperar. Sin embargo, fue durante una de las clases del doctor Mendoza, Cirugía de Trasplantes No Invasiva, donde todo se complicó de verdad.

El doctor Mendoza explicaba una vez más la historia moderna de los trasplantes mientras Daniel fingía que le interesaba y trababa de ocultar que le asqueaba lo que oía. Empezó hablando de los nuevos avances científicos y las nuevas técnicas quirúrgicas desarrolladas en Inglaterra y Francia desde finales del siglo XIX. Después, gracias a todo lo que se había aprendido de medicina durante las guerras mundiales, pasó a explicar cómo se derivó la aplicación de los trasplantes, ya en tiempo de paz, a la cirugía estética. Así todo el mundo podía hacerse trasplantes por cualquier cosa ya mediados de siglo XX. Él mismo había conseguido su puesto de docente gracias a sus ojos, extraídos de un esclavo negro de vista prodigiosa. Ahora contaba con unos ojos que le permitían no perder detalle durante las clases — y durante los exámenes —, y había pagado un poco más porque se decía que aquel negro podía ver mejor que nadie cuando trabajaba en las minas, casi en total oscuridad. Y no se había arrepentido de comprarlos.

Además, ya que había tenido que apretarse un poco el cinturón para conseguirlos, había aprovechado para recuperar un 20 % del gasto vendiendo sus originales a una casa de subastas. No paraba de repetir aquella historia una y otra vez.

'¿Por qué no pregunta eso en el examen, ojo de halcón? Sacaríamos todos matrícula de honor, de tantas veces que lo hemos oído,' gritó un muchacho desde el fondo de la sala.

'Guarde silencio, por favor,' se limitó a decir el doctor, alzando las palmas de sus perfectas manos de escritor. Daniel se preguntó si serían originales. Nunca había hablado de ellas. Sólo contaba lo de sus ojos. 'De no ser por estos avances científicos usted no estaría aquí. Su padre nunca habría podido amasar la fortuna que ahora le permite a usted estudiar Medicina.'

'Mi padre no se dedica a los trasplantes. Tiene una empresa de minería.'

'Me temo que se equivoca, señor Martínez. El cuerpo humano tiende al deterioro y siempre acusa algún fallo. Siempre. Seamos nobles o plebeyos, ricos o pobres, españoles o esclavos, todos vivimos sujetos a esa premisa. Nosotros lo subsanamos gracias a los trasplantes. Y su padre se beneficia de ello vendiendo a precio de oro a los esclavos más sanos de los que trabajan en sus minas. Y con los beneficios de las ventas puede aumentar sus beneficios año a año, ¿no es así? Todo debido a la ciencia de los trasplantes. A la producción y venta de materia para trasplantar.'

'Y has tenido mucha suerte, Martínez,' se rio de él un noble Borbón. 'De no ser por las técnicas de decoloración, que permiten que la piel del donante se adapte a la del comprador, jamás le comprarían nada a tu viejo.'

'Ya ven lo importante que son estos avances científicos para sus vidas, señores,' continuó el profesor, mientras todos reían. 'Están más presentes de lo que ustedes creen. Y todo gracias a que nos permite corregir nuestras taras o añadir lo que nos falte y estar así contentos con nosotros mismos.'

'No siempre, por lo visto,' rio otro muchacho, señalando con la vista a Daniel. 'Ahí, el señor chocolate parece tener todo en su sitio.'

Daniel se encogió en su asiento, enrojecido y con las sienes a punto de reventar.

'¿De qué habla, muchacho?' preguntó el doctor, extrañado. '¿A qué se refiere?'

'A que el señor Beltrán es un hombre sano y contento consigo mismo desde la cuna. Al menos, eso parece.'

'Cuna que, por lo que parece, debía de estar en la selva …'

Toda la clase rio, arengada por aquellos dos muchachos perfectos. Los dos eran muy parecidos uno a otro, a pesar de no ser parientes. Eran rubios, de ojos azules, con barba implantada porque la suya no acababa de salir, nariz, ojos, pelo, cejas, manos … y con los abdominales más perfectos que se hubiesen visto nunca. Daniel se había preguntado más de una vez si todavía les quedaba algo suyo dentro de aquellas cáscaras artificiales que se habían formado alrededor de sus diminutos cerebros.

El doctor Mendoza alzó sus dos manos de nuevo, tratando de hacerlos callar, mientras se acercaba a la mesa de Daniel.

'¿Es eso cierto, Beltrán? ¿No ha sido usted operado nunca?'

'Nunca, doctor,' murmuró él, sintiendo que la tierra se lo tragaba.

'¿Nunca? ¿Por problemas de dinero, quizá?'

'No, doctor,' continuó Daniel, escueto.

'Señor Beltrán, no les haga caso. No dicen más que sandeces. Pero le agradecería que se dirigiese a mi despacho al terminar la clase, por favor, si no es molestia.'

Daniel accedió, sin ser capaz de prestar atención al resto de la clase. No despertó de sus meditaciones hasta escuchar la sirena que marcaba el fin de la jornada, para dirigirse al despacho del doctor Mendoza.

*

'Así que … nunca ha sido usted operado.'

'No, doctor. Mi padre sí. En cambio, yo …'

'¿Y ese color? En fin, no quiero ser grosero con usted; pero creí que ese bronceado …'

'No es bronceado, doctor Mendoza. Es mi color natural, heredado por parte de madre. ¿Acaso debo avergonzarme de ella?'

'No, claro que no. Disculpe mi atrevimiento,' susurró el doctor, paternal. 'Me cae usted bien. Es buen muchacho y aprende rápido. Será un buen médico. Por eso me gustaría ayudarle.' Mientras hablaba, sacó un formulario de un cajón, y comenzó a rellenarlo. 'Si le escribiese una carta de recomendación, podría entrar usted en un programa especial de trasplante para estudiantes modelo. Yo tendría que supervisar cada una de sus solicitudes, pero creo que el Estado le permitiría un mínimo de, quizá … ¿diez operaciones? Podríamos implantarle ojos diestros, manos de cirujano … creo que no habría problema en conseguirle todas las mejoras físicas que necesitase para ejercer la profesión. Y no tendría que preocuparse por los gastos. Sólo tendríamos que ajustar los créditos que …'

'No, por favor, doctor. No.'

'¿Hay, acaso, alguna mejora física que le urja más? ¿Alguna tara que no haya podido corregir? Porque también podríamos…'

'No,' repitió Daniel, nervioso pero firme. 'No siga hablando, por favor. No quiero operarme.'

'Señor Beltrán, no se avergüence. Este programa de ayudas se creó para estudiantes aplicados como usted. Si el problema es que no tiene dinero …'

'No es por eso, doctor. Es que yo no necesito nada.'

'Pero ¿algo querrá mejorar?'

Daniel no podía dejar de pensar en su problema cardíaco. Su pecho golpeaba con fuerza. Con su fuerte golpeteo, su corazón parecía querer contar su historia a gritos … pero su mente reaccionó a tiempo:

'No, doctor. Estoy bien así. Me siento contento conmigo mismo.'

'Piénselo bien, muchacho, por favor. Le ofrezco las manos y los ojos de un cirujano. En cuanto muera un profesional de su campo, el Estado se encargará de guardarlos para usted.'

'No serían mis ojos ni mis manos.'

'Pero le darían un aval que no puede rechazar. Imagine lo que sería: Cuando acabe la carrera podrá usted añadir en su currículum que hizo las prácticas en la Universidad con ellos ya implantados. Podría llegar a ejercer en los mejores hospitales de Hespéride, de cualquiera de las colonias o incluso de la Tierra. Donde usted quisiera.'

'¿Cuál sería la diferencia con hacer trampas en los exámenes?' El doctor Mendoza dejó el formulario a un lado, suspirando. 'Señor Beltrán, ¿por qué eligió usted esta carrera? ¿No tiene intención de ejercer cuando se gradúe?'

'Sí, doctor,' respondió, no muy convencido. 'Eso es lo que quiero.'

'¿Y cree usted que alguien se fiaría de un médico que nunca ha sido operado? Por Dios, Beltrán, si no le parece justo recibir ya los órganos de un cirujano, al menos acepte alguna otra mejora; cualquier cosa. Si a usted no le pasa nada, si está sano y contento con su cuerpo, está rompiendo la norma básica de su futura profesión. Está atentando contra la Medicina, contra la economía, contra todo el sistema. Y si no registra ninguna operación en su currículum, créame, por muy buenas notas que siga sacando, no logrará nunca un trabajo a su altura.' Daniel no respondió. 'Piénselo unos días, ¿de acuerdo?'

'¿Me puedo ir ya?'

'Sí, váyase,' terminó Mendoza, rompiendo y tirando a la basura el formulario. 'Váyase.'

Daniel regresó aquella noche a casa en silencio y se fue a la cama sin cenar, diciendo que tenía mucho que estudiar. Sin embargo, no hizo más que pensar en su futuro. Si sólo se operase del corazón … Al fin y al cabo, no era ningún capricho; sino una operación necesaria. Un trasplante corregiría su cardiopatía congénita. Pero ¿cómo cerrar los ojos al origen de lo que ellos mismos llamaban "materia prima"? ¿Cómo podría rechazar la historia que su corazón cantaba en cada latido?

Poco antes de nacer en la Tierra, no hacía mucho que la capital de la Guinea Española, fundada como *Port Clarence* por los ingleses, había sido rebautizada como *Santa Isabel*. Habían pasado ya unos años desde que España había logrado echar a Inglaterra y hacerse con el control definitivo sobre la colonia; y sus viejos negocios volvían a aflorar. La población de colonos creció y las empresas españolas volvieron a ganar presencia en la zona. Su padre había sido destinado como capataz por una de Madrid dedicada a minería y extracción de diamantes. Tenía un buen sueldo y una buena posición y era respetado entre todos los colonos; hasta que conoció a la guineana que se convertiría en la madre de Daniel.

En contra de las normas de la empresa y en secreto, Beltrán movió algunos hilos a base de sobornos para poder rescatarla del comercio de esclavos y casarse con ella.

En cambio, todo se complicó con la llegada de Daniel. Su madre estaba dispuesta a dejarse morir con tal de darle la vida; y así lo hizo, a pesar de saber que nacería con una enfermedad congénita y con su oscuro color de piel como herencia. ¿Acaso no le debía él algo a cambio? Su vida, su libertad, su integridad… ¿Acaso no se lo debía todo a ella?

Los ricos y nobles marcaban el precio de la nueva carne según las modas de cada temporada; y vendían la vieja como si se tratase de ropa usada. Los esclavos negros, de hacer trabajos forzados, habían pasado poco a poco a las granjas para formar rebaños, como ovejas, con los que mantener la demanda y el sistema comercial. Y la clase media y la clase trabajadora, para poder seguir a la sombra de los Grandes de España, recurría al trueque como lo más normal del mundo.

Daniel todavía recordaba el día en que su padre se había intercambiado las manos con el vecino del piso de abajo. Apenas contaba tres años, pero lo recordaba como si hubiese sido aquella misma mañana. Por aquel entonces, todavía le daba miedo bajar solo las empinadas escaleras de la casa. Pero cuando caminaba de la mano de su padre no le temía a nada.

Aquel día, su padre lo soltó sólo durante un segundo para saludar a un vecino que subía.

'Es Manuel, ¿sabes?' le explicó, tendiéndole la mano de nuevo. 'Vive aquí, en el cuarto, y es joyero.'

Sonriendo, el hombre le pasó la mano por la cabeza a Beltrán, sin decirle nada. Era tan fuerte y rudo que no pudo evitar hacerle daño.

'Pues parece que tiene manos de obrero,' murmuró él, sin apartar la vista de la manaza del vecino. 'No son como las tuyas.' 'Tiene razón,' rio el joyero. 'Con estas manos, cada día me cuesta más trabajar las joyas. Me temo que cualquier día perderé el empleo.'

Así, de una forma tan inocente, la mano de su padre se soltó de repente de la suya. Daniel no podía recordar más. Sólo sabía que la siguiente vez que lo vio, su padre parecía diferente. Sonreía. Necesitaba manos de obrero, grandes y fuertes, y gracias a Daniel las había conseguido. Las manos que siempre le habían ayudado a bajar las escaleras y a no temer ningún peligro, en cambio, estarían a partir de entonces en el piso de arriba o engarzando joyas en la tienda de la vuelta de la esquina.

¿Qué diría su madre si supiera que todo el mundo quería que él tirase a la basura el corazón por el que ella había dado su vida, el corazón que ella misma había creado en su interior para él? ¿Qué sentido tendría arrancarle el corazón a otro guineano y quedárselo para sí? No. Seguiría los pasos de su madre. Y si tenía que morir por no mancharse las manos de sangre, que así fuese.

*

Tras el primer año de Medicina, Beltrán creyó que el verano y las vacaciones serían para él como un bálsamo y una liberación. Pero, después de lo que había aprendido durante el curso, paseaba por la calle sin poder evitar analizar los trasplantes e implantes de cada cual. Ojos saltones, nariz respingona, melena rubia, piernas de futbolista, manos de pianista … Y, por extraño que pareciera, las personas con implantes mecánicos que deambulaban por las calles o pedían en las aceras eran a sus ojos más personas que todas las demás.

Siempre se topaba con un hombre en la misma esquina, que adaptaba piezas de Dionisio Aguado al violín. A pesar de su mano de metal, manejaba el instrumento con gran maestría. Tenía un pantalón raído, con una pernera arrancada desde la ingle para poder contener los mecanismos de las articulaciones de su pierna artificial. Sin embargo, apenas movía la pierna lo imprescindible. Cada mínimo movimiento del sistema hidráulico requería una descarga de vapor que, en pleno verano, asaba al hombre y le hacía sudar como si acabase de salir de un horno. Los gatos de la calle se le acercaban durante el invierno hasta que él los echaba a patadas de su lado, pero en verano no había quien se le acercase. Y si quería regresar caminando a casa, tenía que llevar el brazo recogido a la espalda, para que el vapor no se lo agarrotase. Así y todo, parecía más humano que cualquier trasplantado. Ni siquiera su padre le parecía ya su padre.

De repente, un frenazo y un agudo silbido de vapor hicieron que Daniel despertase de sus pensamientos. De la nada, se le vino encima un coche de mercancías cargado de frutas y verduras. La caldera y el violín se acompasaron en un único alarido de espanto. Un punzante dolor en una pierna y una presión en el pecho lo cegaron. El mundo se le volvió negro. Se le apagó la luz.

*

Cuando recuperó la consciencia, estaba en una sala enorme llena de camas a ambos lados de un estrecho pasillo. Apenas había enfermeras atendiendo a los pacientes. Las cortinas, tan roídas que ya no servían de nada. La ropa de cama, llena de lamparones de sangre y esputos. Y el suelo con charcos de serrín aquí y allá. El dolor en el pecho era tan fuerte que le impedía incorporarse.

'Eh, estás despierto, muchacho,' sonrió su padre. 'Relájate.

Procura no moverte. ¿Quieres que llame a la enfermera?'

'No …' murmuró entre toses. 'No hace falta.'

'¿Le pido un calmante?'

'No. Sólo quiero saber qué ha pasado.'

'Un camión volcó y se te vino encima justo cuando pasaba a tu lado. Tienes una contusión en el pecho y una pierna rota. Pero no te preocupes, en cuanto termine de rellenar este formulario todo estará arreglado.'

La pluma entre los dedos de su padre semejaba un aguijón que no dejaba de verter veneno.

'¿Para qué es?' preguntó dolorido.

'Para ponerte una pierna nueva, claro. ¿Para qué va a ser? Han encontrado una casi idéntica a la tuya en una granja cercana. La amputarán y traerán en cuanto firmes. Y de paso, van a extraer una caja torácica, para que no tengas que sufrir los dolores del golpe y podamos resolver de una vez tu problema de corazón. Es caro, pero podemos pagarlo. El único problema, según me han dicho, es que el donante es mucho más oscuro que tú, negro como el carbón,' rio, 'y la decoloración será cara. Pero si ahorramos durante unos meses …'

'¡No, papá! ¡No quiero!' gritó, asustado, tratando de incorporarse con todas sus fuerzas. 'No es mi corazón el que está mal. Es el tuyo.'

'No pasa nada, Daniel. Tenemos dinero. Sólo tendremos que ahorrar un poco para la decoloración. Nos han hecho un plan de financiación que …'

'¿¡Estás loco!? ¿Cómo puedes decir eso? ¡No me importa la decoloración!'

'Pero la pierna.'

'¡La pierna es mía! ¡Y no pienso permitir que nadie me la quite!'

Las ásperas y rudas manos del vecino se aferraron a los hombros de Daniel, aplastándolo contra la cama. La presión en el pecho era tan fuerte que apenas podía respirar.

'¡Tranquilízate, Daniel! ¡Tranquilízate! Voy a llamar a la enfermera para sedarte, ¿de acuerdo?'

'No, por favor.'

'Es lo mejor. No puedes ir a ninguna parte con esa pierna rota.'

Aterrado, observó cómo se alejaba su padre, a través de los agujeros de la cortina. El corazón le latía con fuerza, como si intentase escapar a su muerte. Y el miedo pesaba más que el dolor. Despacio, se incorporó. Se tragó la tos que le invadía para no hacer ruido y, mordiéndose la lengua, se puso en pie. Podía verse el hueso sobresaliendo por fuera del pantalón roto. Apenas podía apoyar la pierna en el suelo. Pero no iba a perder ni un segundo más allí tumbado.

La ventana abierta daba a un callejón oscuro. A pesar de estar en un piso bajo, cruzar el hueco y saltar afuera sería un suplicio, pero su única oportunidad. Se lanzó con todas sus fuerzas hacia la calle. El dolor en el pecho casi le hizo perder el sentido. Pero era su pecho. Respiró hondo y se levantó como pudo, arrastrando la pierna. Pero era el dolor de su pierna. Y lo arrastraría consigo el tiempo que hiciese falta.

No supo a dónde ir. No supo qué hacer. Sólo entendió que jamás volvería a casa. No podría fingir que seguía siendo parte del sistema y continuar con sus estudios. Si ni siquiera podía acudir a un centro de salud sin miedo, ¿cómo podría llegar a dedicarse él mismo a trabajar en un centro así? Allí ya no quedaba nada para él.

Tras media hora de camino, casi sin sentido, adormilado y delirante por el dolor que le recorría el cuerpo, se sintió paralizado y cayó entre cartones y basura, víctima de una especie de apoplejía, como si estuviese atado a una camilla. De la nada apareció el doctor Mendoza. Vestía como un soldado español de ultramar, manchado por el barro, el sudor y la lucha; pero lucía un impecable collar de diamantes en el cuello. Sonreía con malicia, blandiendo un bisturí como lo haría un director de orquesta. Daniel lo miraba sin poder hablar. Sólo podía expresarse a través de sus ojos de terror, como si suplicasen no apagarse.

Despertó de repente, apartando las imaginarias manos de cirujano que lo sujetaban aquí y allá, cortando, rasgando, arrancándole la piel …

'Tranquilo, muchacho,' susurró una voz amigable, sujetándole los brazos. 'No pasa nada. Estás a salvo.'

Daniel miró en derredor. Estaba en una habitación que no conocía. No era una enfermera. Y aquello no era un hospital.

'¿Dónde estoy?' murmuró tocándose las vendas del torso. '¿Qué me han hecho?'

'No te preocupes. Todo está bien. Estás a salvo.' Sintiendo un escalofrío, intentó incorporarse. 'Espera, que te ayudo,' dijo ella, acomodándole la almohada.

Al sentarse, Daniel sintió dolor en la pierna. Si se la hubiesen cambiado no sentiría nada. Estaría curado. En cambio, ahora la tenía entablillada, y la molestia de la fractura seguía ahí. Sonrió.

'No me han trasplantado.'

Una vocecilla infantil rio a su lado. Había dos niños con la mujer. Uno de apenas cinco años, que se llevó un coscorrón por reírse de su comentario, y otro poco más joven que Daniel. 'En esta casa no tenemos dinero para eso, muchacho. Lo siento mucho,' dijo la señora, acomodándole la ajada ropa de cama. 'Puedo acogerte y curarte al estilo tradicional; pero si quieres operaciones caras, tendrás que pagártelas tú mismo.'

'Muchas gracias, señora,' murmuró Daniel, con lágrimas en los ojos. 'Muchas gracias.'

*

Sin tener otro lugar a donde ir, Daniel convivió con aquella familia durante el tiempo que duró su convalecencia. Se dedicó a observar desde su ventana a las personas que conformaban aquel barrio, uno de los más pobres y degradados de la sociedad española que se había montado en Hespéride, y a aprender más de ellas que de todos sus años de estudio.

Una tarde, ya casi anocheciendo, Luis, el mayor de los hijos de la señora, entró como una exhalación en el cuarto con una muleta en la mano.

'Vamos, Daniel,' exclamó, lanzándosela por el aire. 'Esta noche vamos a salir.'

'¿De dónde la has sacado?'

'Se la compré a un viejo al salir del trabajo con parte de lo que me pagaron hoy,' respondió Luis, sonriendo. 'Era de su difunta esposa y me la tenía reservada desde hace días.'

'¿Y el dinero?' preguntó Daniel, mientras le veía apartar un ladrillo de la pared con un cuchillo afilado.

'No se lo digas a mi madre, pero hoy fue día de cobro.' El joven sacó una caja de metal del ladrillo hueco y la abrió para contar todo el dinero que había en ella. 'Llevo un tiempo ahorrando sin que lo sepa. Además, cuando mi padre murió y tuvimos que venderlo a piezas ella misma me dio una parte de los beneficios. Pero piensa que lo gasté todo.'

'¿Tu padre?'

'Sí. Quería quedarme con sus brazos. Era muy fuerte, ¿sabes? Pero yo era tan pequeño que aún no me servían. Y los de mi edad eran muy caros. Así que mi madre decidió darme a mí lo que ganamos con ellos. Y, ahora, con la inflación, ni siquiera puedo permitirme unos de adulto. Pero con esto …' se explicó, pasándose el dinero de una mano a otra, 'con esto ya podemos salir y lograr algo grande. Levántate, venga. Que llevas aquí casi un mes y necesitas salir.'

Y sin decir más, emparedó de nuevo su caja de caudales y acompañó a Daniel a la calle.

*

'El siguiente artículo fue adquirido en la liquidación de bienes de una empresa que quebró hace apenas unos días. Está en perfecto estado de conservación,' dijo el subastador. 'El precio de salida es de mil pesetas.'

'¡Mil pesetas!' murmuró Luis, tratando de ocultar su emoción. '¡Es una ganga!'

'Creía que íbamos a cambiar tus brazos …'

'¡Pero mira qué precio, Daniel!'

'Si no la necesito. Mi pierna ya casi está curada. Te podrías haber ahorrado hasta la muleta.'

'¡Mil quinientas!' exclamó Luis. 'No digas tonterías, Daniel. Sin la muleta no habrías podido salir de casa. Además, ahora eres como mi hermano. Déjame que haga esto por ti, por favor.'

'¡Dos mil!'

'No, mira a tu alrededor. ¿Ves cuántas manos levantadas? Este lote interesa a mucha gente y la casa de subastas lo sabe. El precio de salida es bueno para que más gente se anime a pujar. No te dejes engañar.'

'¡Tres mil! Por eso tenemos que actuar rápido. No puedes echarte atrás ahora. Mira la pierna. Mírala. Está ahí, sobre la mesa. Y puede ser tuya.'

'¡Cinco mil!'

'Lo único que hacen es engrosar el precio,' respondió Daniel, cada vez más nervioso.

'¡Cinco mil doscientas cincuenta!'

'¡Seis mil!' continuó Luis. 'Daniel, tienes que ser más optimista. Podemos conseguirlo.'

'¡Seis mil setecientas!'

'No, por favor. No me interesa,' se quejó Daniel, sintiéndose desfallecer. 'Déjalo, por favor, déjalo.' El corazón le dio un vuelco de repente, obligándole a recostarse contra su asiento.

'¡Siete mil!'

'¿Qué te pasa, Daniel? ¿Estás bien?'

'Sí, sí, no pasa nada. Es sólo que hace mucho que no salgo y estoy fatigado. Voy fuera a tomar el aire.'

'Está bien. ¡Ocho mil! Pero yo me quedo.'

'¡Nueve mil!'

'No. Ven conmigo, por favor. Ayúdame.'

'¡Diez mil! ¿Estás loco? Estamos a punto de lograrlo. Sal tú. Ya te iré a buscar para firmar los papeles.'

Al levantarse, Daniel se puso pálido. Caminó a través del pasillo viendo los ojos codiciosos de los pobres que gastaban sus ahorros para mejorar su aspecto físico, las miradas de dolor y sufrimiento de los cojos que necesitaban aquel lote para mantener sus trabajos y los rostros indiferentes de aquellos a los que no les interesaba quién se llevase a casa aquella pierna. Once mil … Doce mil … Trece mil … La cifra no dejaba de aumentar. Las voces se quebraban. Quince mil … La voz de Luis no volvía a alzarse.

'¡Veinte mil!' gritó un anciano, casi suplicante. '¡Veinte mil!'

Al llegar al fondo de la sala, donde la gente se agolpaba de pie, Daniel notó el roce de su pierna contra el metal. Un muchacho se había tropezado con él, haciéndole trastabillar. Parecía nervioso, pero reaccionó a tiempo para ayudarle a mantener el equilibrio.

'Lo siento mucho. ¿Te encuentras bien? Es que a veces no soy capaz de controlar esta …'

Avergonzado, agachó la cabeza, como un muñeco roto. Daniel se quedó helado al ver el engendro que tenía por pierna, gastada y sin suela; una oxidada masa de metal deformada, más corta que la otra, que hacía años que había dejado de funcionar. A su lado incluso la pierna del viejo violinista funcionaba mejor como implante.

'Tranquilo. No pasa nada.'

'¡Veinticinco mil!'

'A la una … A las dos … ¡Adjudicado al caballero por veinticinco mil!'

Daniel se giró con el murmullo de decepción que llenaba la sala, para mirar al subastador. Sonreía. El anciano que sólo valía veinte mil se echó a llorar desconsolado.

Frente a Daniel, el joven perdió las fuerzas. '¿Y tú, muchacho? ¿Estás bien?'

'Sí … No te preocupes. Tampoco tenía dinero para comprarla,' sonrió, nervioso, tratando de fingir que no estaba afectado, a pesar de tener el rostro más rojo que el del viejo violinista en una caminata de verano. 'Me quedé fuera tras los tres mil que ofreció tu hermano, así que …'

'Oh, no es mi hermano. Es … Oye, iba a salir a tomar el aire. Me siento bastante agobiado.'

'Sí, creo que también me hará bien salir un rato.'

'¿Necesitas …?'

'No, no hace falta,' murmuró el muchacho, agachando la cabeza y rechazando su brazo. 'Todavía puedo andar solo.'

Mientras caminaba tras él, Daniel estuvo a punto de echarle la mano en un par de ocasiones. El chico estaba nervioso, cojeaba hasta perder el equilibrio, y su pierna se agarrotaba y se tropezaba con la gente casi a cada paso.

'¿Cuánto hace que …?' le preguntó Beltrán, ya en el exterior, señalándole a la pierna. La noche se reflejaba en los ojos del joven. A través de ellos se adivinaba una profunda oscuridad interior.

'Nunca fue de otra forma,' respondió, escondiendo la vista y apoyándose contra una pared repleta de una infinidad de carteles, unos sobre otros, convocando a revoluciones que nunca terminaron de llegar. 'Nací sin ella y ya perdí la cuenta de las veces que la cambié.'

'¿Nunca tuviste una de carne y hueso?'

'Nunca nos alcanzó el dinero. Las de metal no crecen a medida que lo hacen las de verdad, así que son mucho más baratas, pero hay que cambiarlas con frecuencia. Así y todo, antes podíamos permitírnoslas. Ahora, desde que murió mi padre, cada vez es más difícil. Mi madre apenas gana para darnos de comer y yo no logro mantener un trabajo,' se explicó, golpeando nerviosamente el metal con los nudillos. 'Esta se la tuve que comprar hace varios años a la madre de un amigo que...' El aire venía frío y cortante. Beltrán se escondió entre las solapas de su abrigo. Toda la colonia estaba tan congelada que ya no sentía nada. 'En fin, ya estaba usada; y me vino en muy mal estado.'

Dolor. Remordimiento. Miedo … ¿Quién va a querer sentir nada en un mundo tan corrompido? La brisa, cargada de polvo y suciedad, le hizo soltar una lágrima. Hizo un esfuerzo para que nadie la viese resbalar por su mejilla.

'¿Qué edad tienes, muchacho?' murmuró, acercándose a él. 'Diecinueve … acabados de cumplir.' Daniel se colocó a su lado, con la madera de su pierna entablillada pegada al metal de la pierna artificial del joven. '¿Qué estás haciendo?'

'Podría servir … No creo que te fuese mal. No tardaría en alcanzar tu constitución. Y en unos meses se adaptaría a tu ritmo de crecimiento.'

'¿De qué hablas?'

'De donarte mi pierna. Te serviría mejor que a mí.'

'Deberías esperar a ver si tu hermano logra hacerse con una nueva… Además, tu pierna rota es la derecha, no la izquierda.'

'No quiero una nueva, muchacho. Nunca la quise. Ya ni me importa lo que me pase. Sólo quiero entregarte mi pierna, mi pierna sana, mi pierna izquierda.'

Daniel no oyó nada más. No fue capaz de encajar nada de lo que el joven le decía. Sólo unas pocas palabras rebotaron contra su mente embotada, haciéndole sonreír: "Ojalá tuviese su mismo color de piel. Así su pierna encajaría mejor conmigo."

*

En pocos meses, estalló una revolución de las clases bajas contra la metrópoli en varios planetas. Daniel sintió un remedo de esperanza en su enfermizo pecho; una sensación tan desconocida que ya no recordó cómo mantener dentro. España no tardó en lanzar una ofensiva contra un planeta lejano invadido por Inglaterra cuyo nombre nadie sabía pronunciar con intención de desviar la atención. Todas las colonias se unieron a la metrópoli en el mismo sentimiento patriótico que la prensa creó para ellos. Los ricos lo leían en voz alta en los cafés. Los pobres sentían su calor en los periódicos que usaban para taparse por las noches. Y a partir de entonces los oídos de Daniel se cerraron al mundo y sus ojos se cegaron a la realidad. Se cruzó por la calle con un muchacho sollozante y tembloroso. Se le había curado tan mal un brazo roto que no le permitían alistarse. Daniel se miró el dorso y la palma de la mano y sonrió. Ni siquiera se preocupó por recuperar el sello familiar que llevaba en el dedo cuando se deshizo del brazo entero.

Meses después, con el pueblo orgulloso de las victorias españolas contra el extranjero y las ya olvidadas y sofocadas revoluciones, rescató a otro muchacho de bajo un coche con ayuda de su único brazo. No tenía padres. Iba a trabajar para ganarse la vida y no tenía más familia. Daniel lo acompañó al hospital, cojeando sobre su muleta.

El médico dijo que el muchacho perdería la pierna, nunca volvería a caminar; así que, desde entonces, Daniel no pudo volver a salir de casa. Una sola muleta no era suficiente para hacer andar a un hombre sin piernas.

Pero los vecinos no se habían olvidado de él ni de su generosidad. Nunca se olvidaron de él.

*

Gabriel Beltrán extendió un brazo tembloroso hacia la caja. Se sentía avergonzado de no poder usar su propia mano para tocar a su hijo por última vez. Dubitativo, le tocó el pecho, que aún albergaba un órgano roto. El contraste de la mano blanca y torpe del vecino del piso de arriba sobre aquel pecho mulato, tan oscuro, era mayor incluso que el de la vida frente al de la silenciosa muerte.

Gimió y lloró por no poder mirarle a los ojos, por no poder ver su rostro una vez más. Ya sólo quedaban como testimonio de su corta existencia aquel corazón y su historia, dentro de la caja en la que su madre los había dejado tanto tiempo atrás. Un corazón demasiado grande para que nadie lo quisiera, demasiado grande para que este mundo supiese valorarlo; pero fiel a sus ideales hasta el fin.

UNMADE

Scotland & India

UNMADE

By Suna Dasi

Nausea.

That's all the explosion was to me.
No flying through the air, no flash of light: just the stolid "Dhoomp!" that overwhelmed my body and emptied my stomach.
No noise. No smell of burning.
I don't remember my hand being ripped off. Nor my leg.

Then light. A tugging, pinching, tapping and plucking by shady forms that never quite congeal into reality before my one-eyed gaze. The smell of hot iron filings.
Someone on the edge of my hearing is peppering the air with expletives and short bursts of raw, bestial yelping, until something muffles my face and my mouth fills with Kloro-vapour.
Dimness.

Afterwards, being seasick during transport was pleasant by comparison.

Sutherland Plantation, Orange Hill, St. Vincent,
Tuesday September 10th, 1872

The heat has its way as the sweat from my armpits and loins rills into my plate joints.

I quickly try to flex my hand and knee, but too late. A teeth-razing squeal and I've jammed. Again.

I wrench my Meka arm against the snagging ball joint and shift the cart handle onto my shoulder. As I make my way up the slope, the leg shrieks with every lopsided step and bites into my inner thigh with every impact.

Stupidly, I left my lube can behind instead of tucking it into my utility belt.

I close my ears to the snipes from the Keeper's boys who are lounging on the nearest woodpile and mulishly concentrate on putting one foot in front of the other.

Step, Skree, clunk. Step, Skree, clunk.

Even when I inevitably trip upwards on the incline to the storehouse and I nearly lose control of the cart as it tries to jounce back downhill, I manage not to look at those ruddy-drunk, sunburnt faces, now extra glossy with mirth at my ungainly progress.

Once in the storehouse, I oil my limbs, pocket the can and stare miserably at the heaps of coconuts and crates of bananas.

Then, with depraved fatalism, I look up at the big house.

The smoke from the laboratory curls around the tops of the palm trees, scorning me, reminding me of the life that is now forfeit. Yearning rips through me and I stifle a whine.

My laboratory days are over and I miss my old tools like a real woman would miss her lover's touch.

I barely maintenance myself these days. If it weren't for the Plods I might have done myself a mischief.

I stomp off to work, knowing my sullen scowl will invite more verbal digs, but I'm unable to adjust my face. At least I've become – oh irony – literally untouchable to them.

I wasn't so lucky on my first day.

The moment I arrived, the Sutherland sons pressed close and took my *saree*.

It was the last thing left I could call mine.

They gibed, leered, egged each other on to touch me and finally crushed my bare flesh between clammy fingers. The oldest held me down while the younger lads, doubling over with laughter, flexed and stretched my Meka limbs and proceeded to play 'Strip the Willow' on my leg with sticks.

I was certain they would rape me, but they didn't.

I was naïve to expect it: real men put their manhood in real women, not into such as I, who barely deserve the term female anymore.

When they finally got bored they sent me to Rola, who dumped me into a steaming tub without comment. The vapour smelt of hot cedar.

After being scrubbed, deloused, trimmed and clipped, she took my burnt umber hand in her sloe-black one and pulled me so close I could smell the fermented Demerara on her breath.

For what seemed years, she scrutinized my face.

Then the younger woman wrinkled her nose at me in derision.

'Bad investment. You'll rust. They thinking?'

She threw me a cotton blouse, petticoats and a brown overskirt.

No attempt to help me put them on, even though it was obvious that the putrid infection running round the crease that joined my thigh to my torso made it almost impossible for me to bend down without fainting. She just watched.

The tartan sash was next and then I was done.

Maker to Made. Autonomous to Owned.

They didn't even bother to register me under their family name, as was common with Indentureds. I was less human than they.

I was twenty three.

*

As the seasons spin and are measured by humid mud or feverish deluge, I am breaking my back hauling coconut carts, timber and other hefty cargo with my specialised limbs, often doing more intensive lifting in a day than some of the men in the fields do in a week.

The blooming round form of Kofoworola barely turns my way during this time.

She hasn't looked directly at me since the day she subjected me to her louse-comb.

But I am constantly aware of where she is. Even with my back turned, it's as if she transmits a signal that resonates like a gong in my gut. I gaze at her with the caution of a pygmy shrew trying to avoid an owl.

I don't see much of the other Indentureds: the women all work inside the manufactories, processing the sugar, desiccating the coconuts, drying and packing the bananas in crates.

The logging and harvesting teams dump their loads by the side of the plantation tracks for my gang of seven haulage Plods to pick up.

Black workers have their own quarters. Indian workers have theirs.

And never the twain may meet. I belong to neither and live in the Plodder depot on the edge of the Indian quarter.

There, I am endured because it means I take the maintenance of the 'jiggers', as they resentfully term Plods, out of their hands. I'd never admit it, but their upkeep is my saving grace.

Other than that, I'm tolerated at the shrine and the well.

But they will not eat their meals with me. It's not as though the wretched slumgullion that bubbles away in their stewing kettles is worth eating, in any case.

I trap my meat and roast it in the tiny furnace that's meant for small smelting and joining jobs to do with Plodder repair. There is fruit and there is Demerara.

I certainly don't starve, but I would cheerfully commit gruesome murder for a proper cup of *chai*.

In our own way we've installed rules and ways of being that set us apart from our owners and thus retain some sense of individual meaning.

Including, apparently, an aberrant specimen to ostracise, in the person of myself.

But some of the most rigid aspects of caste division have broken down among the Hindoo Indentureds. Leaving Bharat soil, combined with the sea crossing, allowed caste status to be mainly neutralised: however, thousands of years of social hierarchy are not to be fudged out in a mere decade.

Pooja is performed each morning, with crude incense made from coconut fibre dipped in oil, infused with swamp-apple blossoms and burnt in conch shells.

Garlands of wild rhododendrons are hung with much chanting of '*Jai Maha Devi, Devi Ma Jaya*' around the spindly neck of the rickety clockwork effigy of Durga, which was smuggled onto the plantation by a long-dead *poojarini* from Bhopal.

The statue is meant to majestically swing one of its swords in a circular motion over the tiger's head while the other arms form crude *mudhras*, but it's so flimsy that Durga appears to perpetually tap the tiger on the head with the sword-tip.

I long to repair it, but some of the elder folk spoke against me touching it.

Their resentment of my mechanical limbs prevents me from fixing their mechanical goddess.

I dance the Bharat dances I was taught as a child in a secluded clearing after dark; the same clearing where the Southern men practice their *Kalaripayatt* at dawn.

Erratic though my movements are, I still get pleasure and comfort from the structured patterns and gestures.

I can just make out the stringed veena and the flute from where the main community gathers after the evening meal.

Devi-Ma, I miss my workshop.

In the deep of night, Rola's folk will start their haunting drums and their hoarse ululations; those half-chanted, half-shouted harmonies that sound so flat to my ears but to which I cannot stop listening.

They weave strangely patterned mats and hangings from cotton fibre, carve their own idols from teak and tell their children about Anansi, the spider-trickster.

The children who dare creep closer to listen also whisper of sacrifice: not just of birds, but of the small *agouti* rodents which populate the island. I shrug at this, remembering the gurgling tributaries of goat blood running down the steps of the Chennai Kali temple.

Life here is hard, but there is no camaraderie of suffering.

Minor defiances, transgressions and crimes that result in punishment are not mutually bonding experiences. They are deeply personal moments of blind pain that renounce all awareness of each other's existence.

It helps that the whites aren't entirely unpunishable, as two Sutherland nephews found out with anger and disbelief two weeks ago. The Demerara devil entered their already heat-twisted minds, corrupting them into something more cruelly deviant than usual.

It is, perhaps, true that 'real men' don't degrade themselves on a Meka freak like myself, therefore I don't see much of that particular hell that hides itself in some men.

These two staggered into the depot and, with a warped lust I shudder to imagine, rode out three Plods like monstrous giant toys and raped one of the Yoruba girls.

The poor thing never stood a chance; they tied her to a palm tree and had the Plods insert their hideous, cold limbs into her cavities. When they grew bored of that, they fitted the Plods with other objects: branches, tools from the depot and anything else they could find.

They ravaged her appallingly, fatally.

As dawn stared in judgement they dragged her mutilated body to the edge of the swamp, urinated on her as a parting gesture and stumbled back to the big house, where they passed out on the verandah.

She was found, hours later, by Keepers, who had imagined that she had run away.

The Earl was apoplectic with rage when he'd found out that his little niece had witnessed some of the horrific scene. He called for immediate disciplinary action, which was his sole prerogative. Had he not been furious, his discretion may have gone the other way, the way of all the other terrible family secrets the world shall never know.

They're in gaol now. Well, one of them is at any rate.

When word of riots on the other plantations reaches us, we keep silent while our owners and foremen survey us like hawks for weeks afterwards, to see if we too might rise up.

They need not fear. We are all too eager to prove ourselves better and more sophisticated than our fellow Indentureds, but at the final reckoning, the sum of our existence is that we all belong to the braying, bellicose Scot in the big dwelling.

His wife is a McGregor and from the little I see of them, this nominal difference seems to matter as much to each family as does our African and Indian urge to separate ourselves from each other and paint each other's origins in derogatory colours.

We female 'Wogs' unpick the seams of our skirts and combine the fabric with the Sutherland tartan to make a type of *saree*.

The female 'Spear-Throwers' wear their tartan on their heads, making elaborate *Gele*.

The 'Jocks' wear their kilts, thick woollen stockings and Harris tweed waistcoats, no matter how absurdly suffocating and intolerable the weather.

The more I stand on the outside looking in, the more preposterous we all are.

If there is one thing that does unify us, it's the dizzying Demerara. It baptises and drowns, day and night. Though I can never entirely submerge my dreams in it.

*

I am whole. I am working.

The machine valves, alembics, glass retort bottles and copper receptacles are all gleaming around me and my hands deftly perform their delicate work.

Part of my task is to ensure that the temple engines, which operate the portals and the colossal Shakti statue in the main hall of worship, run smoothly.

I urge Priti to keep an eye on the boilers and regulate the pressure so I may fully devote my attention to the internals of the icon under my fingers.

The oiled ballet of precision that is the clockwork makes my heart smile.

Engrossed, I forget my surroundings until I hear Priti's horrified shout, a split

Nausea…

*

With a nasty shriek of metal I jerk upright.

Before I am properly awake, I am using the cotton rag that lies next to the mat just for these moments and I wipe off the sweat that trickles eagerly to pollute my plate joins and sockets. Pointlessly, I'm crying.

Two huts down the path I can hear Hugh, the middle Sutherland boy, huffing and honking like an asthmatic goose. He's at Seema again. She doesn't sound at all displeased.

That is not going to end well.

I shake my head as I pull my *saree*-skirt towards me.

The last time any of them had a go at me, I'd lost my temper and broke his wrist in seconds. All I had to do was keep squeezing gently with my Meka hand to destroy it, permanently.

How he had wailed and blubbered. Even the whipping, which had laid me down for a whole fortnight, had been worth it.

There had clearly been a decree from on high to 'let the tin girl be' since that time. Alas.

I scramble upright, throw the tartan *pallu* crosswise over my left shoulder and try to muffle my clunks as I pad to the door of the hut, where I pick up my utility belt.

The moment I set foot outside, most of the dream about Priti falls away from my oppressed mind and my body harmonizes with my slowing heartbeat.

The tops of the palm trees are waving in the air against the backdrop of the vasty night, like lazy, upside-down jellyfish. Bats jitter overhead and the swamp is filled with the tinnitus of whistling frogs. The sweaty balm of swamp-apple blossom, married to the perfume of wild jasmine, drifts past my nose. Underneath it all is the inescapable, silt-slick aroma and sonorous booming of the Sea of Atlas.

When I first arrived, the latter made me queasy within seconds; a combination of my body remembering the horrendous crossing, caged up in a crate lacking air holes and the heartsick knowledge that my motherland lay thousands of miles behind me.

But now I love it. It is hard not to acknowledge the eternal beauty of the ocean and her many faces.

She is visible in every direction from the top of Orange Tree Hill; a cruel irony for most of those who look upon it but may never cross the boundaries of the estate.

But not I. Not any more.

I allow her to fill me with a sense of space and infinite movement, a salve to my wrecked body and crippled, lonely mind.

The rhythm of the ocean is what first brought me back to dancing, such a seeming impossibility after the procedure that replaced my supple limbs.

Concentrating hard to dampen my metal noise, I quietly jerk towards the Plodder depot and slip inside before I'm noticed by any patrolling Keepers.

Though they are most likely at the Demerara and dice in the gatehouse and listening to badly played bagpipe music on the wiregraph.

The moonlight stabs into the depot casement and throws a beautifully chill glow on the row of Plods bracketed into the wall, the cylindrical housings in their chest cavities dark and empty for the night.

Many of my former colleagues used to be dismissive of them, snorting that they were aesthetically unpleasant. But I find a crude beauty in their upturned, eyeless bucket heads, their cash-register underbites and the soft thrum of their capacitors when the solar cells are running.

They are certainly coarse, but I have a deep affection for them.

I prise open the floorboard where I keep my secret stash of spare solar cells, the discards which I've repaired and which I charge in a small clearing deep in the swamp during the day.

I alternate days and sometimes I leave week-long gaps, so there is no discernible rhythm to my comings and goings.

Tonight I'm in better luck than usual: in spite of the late hour, some of the musicians are still playing by the fire.

The distant sounds of *Dhol* and *Nagara* drums blend with the agile tones of Ravi's flute.

The lad is painfully talented and should be travelling through Bharat, performing with the great musical *pundits* of our time.

But his hands are wasting to blisters in the fields and his lungs are being ruined inhaling the heavy Demerara fumes. Yet, his callused fingers and shortening breath stubbornly work his bamboo treasure to send its notes into the deaf void.

At the big house they think Ravi is just a darkie grunt, his flute regarded as a barbaric tribal instrument. Obviously.

I unlock the clamps holding the Plods in place, insert my cells and soon they stand in a row on the depot floor, their clangorous purr dispersing the last wisps of my nightmare.

Walking around them, I take my precious seven silver beads from my utility belt.

There was a large party at the big house last year and some very foolish, tipsy young folk dared each other into the swamp.

I was called upon to rouse two Plods and haul them out after they found themselves hopelessly stuck and sinking. Once rescued and being bedamned for their youth by their livid elders, they were shoved into a cart and taken back to the house.

One of the young girls fell behind as the others were being helped up. She looked a fright: her teeth were chattering, her ginger locks pasted to her forehead, her fine muslin gown sodden with swamp muck and her legs covered in leeches.

She gripped the rods of my steel wrist – her fingers trembled as she pushed her beaded bracelet into my palm. Her sapphire eyes seemed to flare briefly, then she ran like a colt to her brusque Papa.

With a flick of one of my bolt-drivers, I dislodge the housing in the small of their backs and insert the beads.

It did not take me very long after I arrived at the plantation to work out that jamming the metal punch card in the Plod's housing reset them to manufactory mode.

In this state of *tabula rasa*, their sensors can be set to detect, process and reciprocate the movements of the user.

It's a painfully primitive system compared to the complex domestic and scientific Bionics employed most everywhere nowadays. But they'll do.

I walk and they follow. I stop and they silently stand in the moonlight outside the depot, humming quietly.

I stand before them and raise my arm; they raise theirs in unison and then I forget myself for several blissful minutes as I perform a slow version of one of my Bharat dances, the Plods cumbrously joining in my every step and *mudhra*.

The music in the distance transports me briefly home and I can almost feel the cool courtyard flagstones of my family home under my feet, smell the fresh warmth of *chapattis* wafting from the kitchen and hear my little sister's finger cymbals guiding the rhythm.

Then Rola's there, behind me.

I have no idea for how long, but she's been there a while. It's the first time I haven't noticed her presence straight away. Or is it?

I stop dancing abruptly, my arms and the Plods' dropping by our sides in a defeated slump. Slowly I turn towards her and I can hear the Plods feet crunch softly in the sand as they, too, turn in the same direction.

She's staring over my shoulder at the metal creatures and wrinkles her nose the way she did at me when I just arrived.

"Been dreaming again?"

I nod stupidly and let my eyes flit everywhere but to hers.

"Poor thing was in the worst of places at the worst of times. Took your girl to your workshop often?"

Caught unawares by her directness, I start to answer: "Ever chance I…."

Then I suck in my breath. "Now hold. Your hut is nowhere near here. Are you lurking out there *listening* to me talk in my sleep?"

To my great shame and deeply resentful surprise, Rola nods, completely unapologetic.

"Ever night. Ever when you arrived."

Open-mouthed, I stare at her and don't know where to put myself.

"That was *two years* ago!" So much for my imagined sensory skills.

Then the right question finally percolates through my mortification.

"But. What for?" I narrow my eyes in suspicion. "The Jocks put you up to this?"

She snorts angrily. "For shame, you."

I flinch. I feel like I've been slapped. She's right, I know there must be a better reason.

But… the same reason I've been watching *her*? Not likely.

Rola is incredibly proud and regal, her stocky build and heavy tread notwithstanding.

And I am… a mess.

"No tears. You'll rust again." Rola says and I can hear the smile in her voice.

"I'm not…" I start to say, still doggedly trying to save face. But I am.

I can't even finish speaking. A mewl of distress is wrenched from my throat and I start blubbing loudly. I'm pathetic and she knows it.

I turn away from her to face my seven Plods, all with their metal fingers in front of their faces, wobbling their bucket heads and rocking slightly in a ludicrous parody of my grief.

Rola lets out another snort and I sneak a tear-blurred glance at her. Her shoulders are heaving with laughter.

I can feel an indulgent, destructive rage ready to erupt within me.

I want to throw vicious, hurtful words at her for laughing and I want to turn her away, for looking at me, for seeing the hobbling pile of flesh and metal that is my wretched self. But I don't.

Instead, for blessed reasons which I cannot comprehend, the world seems to still itself for a single beat and a strange calm washes over my agitated mind.

I pull a deep, trembling sigh and swallow my pride. I rub my face with my filthy sleeve, the Plods repeating the gesture with a clanking sweep of their arms. I look at her askance, trying to grin.

She nods at me and I can sense she recognises my small victory over self-pity.

Durga-Ma, how I want her.

"I suppose I'd better put them to bed." I start searching my utility belt for my bolt-driver, relieved to have something real to do.

"Girl, wait! I see them dance again. You show me."

Rola puts a hand on my arm and, at the sudden touch, I can't repress a shudder that runs all the way to my loins. She stiffens, clearly thinking it's revulsion on my part.

She makes to withdraw. Quick as a viper, I put my hand over hers, trapping it.

I meet her eyes unswervingly for the very first time.

What smoulders there could not be mistaken by a Plod.

Kisses are a strange thing.

In my, albeit moderate, experience they are either urgent and famished, or languid and gradual.

When Rola puts her cushy lips to mine and my mouth opens to receive her tongue, there is a decisive fluidity to our movements that will not tolerate any awkwardness on my part or any aloofness on hers.

We slip into and against each other in a manner most definite and right, our tongues twirling, crushing and enfolding each other's in a dance we both seem to know like our own flesh.

Her hands rough slowly down my blouse until they find the edging of my skirt and, with a sharp tug and a sly move, they are on my bare breasts.

My breath swirls into her lungs at the touch. Clutching her, I arch my back and drive my human thigh into the humid recess between her legs.

My metal foot drives down into the sand to steady us and strikes a rock, shattering it.

Rola makes a lewd noise in her throat as she tugs at my lower lip with her perfect teeth.

The smell of her sweat deepens.

A dull clang brings us up sharp and I pull away too fast, the taste of blood replacing the sweetness of Rola's mouth.

"Bugger!"

Rola tuts at me for the expletive. I shrug, smack my lips and look toward the racket.

The Plods are still there. Still mimicking my every move. The clanging noise was copper heads and iron bodies banging together in a semblance of our embrace. They now all stand, with hands over where their mouths ought to be, like nothing so much as disapproving aunties.

I waste no time in putting them back in order, removing the beads and pushing all seven of them into their brackets in the depot. I'm in a tearing hurry as, for once, I have something so much better to do.

Rola is waiting for me when I step back outside, her exuberant, naked body luminous in the indiscriminate glare of the moon.

My life acquires an unutterable brilliance in the space of an hour as we enjoy the lack of inhibition known only to the absolutely powerless.

Two months later, we are discovered.

Epilogue

Alexandra McGregor sits at her father's desk, apathetically trying to concentrate on her lesson.

He had grudgingly allowed her to continue studying mathematics, but today it is too hot in the study. She has to make as if she is working or else he will certainly take the privilege away again.

A creak in the corridor makes her bend her head over her book in an affectation of deep thought, but the person who softly slips into the room is Stuart, clutching the day's broadsheet.

Instantly, she knows this is not the regular brother-bother.

Something is the matter; his vibrant nerviness infects her as he approaches the desk.

She whispers: "What, Stu?"

He lays the paper over her algebra and hisses back in a fierce, triumphant voice:

"That barmy Meka-girl. Who got you out of the swamp at the Sutherland's? Look, Alex, look!'

He steps back to watch the full impact on her face as she reads:

THE VINCENTIAN DAILY HERALD, St. Vincent, Monday the 11th of November 1872

Bizarre deaths at Orange Hill, fugitive Sutherland Indentureds presumed stowaways on East India Dirigible

In an unprecedented and coldly calculated act of slaughter, two Indentured workers of the Sutherland Estate, currently owned by Earl Robert Sutherland the 3rd, are thought to have poisoned several guests and members of the household during the plantation's famed annual Fancy Dress ball.

The constabulary cites the use of Rhododendron honey; Dr. Willow McGregor of the Layou Laboratory has confirmed that both the festive punch and all the sweet pastries were thoroughly infused with the substance.

The unfortunate victims include the Earl's wife and their three sons.

The Earl himself, along with four and thirty guests, has been transported to Kingstown Hospice. His exact condition is unknown at the time of going to print.

The arc of events is being hotly disputed, but the following is widely known: in a case of what may perhaps be called a peculiar sense of Scottish humour, the Earl incorporated both the Estate's only Bio-Meka and seven haulage Plods into the Ball's entertainment.

The Earl had them perform certain capers for his guests' delectation.

According to eyewitnesses, the performance was accompanied by a rendition of Charles-Camille Saint-Saëns' Danse Macabre, a grisly detail made all the more poignant by the dissolution which followed.

The constabulary is at a loss to explain how either of the two scoff-laws might have had access to the plantation's Rhododendron grove to collect the wild honey for their baleful purpose, let alone introduce it to the victuals.

They are both said to have been separately confined and under the strictest surveillance following a recent shameful incident, the exact details of which witnesses have been reluctant to divulge.

Alexandra slowly lowers the broadsheet, her eyes glinting in the lamplight. "Stu, that's…."

Her brother nods enthusiastically, almost stamping with excitement. "Gripping, isn't it? So gruesome. Such an adventure!"

His sister shakes her head: with his twelve years, Stuart hasn't quite grasped the whole picture.

She knows exactly what will happen to the fugitives if they are ever caught and she does not wish any of it upon the Meka girl who saved her life.

Perhaps this will instigate some movement towards more humane circumstances at the plantations, she muses. But she keeps silent on the subject; she is the only abolitionist in the family.

Alex frowns, her eyes roving over the article again, trying to read what is not being said and silently wishing the two women well.

Out loud she wonders: "Where do you suppose they are now?"

*

170

I scrabble my way out of the whorls of desiccated coconut and break the lid of my crate with a violent crash of my steel shoulder. I spit out miniscule fragments of the dried, oily-sweet fruit.

I will never be able to eat, or even smell, this stuff again. I glance around nervously for Rola's crate.

There… the bananas.

The irony of being nailed into Sutherland export crates has not escaped me.

But we have been exported, and very efficiently.

After making a great pretense of stowing away on one ship, Rola bartered passage on the one and only dirigible that could actually guarantee a chance of true safety.

How exactly she is acquainted with its Captain, a slight firebrand of a woman named Gita, I have yet to wheedle out of her.

I stalk over to the crate that holds my beloved and push one steel finger under the lid.

With a slight mechanical hiss of minimal effort my hand shreds the cheap wooden casing.

I'm not entirely certain where we will disembark, but one thing is as clear as the brightest star: we are free and our destination is entirely irrelevant.

Grinning from ear to ear, I proceed to demolish the rest of the crate.

Soon, I shall change the nature of Rola's muffled cursing and grunts for caution into sounds of a very different kind.

LA MALDICIÓN DE LA ESPINA

Cuba

LA MALDICIÓN DE LA ESPINA

By Elaine Vilar Madruga

¿Quieres una confesión, Lis? ¿Un mea culpa? Lo hice. Convertí tu cuerpo. Sacrifiqué a tu madre. El arpón escapó de mi mano antes de saber que estabas cubierta por sus gritos y escamas. Ningún perdón puede lavar mis manos, manchadas aún por la sangre de aquella que te dio la vida.

Pero, ya ves, su venganza llegó sobre la cabalgadura de los años, cuando ya nos creía a salvo. Es tonto pensar que el amor es todopoderoso.

¿Quieres una confesión? Eres la venganza de tu madre; el arpón que entierra con todas sus sonrisas en el medio de mi espalda.

Sí, eso es cierto. Solo hay un culpable. Ni ella, ni tú.

Ciclo 8, año ijnno dossi. En altamar.

Ayer abandoné tierra firme. Puerto Escara se alejó con sus máquinas de vapor, la magia de los solipdistas y la risa de los niños que querían ver partir el barco. Una santacantaora levitó sobre los mástiles mientras dibujaba en el aire ciertas marcas de humo, signos de buena suerte.

Luego, fue el mar.

Por mucho tiempo, no me había sentido tan vivo. Los años que viví lejos del agua dejaron cicatrices en mis huesos. Fue estúpido pensar que no volvería a tripular una nave. Hoy, la Neuf es mía y siento felicidad de las décadas que ya pasaron, cuando era apenas un polizón en uno de los barcos que surcaban las aguas.

Recuerdo la primera guerra. Cinco años sin ver tierra firme. Tantos que comencé a odiar las palabras mar, algas, eslora, palo mayor, vigilante, nudos y, sobre todo, ese maldito llamado de alerta que estremecía las noches: sirenas. Eran las culpables de que no pudiera volver al puerto. Culpables por obligarnos a pelear por el control de las rutas marítimas y la pesca. Por no pagar el diezmo que nuestro rey exigía.

Diez años de guerra. Y el precio doloroso de siempre. Marineros muertos. Nuestro navegante enloqueció al saber de la ola gigantesca que había acabado con su pueblo pesquero, y ahogado a su mujer y a su hija recién nacida. Hambre. Mucha hambre. Las ciudades abastecían poco combustible. Era arriesgado pilotear el barco tras el toque de queda, entre las nieblas artificiales que vomitaban las sirenas. El riesgo se reducía si la nave tenía reservas de *criovapor* para volar sobre las aguas. Sin embargo, la paranoia era un mal demasiado extendido, y muchos barcos fueron atacados por fuego hermano. Las excusas se repetían una y otra vez. Nadie parecía ser culpable porque, bajo la niebla, cualquier cosa podía ser un engaño de las sirenas.

Sus cantos: programados para engendrar deseos de suicidio y asesinato. Nos ofrecían conchas envenenadas, que algunos locos todavía recogían cuando se enredaban entre las redes del barco, con la esperanza de encontrar una perla, un tesoro, cualquier otra maravilla que apartara la pobreza del mar y de la guerra. Pescados podridos que pronto dejamos de comer. Asedio. Bloqueo. Los hombres se ahogaban a la luz de la luna, cuando nadie más veía. Accidentes.

Eran difíciles de cazar las desgraciadas. Nadaban en manchas. Atacaban juntas y coordinadamente. Parecían máquinas de matar, torpedos de escamas que nunca salían del agua excepto cuando buscaban el punto débil del adversario. Una guerrilla silenciosa vivía debajo de los barcos.

En aquellos años tuve pocos buenos sueños. El insomnio era mi compañero. Solo podía dormir cuando el navegante encendía los motores de *criovapor* para que la nave se elevara en el aire, lejos del alcance de las sirenas. Otra vez la paranoia. El *criovapor* se consumía a mayor velocidad que el pan.

Unas horas de sueño tranquilo por decenas sobre las aguas engañosas.

Ciclo 11, año ijnno dossi.

Las cazábamos con redes y arpones: una tarea ingrata. A veces, se arrojaban bombas sobre el agua, con la esperanza de que una mancha vigilase cerca de la superficie. Casi siempre fallábamos. Sin embargo, un día la suerte nos sonrió. Era una solitaria.

Nadaba sin pareja, quizás en busca de alguna baratija que los marineros de menos experiencia cambiaban a las sirenas por el oro mohoso de los barcos hundidos. Fue el navegante quien arrojó el arpón.

Aun no estaba loco. Su mano era certera. Tenía la vista envidiable del lobo de mar. También tuvo suerte, no lo niego: la solitaria había olvidado cubrirse las vulnerables escamas de la cola con las mallas de hierro. El navegante la ensartó limpiamente.

Nunca podré olvidar sus gritos. La sangre sobre el agua. La red que envolvió a la muchacha pez. Cómo la alzaron sobre la cubierta. Los golpes. Otra vez los gritos: nuestros. Las patadas. Ella parecía suplicar en su lengua de chillidos. El navegante buscó su vientre, y rio cuando la sirena — de forma instintiva — lo cubrió de escamas, estas sí duras y cristalinas, a diferencia de las de su cola. Alguien la golpeó en la cabeza. Las agallas en su torso desnudo temblaron. Comenzaba a sentir asfixia. Las escamas del vientre fueron tornándose azules.

El navegante las arponeó, una vez y otra. Y una tercera.

Alguien dijo: *Comeremos pescado, no hay plato mejor*, y todos reímos hasta sentir dolor en el pecho.

Ciclo 12, año ijnno dossi.

Le decían la maldición de la espina.

En tierra firme, consulté a los mejores magos y *medcs*, con la esperanza de escuchar una palabra distinta de las que ya conocía: 'No se puede hacer nada.' La culpa era de ella. De la solitaria que engullimos aquella noche como niños glotones que celebraban una fiesta. Su sabor era inolvidable.

Sí, ciertamente.

En las siguientes veinte ruedas de sol, los marineros comenzamos a desarrollar el mal. A algunos se les secaron las piernas y los brazos: en pocos años, se convirtieron en mendigos que solicitaban una limosna en Puerto Escara para no morir de hambre. Otros, los más, tuvieron fallas orgánicas internas: corazón, pulmones, estómago. Los escuchaba agonizar sobre la cubierta del barco, recluidos en montones temblorosos que esperaban el desenlace, la lejanía del dolor. Miles de veces tuve ganas de arponearlos para que terminaran los susurros, los gritos, las lágrimas.

¿Yo? Sufrí un mal pequeño, en comparación con el de tantos: fue mi semilla, condenada a la esterilidad y la muerte. A lo largo de los años, magos y *medcs* han examinado mi cuerpo, rezado oraciones, pinchado innumerables veces y la respuesta es siempre: 'No se puede hacer nada.'

Es lo que los dioses quieren. La maldición de la espina navegó dentro de mí y secó mi hombría para siempre.

Antes, solía pensar todo el tiempo en aquellos hijos que nunca tendré. Pero, quizás sea la costumbre, ya casi nunca lo hago.

Ciclo 20, año ijnno dossi.

Quién lo duda: la paz es un juguete extremadamente delicado. Se rompe enseguida. Solo basta con respirar encima de él y los pedazos explotan, vuelan, se desintegran.

Quince años de calma se iniciaron con un tratado de no agresión mutua, firmado sobre las masacres en el mar del oeste. Los cadáveres aun flotaban sobre las aguas. Una pierna humana. La cola destrozada de una sirena. Dedos. Branquias. Arpones. Perlas envenenadas.

Paz y utopía, qué palabras tan estúpidas.

Con grados de capitán, una pierna de menos y la renta de los veteranos de guerra, abandoné las aguas. Al cabo de diez años en que ahorré cada crédito, pude costearme un miembro criocultivado en los jardines de órganos de los *medcs*. Viví en Puerto Escara, ese lugar infame que debería ser barrido de los rincones del reino. Era el viejo lobo a quien los ladronzuelos de nueve y ocho años — muchos de ellos huérfanos por la guerra — solían preguntar: ¿Cómo son las mujeres pescado?, ¿existe de verdad la maldición de la espina?, ¿alguna vez cazaste a un bicho de esos?

La Neuf no es un buque de guerra que valga mi vida, ni siquiera la de los pobres diablos que me acompañan. Es un barco viejo, casi en desuso… quizás por eso decidieron entregármelo. Un cachivache para Eder´ym el recompuesto, el maldito por la espina, el veterano de la primera guerra que todavía sueña con el mar.

*

¿Quieres una confesión, Lis?

La noche era oscura, y la Neuf casi había zozobrado unas horas antes. Sentía el pecho comprimido por el odio hacia las sirenas… pero también hacia el maldito rey que nos había otorgado una miseria de créditos para comprar *criovapor*. Teníamos que dormir sobre las aguas como animales a merced de la mordida de un depredador silencioso. El pez grande se come al chico, dice la sentencia de las santacantaoras: es una de las pocas que creo sin poner en duda ni un segundo.

Volar en las noches sobre las aguas es la única garantía de vida en esta guerra.

Dormir abajo: la muerte.

Fue la ola. Artificial. Enorme. Había sido creada para hundir el barco. Se alzó por encima de la Neuf y lo supe de inmediato: éramos vigilados por una mancha de sirenas.

Los dioses del mar no quisieron mi muerte, Lis. Debes creerlo. El *criovapor* estaba consumido. La Neuf era demasiado pesada para alzarse sobre las aguas a tiempo y volar por encima de la ola. Recé. Aquella mole de oscuridad y agua se acercó a la endeble masa que era el barco. Justo cuando iba a hundirlo como si fuera un palo de madera que flotara a duras penas, ocurrió el milagro: la ola se detuvo. Tan cerca que bastaba con extender la mano para sentir la humedad.

¿Una confesión, Lis? Lloré. Y de qué manera. La ola se retiró hacia el oeste y de inmediato supe que allí se libraba una batalla decisiva. El horizonte comenzaba a teñirse del naranja del fuego y la muerte. La mole oscura se alejó de la Neuf en busca de platos más suculentos. Respiré tranquilo. Junto a la ola, se marcharían también las sirenas. Los míos tendrían una noche más de vida.

Cuando llegó la mañana, la luz, hice que la Neuf navegara hacia el oeste con la esperanza de que quizás algún barco pudiera haber sobrevivido al caos de la ola. Tú, que no recuerdas la guerra, hija mía, no puedes saber lo que vi. La destrucción. Las maderas que flotaban a la deriva. Los cuerpos de las sirenas, bultos de escamas petrificadas que chocaban contra los despojos de las barcas. Arpones. Sangre. Esquirlas de hueso y metralla. La sombra de un hechizo, Lis, había congelado un fragmento de ola: se erguía como un trozo de hielo, la mano de un dios sin clemencia, por encima del mar hecho pedazos.

Iba a ordenar la retirada porque los ojos aterrados de los marineros comenzaban a escocerme como heridas. El miedo a morir se había sembrado en el corazón de aquellos pichones de tierra firme… ¡pobres muchachos sin esperanza! Y entonces la vi. Escondida tras la ola congelada. A la sirena. Una rezagada, pensé, pero entonces vi la herida en el vientre, el arpón que la atravesaba y la unía a la superficie de la ola. No podía escapar. Sus escamas se habían petrificado en torno al arpón, haciéndole imposible huir de su abrazo. El arma poseía algún hechizo o truco de solipdista que le impedía escapar.

Ella nos vio. Me vio, y comenzó a chillar como hacen las sirenas cuando sienten la cercanía del fin… Aquellos gemidos de animal se cuelan en los tímpanos y ensordecen tu cerebro. Cada vez más.

'Vamos a matar al pescado, dije, y mis pichones cobardes sintieron cómo nacía un rayo de valor en aquel lugar que hasta entonces había estado ocupado por el miedo. 'Vamos a enseñarle a esta sirenita cuánto vale una ola.'

Tu madre se revolvió, Lis, hija mía. El arpón era su jaula. ¿Quieres la verdad? Gocé con su sufrimiento. Reí cuando intentó, inútilmente, suavizar las escamas para intentar escapar. Continué haciéndolo cuando la petrificación de su cuerpo le hizo arrojar sangre por la boca. Sus ojos se clavaron en los míos, y volvió a chillar.

'Cállate, pescadita…'

Mis marineros, desde la borda, comenzaron a pincharla con arpones y palos. Uno le escupió el rostro.

'¿Dónde está la ola que te salva? ¿Y tu mancha? ¿Te dejaron atrás, sirena, cuando vieron que no podías escapar?'

¿Quieres una confesión, Lis? La odiaba. Su raza había masacrado a mis hermanos de armas, a los padres de los niños ladrones de Puerto Escara, a la hija y a la mujer de mi navegante. Su raza me había negado el amor y el placer.

'Ahora vas a saber qué es la maldición del arpón,' le dije.

Ella volvió a mirarme, Lis. Pedía clemencia. Pero esa es una palabra que no me importaba entonces. Fue mi arpón el que atravesó su cuello en el preciso instante en que sus ojos — siempre sus ojos — lanzaban una última súplica.

La vida huyó de su cuerpo en un buche rojo. De inmediato, las escamas petrificadas volvieron a convertirse en telillas cristalinas.

'Cojan el arpón,' pedí. Las armas mágicas no podían ser desechadas en la guerra.

Uno de mis muchachos retiró el cuerpo de un golpe y lo arrojó al agua, y en ese momento encontré los ojos — tus ojos — mirándome.

Te habías escondido entre el cuerpo de tu madre y la ola congelada. No llevabas escudo. No tenías más de tres *declas*. No habías mudado los dientes. Tus escamas todavía no aprendían a petrificarse. Estabas sola, junto a los dos arpones que habían dado muerte a tu madre. Su cuerpo se hundió y, por un momento, pensé que nadarías hasta el fondo con él, pero no lo hiciste, hija mía, porque no conocías las palabras odio, peligro, guerra, masacre, venganza.

Chillaste como lo hizo tu madre, pero no era un llamado de miedo, sino de bienvenida, como si nosotros — los asesinos — fuéramos los miembros de esa mancha que te había abandonado junto a la moribunda. Parecías indefensa y pequeña, como los tantos niños que las sirenas ahogaron en las playas y puertos del reino.

El cadáver se hundió y no escapaste, Lis. Estabas dentro de mis ojos, y la venganza — la verdadera maldición de la espina — se clavó en mi corazón como el arpón en el centro de tu madre.

Ciclo 39, año ijnno dossi.

Dentro del camarote, al menos tres veces al día — cuando la responsabilidad del combate o el desarme de una zona no exigen de mi tiempo —, me contento con verla. Puede respirar si la saco de la pecera, pero comienza a sofocarse a los pocos minutos. Trato de que hable, pero la sirenita es caprichosa: solo escucho los sonidos de siempre.

Mis hombres me miran con rencor. Los entiendo. Muchos están aterrados ante la idea de tener a bordo una abominación que puede, en cualquier momento, escupir niebla, crear olas artificiales o secretar aquella materia blanca que forja perlas venenosas. No entienden: ella es solo una niña.

Será la lástima en mi pecho, el remordimiento… no lo sé… pero abandonarla en medio de la guerra es un crimen.

He mentido mucho en estos días. Pienso que los hombres todavía me creen, pero las horas pasan y cada vez la confianza se va quebrando en pedazos más chicos. La *venderemos*, les anuncio. *Cualquier mago o solipdista daría lo que fuera por estudiar a una sirena. No son muchas las que atrapan y llegan vivas a tierra firme.*

Mientras, sin que nadie lo sepa, rescato del mar las baratijas y armas de las sirenas. En Puerto Escara conozco a un par de estudiosos que pagarán bien si se las llevo. Perlas venenosas del tamaño de huevos de serpiente, tridentes y hojas cargados de veneno de pez, fragmentos de una cola, tonterías que puedo vender en los lugares precisos para adquirir créditos: ese es mi plan.

Y luego transformar a Lis.

Esta segunda guerra ha vuelto cobardes a los hombres. En la primera, magos y coleccionistas no pagaban ni una moneda roñosa por cualquiera de mis adquisiciones. Ahora son en una rareza, aunque casi nunca llegan a Puerto Escara: los marineros se han vuelto precavidos entre tanta leyenda de maldiciones de la espina y asesinatos nocturnos.

Pocos se atreven a arrebatarle secretos al mar.

Yo tengo cuidado, por supuesto. Existen objetos y prendas desconocidos que flotan a la deriva y que jamás tocaré, los dioses me guarden. Pero las viejas, tontas cosas de siempre… ¡ah, y luego transformar a Lis!

Así se llamaba la abuela de mi madre. Es un nombre hermoso. El sueño de tener un hijo ha sembrado sus raíces en mi esterilidad. Quizás ella sea la respuesta de los dioses.

Solo me falta hacerla humana.

Ciclo 41, año ijnno dossi.

Se puede. Claro que se puede. Los *medcs* cultivan órganos en sus jardines como si fueran semillas que colgaran de las ramas. A mí me dieron una pierna artificial que en nada se diferencia a la verdadera. Los magos realizan sus hechizos y transmutaciones.

Pueden convertirla. Desaparecer las agallas, la cola, las escamas de su cuerpo. Será una niña como otra cualquiera. Crecerá junto a mí. Voy a esforzarme por hacerla feliz, porque nunca recuerde ni sepa de la guerra o de su madre.

Lis, hija mía… se escucha bien.

Ciclo 53, año ijnno dossi.

Carecemos de pan y agua. *¿Criovapor?* Ya no sueño con eso.

He solicitado permiso a la Ura, el buque mayor de la flota, para llegar al puerto más cercano y abastecer a la Neuf con los pocos créditos que quedan. Es la única esperanza. Pero la Ura no contesta. Tal vez haya desaparecido, como tantos barcos, o deambule entre la niebla que han vomitado las sirenas a la espera de un rescate que nunca llegará. ¡Quién se atrevería en estos tiempos a atravesar un cerco como ese! Quizás solo ignoren mi llamado.

El mar es un mendigo asqueroso: te pide todo sin dar nada a cambio.

El hambre trota salvajemente sobre mis marinos. Hoy, alguien propuso que quizás sería bueno comer de la carne de Lis. 'Es pequeña, pero todos podremos compartir un pedazo.' La rabia me impidió hablar. No les recordé que era una niña, una víctima de la guerra: no habría servido de nada. Les hablé de la maldición de la espina, de los hombres que vi morir con los órganos secos, de mis secuelas, y los pobres marineros se estremecieron ante la idea de no volver a abrazar a una mujer en los puertos.

Pero Lis peligra, y el hambre crece. El buque mayor ignora mi insistencia, los mensajes cifrados que envío. Mientras, un puerto se acerca y he tomado la decisión… la única que quedaba. Abandonaré a la Neuf cuando llegue a tierra firme, con todos mis tesoros, junto a mi hija.

Escucha, Lis.

El puerto se llamaba Yugular. Era uno de los más pobres del reino. Sus costas habían sido barridas más de trece veces por manchas tribales de sirenas que creaban sus olas contra los habitantes. Las autoridades portuarias nunca prohibían los desembarcos, aunque la nave careciera de la autorización del buque mayor de la flota. A nadie le importaban esos asuntos.

¿Un barco con lepra, peste, epidemia? Bienvenido sea si puede pagar el impuesto. ¿Marinos rebeldes, fugados de las órdenes del rey? Bienvenidos sean, créditos por delante. ¿Piratas? ¿Contrabandistas? ¿Ilegales? La pobreza obliga.

Yugular era el lugar preciso, quizás el único que nos recibiría a ambos: al prófugo y la enemiga.

El engaño se había convertido en una parte de mi cuerpo: cabeza, tronco, extremidades, mentiras. Resultaba cada vez más fácil mirar a aquellos niños confiados de la Neuf y decir: *Todo estará bien. He pedido un permiso a las autoridades aduanales. Mañana o pasado desembarcaremos, pero antes debo bajar y discutir con el comendador de Yugular. No reciben a muchos extranjeros, son paranoicos. Lo arreglaré todo, haré que nos dejen tocar tierra firme. Cuando vuelva esta noche, traeré toneladas de comida y mujeres necesitadas de cariño. Venderé a la sirena.*

Lis, me creyeron. Infelices muchachos. La Neuf quedó varada a la entrada del puerto, y yo desembarqué contigo y mis prendas, el pago por una vida de guerra que tantas mentiras había urdido. Los marineros se despidieron de mí con una sonrisa. *Vuelve pronto, capitán*, me gritó alguien mientras yo le devolvía un saludo de confianza y apretaba a duras penas la pecera que levitaba a mi costado: en ella estabas tú, hija, más valiosa que el honor y la vergüenza.

¿Por qué te amé de esa manera, Lis? ¿Tan desesperadamente? Nuestras especies eran enemigas… pude haberte matado, nadie iba a reprochármelo. Tal vez fue la maldición de la espina que me arrojó tu madre con la última mirada. Estaba condenado a criarte y protegerte

… o quizás sea solo mi corazón, blando después de ver tanta agua y sangre en esta vida.

Desembarcamos, Lis, y pagué el impuesto con toda la alegría que concede el saberse libre de ataduras. La Neuf se diluyó de mi recuerdo en un segundo. Penetré junto a ti en el laberinto de calles, basureros y mugre del puerto, cada vez más adentro, hasta que el mar quedó desdibujado y encontré la ciudad, aquel tugurio de mala muerte donde sembraría tu infancia. Algunos ojos de curiosos y ladrones se fijaron en nosotros. A primera vista, parecíamos una presa fácil, pero mis tesoros eran más terribles que maravillosos, Lis. Nadie se atrevió a acercarse al maldito por la espina que llevaba, en una pecera levitante, a la sirena.

'Necesito a un mago de inmediato. Pagaré bien a quien quiera ser mi guía,' creo que grité entonces.

Cinco voluntarios salieron de los vericuetos de las calles. Escogí a uno, el que me pareció menos peligroso, un adolescente manco que tosía sangre, sin dudas consumido prematuramente por alguna de las enfermedades del puerto.

Avanzamos, siempre con las miradas sobre nosotros, a través de calles que habían perdido el nombre, atravesando basureros y edificios laberínticos.

La esperanza me hacía confiar. Pronto ibas a ser una niña. Sana. Normal. Como tantas, y la gente no se acordaría del hombre que llevaba a rastras una pecera o de la sirena que miraba las calles de Yugular con los ojos curiosos de quien ha visto otras cosas.

'Aquí es. Anda, paga,' me dijo el joven y extendió su mano para recibir el pago por sus servicios.

'Si le cuentas a alguien sobre nosotros,' amenacé, 'cortaré tu corazón en lonjas. No me gustan los entrometidos.'

'Anda, viejo. Paga. No diré.'

'Más te vale. Soy un lobo de mar y he aprendido a rastrear a mi presa por el olor.' Todas aquellas palabras eran mentira, por supuesto, pero la mirada de asombro y terror del manco me hizo suponer que no iba a traicionarme.

'Anda, viejo, gracias,' susurró, e hizo reverencias cuando le extendí una moneda más. 'Y suerte con el pescado.'

Su única mano me señaló hacia una puerta de madera: 'Anda, viejo, es la casa del mago…'

Solo bastó con pronunciar su nombre: la puerta se corrió y en el umbral apareció un sujeto de edad indefinida. Las marcas de los años podían leerse en su rostro, pero estaban cubiertas por hologramas y cirugías de rejuvenecimiento, hechizos y trucos que le hacían parecer más joven. El olor a formol, a cosa muerta, sacudía el umbral:

'¿Qué tienes para mí?,' preguntó, sin invitarnos a pasar. '¿Pescado fresco para mis pociones?'

Rio, y sus dientes amarillos se asomaron como una jauría.

'Traje algunas cosas de mar adentro que a lo mejor te interesan.'

Le arrojé la bolsa donde cargaba mis tesoros. El mago se entretuvo revolviendo adentro. Rumiaba cuentas. Quería estafarme, como todos los de su especie suelen hacer.

'Bueno, muy bueno… sí… puede que me interese… aunque esto no … tengo demasiadas perlas … ah, un arpón de solipdista, curioso, ¿no?' Luego volvió a mirarme. 'A ver, ratero, ¿cuál buque secaste?'

'¿Quieres el paquete completo?'

'Qué va, hombre. Estas perlas… no me sirven. Eso sí, no lo niego, tienes algunas cosas interesantes… y peligrosas. Dudo que alguien pague más de ochenta créditos por un arpón de solipdista. Es, ¿cómo diría?, inestable.'

'Puedes tenerlo todo si la transformas,' señalé hacia tu pecera, Lis, y el mago abrió mucho los ojos:

'¿A la pescadita? Qué va. Si me la vendes, te pagaré tres veces esos ochenta créditos que prometí por el arpón.'

'No me interesa venderla.

El mago cloqueó: un hipido de borracho y loco.

'Escucha, pillo: Las sirenas son la peor clase de perras que parieron los demonios del agua. ¿No has escuchado de la maldición de la espina? Si comes de ella, te secarás como un árbol sin raíces, idiota.'

'No lo haré.'

'Ja, ja, ja,' rio de nuevo y me palmeó el hombro. 'Así que un amor de tierra y mar, ¿eh? Es un buen tema para los bardos, quién lo duda. Aunque vas a tener que esperar un poco, marinerito, si quieres pescado maduro.'

Tuve deseos, Lis, de romper su cuello de animal podrido. Pero no lo hice.

'¿Eres bueno con los hechizos, mago?'

'Soy lo mejor que podrás encontrar en Yugular, marinerito.'

'¿Has estudiado la transmutación?'

'La temporal sí… No la definitiva.'

Supe que había leído mi mente, Lis. Sabía de mis deseos de

convertirte en humana.

'Soy lo mejor que podrás encontrar en Yugular, marinerito,' repitió. 'Pero no pidas que convierta a tu abominación en una niña. Cosas como esas deberían estar prohibidas.'

'Es mi hija, y haré lo que sea necesario para que pueda ser normal.'

'¿Normal? Ella es lo que ves: una sirena. Si la transformas, solo crearás distorsión… Olvídate de esa que llamas hija, y véndela. Pagaré bien.'

¿Quieres una confesión, Lis?

Debajo de mis ropas había escondido el mayor tesoro. Mi instinto lo sabía: el mago no iba a rechazarlo. Exhibí la carga frente a los hologramas de juventud que cubrían su rostro. La codicia, la posesión, la urgencia: marcas que aparecieron sobre las arrugas de aquel desgraciado:

'¿Cómo conseguiste esos huevos de sirena?'

'Están fecundados,' dije. 'Pueden ser tuyos si conviertes a mi hija en humana.'

Dos huevos que encontré a la deriva, Lis, flotando como boyas en altamar. Hermanas tuyas de especie.

'Perfecto, haré lo que quieras. Mis mejores hechizos, marinerito. Convertiré a tu pescado en niña.'

Extendió las manos como un mendigo:

'Pero tienes que saber, marinerito, que la transmutación no es eterna.'

Ciclo 80, año ijnno dossi.

Lis se recupera bien. Hemos encontrado abrigo en uno de los edificios laberinto. Nuestros vecinos son ancianas sin ojos, huérfanos, gente que no tiene adónde ir. No les importamos demasiado. Piensan que Lis es otra de las tantas mutiladas de la guerra.

El mago lo advirtió con su risa de cínico: *Le dolerá terriblemente, tal vez por el resto de su vida*, y luego dividió la cola de Lis en dos trozos, transmutó, distorsionó, lanzó sus hechizos sobre la carne. Entonces tuve sus dos piernas deformes, a una hija desmayada por el dolor que la magia no podía contener.

¿Sufre mucho?, pregunté. El rastro oleaginoso de la hipocresía resbaló sobre mi cuerpo. Nada de eso importaba si podía convertirla en humana.

Los huesos son lo peor, me contestó el mago mientras lo duro comenzaba a crecer dentro de las piernas de mi hija. Vi cómo el fémur se sembraba en Lis. Hueso tras hueso, y al final el sello de lo culminado: olor a carne chamuscada.

Las cicatrices son espantosas. Se extienden como gusanos por todo el cuerpo de la niña. En cada lugar donde crecía una escama, quedó un rosetón, como si fueran las marcas de la viruela. Las estrías han reemplazado sus agallas y el mago me asegura que podrá hablar, aunque nunca con voz clara.

Le entregué los huevos. Lis es todo lo humana que podrá ser.

Le continuará doliendo, pero cuando pase el tiempo será tolerable, un leve tono de consuelo se escapó de la boca del mago, tal vez porque era feliz con su tesoro. *Pero te diré, marinerito, la transmutación no es eterna. Recuerda eso: algún día las piernas volverán a convertirse en cola, los huesos desaparecerán, la voz se hará chillidos. Una vez sirena, siempre sirena. Comenzará a vomitar niebla y a escupir esa flema blanca con la que crean las perlas venenosas. Algún día tendrás que devolverla al mar o pagar de nuevo porque otro mago realice este mismo trabajo, una y otra vez, hasta que su cuerpo no soporte más la transmutación.*

¿Morirá?, inquirí, de súbito aterrado ante la idea de perder a mi hija.

Peor: se convertirá en lo que odias.

No, eso nunca sucederá. Lo juro. Lo juro. Transmutaré el cuerpo de Lis cuantas veces sea necesario, pero no dejaré que se transforme en pez.

He encontrado un techo para nosotros. No es lo que soñaba para criarla, pero está bien para comenzar, sobre todo porque nadie observa demasiado a Lis, a nadie le parece ajena a pesar de su voz ronca, de sus palabras a media lengua y sus pasos desaliñados. Cuando algún curioso pregunta por la salud de mi hija, le digo que se recupera de un accidente que provocaron la sirenas. Las cicatrices en las piernas y el cuerpo de Lis fortalecen mi historia.

Ella no parece recordar nada del pasado.

*

Casi lo he confesado todo, Lis, hija mía. Asesiné a tu madre, vendí a tus hermanas de especie, te convertí en humana, torturé tu cuerpo para hacerte normal. Engañé. Robé. Mentí. He ganado varios siglos de castigo en la eternidad, pero valió la pena. Por ti todo valdría la pena.

Creciste tan feliz como podías en medio de lo podrido y lo sucio. Mis deseos de darte una mejor casa, un lugar donde soñar, nunca fueron posibles. Los créditos no alcanzaban, Lis. A menos de cinco años de tu primera transmutación, descubrí mientras te bañaba la mancha de una primera escama. Sentí pánico. Miedo. Iba a perderte. Pronto comenzarías a mostrar las agallas, a dejar de hablar, a asfixiarte. Nacería de nuevo la maldita cola que te hacía enemiga de mi especie, distinta de tu padre.

Aquella noche, Lis, tomé nuestros últimos créditos: alcanzaban a duras penas para un nuevo proceso de reconstrucción. Todos los ahorros de una vida en altamar se apagaban, se consumían, con tal de darte unos años más de humanidad. El mago volvió a recibirnos con una sonrisa cínica, pero te reconstruyó los huesos, impidió que la cola creciera, transmutó las escamas y agallas. Volviste a ser normal, Lis, a pesar del dolor de las curas, de las punzadas (*son como agujas, papá*) que se clavaban en tus pies cuando dabas un paso, de las crisis de asfixia que te atacaban violentamente cada noche.

Supe entonces, como lo sé ahora, que esa condena nos perseguiría por el resto de la vida. Cinco. Seis años más junto a ti, ¿y luego qué? ¿Asesinarte? ¿Ver cómo te convertías en un pescado, hija, capaz de escupir perlas venenosas y generar olas que aplastarían pueblos y pueblos, a tanta gente?

Quise ahorrar los créditos, Lis. Envejecí como un miserable que contaba las migajas de pan y reducía los gastos hasta el ascetismo. Envenené el resto de tu infancia.

Yo te amaba, Lis. Te quiero, hija mía, hasta el punto de abandonar los harapos de mi honor al hacerme miembro de una tribu de cobradores de viejas cuentas. Me contrataban para torturar a aquellos que no podían pagar los impuestos y diezmos a los jefes tribales de Yugular. Mi vergüenza se convirtió en un jirón, algo sin importancia que arrastraba como la lepra: debía desprenderme del miembro muerto para seguir adelante y poder ganar los créditos, las monedas, que impedirían el desastre.

Pasaron los años, Lis. A los tres de la segunda transmutación, tuviste una crisis de asfixia que casi te cuesta la vida. Tuve que llevarte en brazos hasta el mar y sumergir tu cuerpo. Volviste a respirar dentro del agua.

'Papá, me siento mal.' Tu voz ronca guardaba una semejanza con los chillidos que escuché brotar desde lo profundo de tu madre: terror, incertidumbre, la cercanía del fin. '¿Qué pasa?'

'Son solo las secuelas del accidente, Lis.'

Habían transcurrido menos de ocho meses de aquel evento cuando te hice recibir la tercera transmutación.

'No volverá a caminar,' dijo el mago con su sonrisa de siempre. 'Los huesos ya no crecen.'

El dolor de las curas fue tan negro, Lis, que una noche especialmente terrible — cuando tus gritos amenazaban con volverme loco — pensé en la piedad de los arpones con los que atravesaría tu cuerpo adolescente, en cómo me agradecerías por ser tan buen padre.

'Duele todo el tiempo,' confesaste después, con los ojos llenos de lágrimas. 'Papá, creo que voy a morir.'

Era la transformación definitiva, Lis, la que no pude evitar a pesar de tantos intentos. La maldición de la espina navega en mi sangre, ¿recuerdas? La venganza de tu madre. Todo eso, todo a la vez.

Dos días después, te incorporaste de la cama. Ya no podías hablar. O no querías. Tus ojos me miraron un instante y supe, Lis, que algún resorte de la rabia y el recuerdo se había disparado en tu interior. Tenías la mirada de tu madre y el odio de las sirenas hacia los de mi especie. Luego escupiste una saliva blanca que redondeaste con los dedos hasta hacer una pelota, un huevo magnífico. Me lo ofreciste… cargado de veneno.

Sabías todo, Lis. Recordabas tu infancia de huérfana. Tu naturaleza engañada. Tu rapto. La miseria de tantos años viviendo en un cuerpo que no te pertenecía. La tortura y el dolor a los que te sometí con la transmutación. Yo era el enemigo, y la piedad del arpón volvió a pasar por mi cabeza. Guardaba uno, solo por seguridad, nunca pensé que tendría que usarlo en tu contra. Estabas postrada sobre la estera y las escamas comenzaban a extenderse por tu vientre y rostro: las solidificaste, Lis. Algo en ti habló y dijo que debías hacerlo porque yo soñaba con matarte.

No lo hice, a pesar de tu odio, de la cola que comenzó a surgir en el sitio donde antes estaban tus piernas. No lo hice a pesar de las branquias y las agallas, del continuo boquear por una asfixia cada vez más cercana.

Una nueva flema. Una nueva perla. Tu mano extendida por un segundo, antes de que la apartara de golpe.

Aquella noche vomitaste niebla. Pensabas, sin dudas, que estaba dormido y así lograrías matarme. No. Eres tonta, Lis, o no me conoces del todo. Olvidas que soy un veterano de las guerras contra las de tu especie. Te vigilaba, hija mía, y leí en ti los símbolos de la urgencia. La niebla no me tomó por sorpresa. Era venenosa.

Corrí fuera de nuestro cuartucho, Lis, en busca de aire limpio. El arpón seguía en mis manos. Esperé afuera del edificio laberinto. Sabía que ibas a salir, Lis, arrastrándote sobre los escombros y la mugre. En busca del mar.

¿Quieres una confesión, hija mía? La verdadera maldición de la espina me ha tocado. Estás bajo mi arpón y chillas con toda tu naturaleza de sirena, de animal. El odio se escapa de tus ojos porque no pertenezco a tu mancha; pero el arpón no desciende, la muerte no baja, mi mano no se atreve.

Este es el mar, Lis, lo que siempre te negué. El mundo que existe más allá del mío: tu mundo. Las aguas llenas de guerra adonde sé que irás en busca de venganza por tantos años de sufrimiento. Serás cruel. Escupirás niebla y perlas venenosas, y forjarás aquellas olas que conducen al desastre a los puertos del reino. Y quizás, hija, encuentres en otro arpón la muerte, atrapada como tu madre entre una ola y su cría.

Este es el mar, Lis. Desaparece ahora y nunca vuelvas a Yugular con la esperanza de asesinarme o hacerme pagar todo el mal que hice. La maldición de la espina que ahora me arrojas con tus ojos no puede ser peor que ver cómo te sumerges, de vuelta al fondo de las aguas.

El arpón se escapa de mi mano y golpea una de las tablas del puerto.

Entre mis pies, encuentro tu último recuerdo: la perla redonda y brillante como una escama de sirena. Y desde el mar, allá a lo lejos, una sombra que no puedo definir.

Se acerca la niebla.

STEAM PUNK

THE GOLDEN APPLE

Czech Republic

THE GOLDEN APPLE

By Petra Slováková

The steam train huffed across an expansive country of woods and meadows, deep within the dreaming Slavic heart of Europe. They say of Moravia that it displays the splendour of ages long past, when the land prospered. The women there were beautiful, the men brave and fearless. Even though the revolution sweeping across the countryside had created factories, monstrosities with belching poisonous fumes, one could still find wild brooks, untamed by dams and dykes. The woods were still feral and untamed, home to wolves that tore into the flocks of sheep by chill wintery night. The progress had brought a new era to the cities, steam cars and trams streaming through their streets alongside horse-drawn carriages, but the villages were yet untouched by the revolutionary hand of industry and mining.

The village of Middle could pride itself on its own train station, humble but still of prime import in the sparsely populated country. The gas lamps illuminated the small platform where John Calder had disembarked. Fog banks rolled around the station; the morning was close, but it had yet to flood across the hills and pierce the clouds and mists. The surly dusk had caught him unprepared. Shuddering, he held on to his shoulders. The wind spared no effort to sweep his tall top hat off his head. With a whistle, the locomotive set out again. The conductors had treated him with a cold and distant manner the entire journey, and now measured and examined him with hostile mien from behind the foggy windows. The fact that he was a foreigner was evident at first sight. He rolled up the collar of his long coat, holding his cane and briefcase close to him to guard them from thieves. Without his documents, he would be lost.

During his train journey, he had again perused the manuscript brought to London by an unknown traveller. It contained a collection of legends of the Czech lands – that's where he had found the mention of golden apples. Given that the Royal Society had long been searching for a means to ensure immortality, he immediately set out to conduct a closer examination. Recently, he had waged an adventurous expedition to Greece in search of the fabled Tree of the Hesperides. Regrettably, not even a team of brilliant archaeologists and scientists had reached the desired goal. The golden apples seemed to be a fairy tale. But still, this writer, this Erben, wrote of them with such conviction and appeal that John at long last could not resist, and departed towards the heart of Europe to see for himself.

Stray dogs circled a ruined building. The fields were overgrown with thistle, and the muddy roads bore no semblance to comfortable motorways. No carriage was in sight; after several failures, he negotiated with a pair of farmers to be taken along on their carriage together with a cargo of grain. The bumpy road took them to another village, to Upper. The locals knew no English, exchanging no words with him, but amongst themselves they chattered and gesticulated vividly. He could not help but notice that he was being observed, the locals pointing at him whenever his attention was lost to stray thought.

His promised guide had been an interpreter once, thus knew the foreign tongue. He came recommended by other travellers and, after an exchange of letters, they had agreed on a mutually beneficial cooperation. As his farm was close to the expected site of discovery, the guide did not object – and John was grateful for any help in a strange and hostile land. He imagined his guide to be couth and well-read. But when an older woman in a head-scarf pointed him to the stables, where he discovered an unshaven farmer misting out the boxes, he doubted the wisdom of his choice.

"You're the adventurer?" the man asked and spat on the floor. He smelled of sweat and beasts. His linen shirt was stained and long unwashed.

"John Calder," he smiled, and offered his hand – but when he was met with no handshake, he reconsidered.

"Josef Máchal," the other answered. "But call me Pepa."

"Excellent, mister Pepa. Allegedly you know of the site described in the books, which my colleagues and I have placed in the vicinity of your village?"

"Yes. To be exact, not directly near our village, but near Lower. That's nearby."

"And you're in Upper?" he asked nervously. He lifted his top hat and scratched his scalp.

"Spot on. This is Upper and there is Lower."

Pepa withdrew a bottle of spirits from the hay and quaffed heartily. Then he offered it to John, who shyly refused.

"You must drink. In these parts, it's the foundation of any friendship," Pepa explained.

"Oh! Then forgive me," John replied and, akin to his host, swung the bottle – immediately gasping for air and coughing, grasping his throat, eyes filled with tears.

"You're not used to it, but that doesn't matter! Soon you'll learn to drink like a man!"

"My sincere thanks, but I am uncertain whether that is my desire," John replied with a rasping voice, continuing to hold his seared throat for the entire time it took his guide to prepare for the trip.

"Take a rifle, in case we come across wolves."

"Wolves?" the gentleman gasped.

"Yup – but don't fear, the beasts usually come out only at night. By day they usually don't have enough courage, unless they are starved to death. What do you want in that ravine anyway? I had you pinned for a treasure seeker."

"I seek an exceptionally rare tree."

"Are you a botanist?"

"Yes, a bit. I am mostly a scientist. I search for a tree that bears golden apples."

Pepa bent over in laughter, holding onto his sizeable paunch.

"What is so humorous about it?"

"What will you do with *apples*?"

"I will acquire splices of the tree, bring them to my homeland, then multiply the plant. Have you never heard of the tree of eternal youth?"

"Nay," the farmer grumbled. "Only in fairy tales my granny told me, the bedtime stories we tell our children."

"I assure you, the existence of golden apples is scientifically proven. They are slightly oblong, almost conical, not round as common fruit. Their taste is exceptional, sweet and strange. They are described in numerous pieces of literature by renowned scholars. Not to mention the legend of Heracles, or the mythological apple of the May Queen, Îðunn, of Scandinavian legend."

Pepa shrugged. Lack of interest such as this was common. John was faced with it frequently. People distrusted lofty goals and visions that were intended to ennoble the world.

"In these parts, fruit is the main source of eternal life," the farmer declared at last, mysteriously, and quaffed from the schnapps bottle again. He gazed at the foreigner through the distorting glass of the bottle and nodded for emphasis.

"Excuse me, but I am not an avid consumer of alcohol."

"Perhaps you mean the wine apple. That's yellow," Pepa tried.

"I do not fathom how it is called in your language," he answered. "At first, we erroneously believed it might be the pomegranate. But those do not have any effect, of course, and also grow on hideous thorn bushes."

"Doesn't matter. We'll take a look in the ravine, and perchance you'll find what you were looking for," the farmer decided. John produced a map with meticulously noted landmarks, commentaries and overlays. He drew a line connecting the villages of Upper and Lower and marked the area of wilderness; Pepa just shook his head, took the pen from the Englishman's hand and began correcting the drawing with resolute strokes and hums of disapproval.

"Thank you for coming with me. I would certainly have become lost. Though I had imagined it differently."

"What differently?" Pepa inquired.

"Well, you. I had believed you were... a townsman," he appended quickly, so as not to insult.

"I've been to the city a few times. Don't think I like wearing fancy clothes. I'm a simple man who had the good fortune of having been allowed to learn a foreign language. My father once met a rich merchant who took me in as a servant. I picked up quite a bit there. But I am still a farmer – I've got fields and the stables. It's not much, but it will not tend itself. So I returned to my roots. I've got a wife here. I'm happy."

"To each his own," John flashed a sincere smile; he knew several gentlemen who had withdrawn from the hustle of London to a simpler rural life.

Royal airships flew overhead. The scientist flinched when they began bombarding hills in the distance. Briefly, the horizon flared red.

"What's happening?" the foreigner inquired, fear in his voice. Pepa just waved his hand in ennui.

"The Royals are chasing traitors and deserters. Don't you know? The Austrian-Prussian war?"

"I have noticed something in the newspaper, yes," John replied.

"Prussia came into power after the Napoleonic wars. They'd like to rule Germany, but Austria wishes to unite the German-speaking lands of the former Holy Roman Empire. Many allies have joined the Austrians – Bavaria, Hannover, Saxony ... many disagree with Bismarck's visions. His politics are blood, I'd say."

"I heard of conflicts with the Danes?"

"Yes, they've been fighting the Danes too. Joint armies of both states defeated them on land, and the squadron of Wilhelm von Tegetthoff sank the Danish fleet off Helgoland. But then the Prussians wanted more. Franz Josef I., our uncrowned king, wanted to swap a part of Schleswig for Holstein, but they didn't bite. Bismarck ran the numbers well, and knew that wasn't a good deal. Since then, they're fighting," he added in a dispassionate tone, as if it did not concern him.

"The situation is not simple. But airships – isn't this excessive force?"

"You see war machines here all the time, artillery and steam tanks. Sometimes they plough through the fields and we have to fix the mess. What else is left? Armies march through here hence and forth. Luckily they don't stay long. They're moving to Czechia, luckily, and will bomb the fields *there* for a while."

"And your monarch, is he virtuous?"

"Fairly alright," Pepa added. "He brought factories to the smaller towns and promotes the industrial revolution. He even spends money on expanding the railways and doesn't come here from his den in Vienna. What more could we wish for?"

John missed the obvious rhetorical question, and breathed in to launch further questions, yet was abruptly stopped.

"You should have a drink!" Pepa offered him the flask.

"Dear Lord, no!"

᛫|᛫

Tenacious fine rain soaked their coats. They had walked for many miles. John hardly managed to place one foot in front of the other. He had held no idea there would be such a long trek ahead. At least he had left, following his guide's advice, any superfluous burden behind and had switched his suit for sturdier garb and footwear. He stumbled ahead on the muddy path; Pepa was waiting for him, mood unspoiled, a song on his lips.

Cows grazed beneath the forest's boughs, startling the gentleman.

"Hideous beasts!"

"Just cows," the farmer replied, and headed up into the hills. "The land's not too varied here, but there's a few mountains. We'll head onwards, uphill, and should be at the ravine soon."

"They tell that the legendary Hesperides were the daughters of a giant. And that a fierce dragon was the guardian of the garden's gate!" John warned, sore and tired from the climb.

"Nonsense! Our girls are normal, and no dragons live here – Saint George murdered them all."

"So we shan't fear for our lives?"

"Certainly not. But if you intend on teetering like a drunk, you may fall and break your legs."

"I am ever so sorry – my head is still a domain of pain from your schnapps."

"Problems after drinking it can arise due to two reasons – either you drank too little, or too much. In your case, I'd wager it's the first option." This said, Pepa forced John to drink another gulp. At first he coughed, but then he felt the brew's fire spread into his limbs.

A thunder of guns in the distance brought them back into the moment. They picked up pace.

"Ha, never mind them, they're just fighting again," the farmer spat. "Armies, bah. Give them new toys and they'll go and break them right away."

"I... I do not understand you at all," John shook, visibly unnerved by the proximity of the battle.

"Doesn't matter. We're used to it. It doesn't matter who wins anyway."

"How can you not care?" the Brit was visibly amazed.

"The bread will not be cheaper. There will always be soldiers who plunder your land and leave. We will rebuild and others will come. And do the same. We're used to it. We have our certainties. We are not dependent upon the state or its officials. So we don't really care who sits on the throne. If they trample our fields, we plough them again. Does this make sense?"

"Not really..." he admitted.

"Then you drink too little."

*

Pepa forced the back-up bottle of liquor into his hand; he sipped slowly, the taste getting better with each lick at the bottle. Before they were at the ravine, he was thoroughly drunk. No wonder he started screaming in panic as fat Bertha burst from the bushes, returning with picked herbs. The giant woman of ponderous constitution shook her meaty fist at him. Pepa just tapped his forehead, to indicate that the poor fellow is not lord over his cognitive faculties, and they headed onwards. Once he calmed the Brit, they descended into the darkness of the cave. They were met with the hissing and claws of a cat protecting her litter. Yelling something of dragons, John would have fled if not for the farmer holding him by his suspenders.

"I have never been to so horrid a place!" John admitted. Solely for the sake of science he advanced, for it was his duty to find the tree bearing the golden apples. His head throbbed with the unfamiliar alcohol.

"Then you haven't seen much yet," Pepa asserted. He took off his shirt, wringing water out of it.

"I trudge across the continent into a forgotten backwater only to save the Empire!" he complained.

"See? At least you have a mission. You've travelled a good deal of the world. What would you do at home? Lounge by the fireplace?"

"Yes, and believe me, it would be time well-spent!"

"These scientists, no endurance," Pepa grumbled.

"Excuse me? I was a member of a polar expedition. In Africa, I have searched for the mines of Solomon and battled in Crimea!"

"I battled with the plough on my field, before they made steam tractors," Pepa replied. John pondered it a while, then nodded.

"The village has no shortage of hard work. I believe you. Very well: I have not reached the pole. Influenza held me back at camp. And I have never reached Africa, for I missed the boat. I have met up with the expedition upon their return, yet my name was on the list of participants. The press swallowed the story."

"Bolster yourself with schnapps, and let's head on. If this is your first adventurous voyage, you should not return empty-handed."

John nodded and had a proper gulp. They passed through a tight crevice further into darkness. The rock parted barely enough for a grown man to pass through. Grunting, Pepa squeezed through tight spots. The meek light filtering from above barely illuminated the dark corners. John stumbled over a tight rope, falling face forward onto the rocks, bracing his impact with his hands at the last moment. Pepa grabbed him by his suspenders again, leaving him hovering above the sharp shards.

"Careful. There can be traps around," he advised.

"Of course! I should have considered this earlier!" he agreed. With his shoe, he brushed the cover of rotting leaves aside to reveal a pit with wicked spikes. Swallowing nervously, he headed on. They measured every step. Faced with an open and suspiciously empty space, they tied a rope around their waists and to a support; upon entering it they were immediately proven right as the floor gave away. They were faced with falling rocks and even a serpent's nest, whose inhabitants were unpleasantly disturbed from their sleep. John saw the tangle as far larger and more ominous in his imagination than in reality. The alcohol had clouded his mind, making problems seem insurmountable.

"It must be here somewhere!" he complained, stumbling across a string at the level of his ankles. The dart, no doubt infused with lethal poison, missed him by a hair's breadth. With a yelp, he recoiled and fell towards the depths as the rock beneath him gave way. Pepa, caught unprepared, was dragged along by the rope connecting them. They rolled down a rock face, grabbing on to a protruding boulder at the very last moment.

"Good Lord!" the foreigner whimpered.

"Climb," Pepa advised, rock-faced. He shoved his colleague upwards, to hurry back up before the precipice supporting them plummets to the depths along with them. They rested on a rocky ledge. John began to cheer. Ahead, in the middle of a ravine, a tree grew. An old, twisted apple tree was richly burdened with fruit. He clapped in exultation, for they were indeed as golden as the sun.

"This certainly must be my prize!" he pointed out his discovery to his guide, who just opened his bottle and took another drink. From their vista, a secure path became apparent and they proceeded between jagged rocks towards the island of green. The tree's boughs were bent and bowed, telling of its age. John reached out in almost religious awe, touching one of the sacred apples.

"Beautiful," he whispered. With shears, he clipped young branches and wrapped them into a wet rag. He plucked even a few fruits, to show. "This will be perfect genetic material. I shall multiply it and immortality will be ours!" he exclaimed in excitement. Pepa just rolled his eyes back. Then they climbed back towards the treacherous passages.

"Go ahead, I will catch up," Pepa said. John advanced slowly. The farmer backtracked a few steps, reached into a niche and withdrew two struggling boys from there by their ears.

"Are you two fooling around again? I told you not to lay traps in caves, who knows who might be passing through and get hurt."

"We just wanted to secure it from the soldiers," one of them opposed.

"I'll have none of this. Head home, rascals," he shook his hand. The boys just showed him their tongues and vanished in one of the many tunnels hollowed out by the water.

Pepa caught up with the Englishman on the field road. They did not converse much; from afar, the incessant pounding of cannons disturbed them. A colourful airship passed by, the pastel motifs indicating that it was carrying civilians, as the farmer explained. Tiny figures waved at them from the bulkheads.

Strengthened with spirits and a dinner, he accompanied John to the train station on his steam dirigible that he used to ferry his farm's produce. John's hair and suit were strewn with straws and grain, his shoes muddy.

The locomotive carrying the Englishman towards his home departed, slowly vanishing in the distance. Pepa finished the second bottle and scratched his head. "Strange, these people. They travel here to find a tree that grows throughout Moravia. If he told so, he could have had a few branches from my own orchard. And a sack of apples to boot. From what he plucked, he'll not distill much."

He began to understand how John meant the ramblings about eternal youth and immortality. He must have been speaking in metaphors. Of course – their exalted speech. Higher social class. *These gentlemen*, he thought. Then, he opened the third bottle and smelled the aroma.

"Perfect. An excellent vintage. The elixir of youth, indeed," he smiled. "When they find out all that can be done with these apples, they will be sending entire expeditions. We might even grow rich!" he mumbled, hope in his voice, and drank deeply of the spicy apple schnapps.

CUAUHTLIPOCA, EL ÁGUILA HUMEANTE

Mexico

CUAUHTLIPOCA, EL ÁGUILA HUMEANTE

By Paulo César Ramírez Villaseñor

'¡Aguanta un poco, todo va a salir bien!'

El hombre apenas si me miró pero pude notar claramente en su silencio que no creyó en mis palabras de aliento. No sabía qué hacer, así que únicamente intentaba darle un poco de ánimo a aquel personaje que se encontraba tirado en el escritorio de mi oficina. Las heridas en su cuerpo eran notorias, una en la pierna y dos en el tronco justo del lado izquierdo, mostrando la carne quemada y la sangre que no dejaba de salir a borbotones; signo inequívoco de que se había enfrentado a los infantes de marina. Los balines calientes eran la munición distintiva del cuerpo élite de Su Alteza Serenísima, que solía ser llamada como "La Orden Imperial del Jaguar". Al ver las heridas de aquel hombre no pude más que sentir miedo y rechazo. No era la primera vez que miraba a alguien herido de gravedad, muchos habían sido ya los cuerpos ensangrentados que mis ojos habían visto durante los últimos meses, resultado de la opresión que las fuerzas policiales y militares ejercían sobre todo aquel que osara rebelarse ante el régimen del autoproclamado dictador vitalicio. Quizá a fuerza de la costumbre fue que en esta ocasión pude por fin resistirme al vahído de mirar la sangre. Me acerqué rápidamente hasta donde se encontraba el teletrófono pidiéndole a la voz de la operadora que me comunicara de inmediato a emergencias.

'¿Operadora? Envíe una ambulancia a las oficinas del periódico "El Constitucional". Hay un hombre gravemente herido. Sí, mi nombre es Inocencio Justo Bueno. Felipe de Jesús Inocencio Justo Bueno de los Santos,' repetí el nombre completo a petición de la operadora para después cortar la comunicación del aparato.

'Sé lo que está intentando hacer, Justo; pero no va a funcionar. En el momento en que cualquier galeno cruce por esa puerta significará que mi tiempo ha terminado,' dijo el hombre con la voz enronquecida, opacada no solo por la mascarilla que le cubría la boca, sino también por la debilidad ocasionada por el dolor y las heridas.

'Vas a estar bien, ya verás. Tu tiempo no ha terminado, no aún. La ciudad todavía te necesita,' comenté acercándome y tomándole de la mano, gesto que respondió en silencio únicamente apretándome ligeramente.

El hombre clavó su mirada en mí y pude ver sus ojos a través del cristal de sus gafas protectoras. Por primera vez desde que lo conocí, hace ya nueve meses atrás, pude percibir en aquella mirada lo que nunca antes noté en aquel hombre que yacía sobre mi escritorio: miedo. Desvié la mirada un tanto consternado con dirección a la única ventana que no había sido clausurada debido a los altos costos de la ley hacendaria de 3 reales por ventana impuesta por Su Alteza Serenísima. Desde mi posición, el cielo de la Ciudad de México parecía más gris de lo habitual, lo que me llevó inevitablemente a recordar aquella mañana de Abril cuando arribé por primera vez a la gigantesca capital del Imperio Republicano Mexicano.

Abril de 1874 Nueve meses antes

El cielo grisáceo de la Ciudad de México fue lo primero que me recibió cuando asomé la mirada desde la ventanilla del dirigible en el que viajaba. Había salido proveniente de Guadalajara para comenzar mi vida como reportero. Mi padre, Facundo Inocencio Bueno Villalpando acababa de fallecer unas semanas antes. De acuerdo al reporte de las autoridades había muerto en un fuego cruzado en un enfrentamiento entre la Orden de Guadalupe y unos rebeldes al Imperio. Mi madre, María Felipa Gracia De los Santos, viuda de Bueno decidió entonces enviarme a la capital para que trabajara con mi padrino Juan Ignacio Paulino Ramírez Calzada en "el Siglo Diez y Nueve", periódico del cual era el Director General.

Como buen provinciano, me pareció completamente inaudita la ausencia del color celeste en los cielos de la capital del Imperio, hasta que observando a detalle me percaté porque la Ciudad de México se vestía con aquel gigantesco velo de oscuros nubarrones de esa manera. Múltiples fábricas se ubicaban en todos y cada uno de los islotes y aún en tierra firme a las orillas de los lagos de Texcoco, Xochimilco y Chalco; además de la cantidad de barcos y botes de vapor que notoriamente circulaban por los afluentes de los ríos y lagos de la otrora gran Tenochtitlán; sumado a ello los trenes que recorrían las calzadas desde Coyoacán a la Villa de Guadalupe, sin olvidar los que se dirigían rumbo a Iztapalapa, Tlacopan, Tenayuca o Azcapotzalco. Con todos esos elementos en cuenta: vehículos moviéndose por las aguas, los cielos y la tierra, todos ellos expulsando vapores, aunados a las grandes fábricas dejaban todo claro; o, mejor dicho, explicaban la vista brumosa. A pesar de ello la perspectiva aérea de la ciudad era todo un espectáculo verdaderamente impresionante. Para cuando el dirigible tocó tierra me encontraba absolutamente fascinado por estar en la urbe más grande de América.

El puerto de las aeronaves no era menos impresionante con sus gigantescos pasillos hechos de tubería gigante y un techo construido de cristales. Erigido originalmente por los antiguos aztecas para servir a manera de acueducto cuando el imperio mexicano se abastecía de agua dulce. Las grandes obras arquitectónicas y de ingeniería de aquella civilización casi se habían perdido con la llegada de los españoles, hacía poco más de 300 años, pero gracias a Agustín I, el primer emperador del México libre de la dominación española, muchas de aquellas maravillas habían podido sobrevivir. Sin embargo había sido por la mano de Su Alteza Serenísima quien le había dado los verdaderos toques de modernidad, industrialización y tecnología avanzada al legado azteca poniéndolo a la vanguardia del siglo XIX. No era eso lo único que había realizado aquel que gustaba de llamarse "el Napoleón de América"; muchas habían sido las veces que Antonio López de Santa Anna había estado gobernando el país y que, por una razón u otra, terminaba abandonando. Ya fuera por el cansancio de la vida política de México o gracias a las constantes luchas por el poder de diversos grupos. Pero al final, estuviese retirado de la silla presidencial por la razón que fuere, siempre regresaba o bien porque algún grupo de políticos se lo pedían o debido a que él mismo se percibía como un caudillo, un verdadero héroe y patriota. El único hombre capaz de conducir al país por un buen camino, lleno de progreso y esplendor.

'¡Alto ahí! ¡Deténgase en nombre de Su Alteza Serenísima, dictador vitalicio del Imperio Republicano Mexicano!'

Los gritos de los oficiales me sorprendieron justo a la salida del puerto de aeronaves, cuando apenas ponía un pie fuera de las puertas. El uniforme de pantalón blanco y chaqueta verde con el pectoral rojo indicaba claramente que eran miembros de la Orden Imperial de Guadalupe. Cuatro de ellos cargaron sus fusiles cortando cartucho apenas a unos cuantos metros de mí. Me quedé pasmado, absolutamente quieto bajo el marco de aquellas enormes láminas que duraban casi cerca del minuto abiertas para que los transeúntes pudieran cruzarlas y que después volvían a cerrarse debido al mecanismo de presión que las controlaba hasta que alguien activara nuevamente la manivela que hacía que la presión las abriera. Escuché los estruendos originados por los disparos de las armas y el olor a pólvora inundó mi nariz, mientras que las enormes puertas comenzaban a cerrarse. Ignoré por completo el ruido de advertencia de las puertas cerrándose cuando mis ojos se percataron del blanco al que los oficiales disparaban: un hombre que evitaba a toda costa los disparos y que llevaba una especie de coraza que le cubría el pecho, brazaletes, guanteletes y lo que parecían ser perneras recubiertas con protecciones metálicas; pero lo que más llamó mi atención era el casco que llevaba sobre la cabeza, una especie de réplica de los usados por los antiguos caballeros águila aztecas, incluso con el tocado de plumas. Las balas seguían siendo escupidas por los cañones de los fusiles mientras el moderno caballero águila se las ingeniaba para evitarlas, al tiempo que se acercaba cada vez más a sus atacantes. Para cuando lo tuve frente a mí daba un giro lanzando dardos hacia los oficiales, haciendo que dos de ellos cayeran al suelo; inmediatamente después desenfundó una extraña arma, similar al *macuahuitl*, la espada que utilizaban los guerreros aztecas, solo que esta vibraba dándole movimiento a las piedras de obsidiana. En un dos por tres arremetió contra los oficiales restantes desarmándolos y destruyendo sus fusiles. El valor abandonó de inmediato a los miembros de la Orden Imperial de Guadalupe, quienes huyeron despavoridos. En un lapso que apenas fue un instante volteó su mirada encontrándose con la mía y pude ver cómo su rostro se encontraba cubierto por una mascarilla antigás y sus ojos por gafas protectoras color jade.

'La puerta va a aplastarlo,' dijo con ronca voz, mientras señalaba detrás de mí.

Giré mi cabeza para observar lo que el hombre de la armadura señalaba y di un paso hacia enfrente con torpeza que pagué tropezando con mis maletas cayendo de bruces. Desde el suelo volteé mi mirada hacia arriba y la visión fue simplemente sorprendente, como si mirara a un antiguo dios azteca.

'Bienvenido a la Ciudad de México, próxima capital de la República Libre Mexicana.'

Después de dicho esto, aquel misterioso hombre-águila me dio la espalda y desplegó un par de monumentales alas mecánicas para alejarse volando, auxiliado de un extraño dispositivo de propulsión.

Mis ojos le vieron perderse entre nubarrones negros y la inmensidad del grisáceo cielo de la Ciudad de México.

Esa fue la primera vez que vi a quien el Gobierno llamaba "un peligroso criminal".

El apretón en mi mano que recibí por parte del hombre que se encontraba sobre mi escritorio me regresó inmediatamente a la realidad.

'Prométame que no dejará que ninguno de los doctores me ponga una mano encima.'

'Pero necesitas atención médica.'

'Necesito atender mis heridas y curarme, es cierto, pero usted sabe, Justo, que los doctores querrán llevarme al hospital e inmediatamente ahí los hombres de Santa Anna volverán inútil cualquier cuidado que haya recibido. Eso suponiendo que no sean los mismos hombres de blanco quienes, por orden del tirano, acaben con mi existencia.'

Iba a replicar el comentario pero caí en cuenta que efectivamente aquel hombre tenía la razón. Antonio López de Santa Anna, Su Alteza Serenísima, había decretado como máxima prioridad capturar al hombre que, según las propias palabras del dictador vitalicio del Imperio Republicano Mexicano, era un verdadero peligro para el país y todos sus habitantes. Ese era el motivo por el que se habían gastado miles de reales de plata, invirtiéndolos en el adiestramiento de dos mil infantes de marina, además del desarrollo de armamento y dispositivos con la tecnología punta; así había surgido La Orden Imperial del Jaguar, que bajo pretexto de atrapar peligrosos criminales deambulaban por las calles, atemorizando a la ciudadanía. Porque el miedo es la mejor herramienta de control que tiene un Gobierno, cuando se tiene una población cada vez más pobre y más descontenta.

'Si no puede atenderte un médico … entonces, ¿Qué sugieres?'

'Necesito llegar al santuario, sé que ya lo he molestado mucho. Con un poco de tiempo puedo ponerme de pie y …'

'¡Por Dios Amado, apenas si puedes hablar!' No continué el resto de lo que iba a decir al percatarme de que le había llamado por su nombre de pila. 'Estás gravemente herido Cuauhtlipoca,' corregí rápidamente, 'y tiempo es lo que menos tienes. Te estás desangrando, además es cuestión de minutos para que llegue la ambulancia que solicité a la operadora.'

El hombre pareció ignorar todo lo que le había dicho. Sus ojos estaban clavados mirándome fijamente. Podía percibir cómo me observaban de lleno, aún detrás de las gafas protectoras de color jade.

'¿Desde hace cuánto tiempo lo sabe, Justo?'

'¿A qué te refieres?'

'Mi nombre. ¿Cómo lo averiguó?'

'No creo que sea lo más importante en este momento …'

'Créame que lo es,' me interrumpió mientras se incorporaba con la dificultad natural que le causaba el dolor. Dirigió su mirada en forma retadora mientras se sentaba sobre el escritorio. 'Si me queda poco tiempo, me gustaría saber cómo y cuándo fue que descubrió mi identidad.'

Julio de 1874 Seis meses atrás

Viajaba a bordo del tren que me conduciría rumbo a las oficinas de "El Siglo Diez y Nueve". Eran las nueve y cuarto de la mañana, conforme al vistazo que acababa de darle a mi reloj de bolsillo. Viajábamos por la Avenida Bucareli y ya muy cerca de la Alameda, un despliegue de uniformados llamó mi atención. Volteé a mirar por la ventanilla del tren tratando de averiguar qué estaba sucediendo exactamente, pero lo único que lograba ver era a los oficiales de la Orden Imperial de Guadalupe moviéndose de un lugar a otro. En los tres meses que llevaba en la capital ya me había acostumbrado a los constantes operativos que realizaban las fuerzas de Santa Anna para, según decía, mantener la seguridad y el orden en el país. Por supuesto éramos muchos los que sabíamos que lo único que hacían los uniformados era perseguir a los enemigos del dictador. Muchos eran ya los desaparecidos que los miembros de la Orden Imperial de Guadalupe se había llevado sin ninguna orden policial; siendo su blanco predilecto los periodistas que hablaban sin tapujo alguno de lo mal que Su Alteza Serenísima estaba conduciendo al país.

En cuanto tuve oportunidad bajé del tren en la estación de la Santa Veracruz y corrí nervioso rumbo al edificio del periódico. Cerca de treinta oficiales de la Orden Imperial se encontraban en posición, listos para irrumpir en el edificio.

'¡Deténgase, no puede pasar!' 'Trabajo en "El Siglo Diez y Nueve."'

El hombre me miró de arriba abajo y pude notar cierto desprecio en su mirada.

'Muéstreme sus papeles,' ordenó.

Obedecí la orden y mientras verificaba mi identificación un sudor frío recorría mi frente. Sin embargo me armé de valor para preguntarle:

'Perdone, oficial; pero ¿qué ocurre?'

'Capitán. Soy el capitán Agustín Guerrero, señor … Bueno,' dijo mientras volvía a mirar mis papeles.

'Usted disculpe, capitán Guerrero; pero ¿qué sucede? Como le comenté trabajo en el periódico y este despliegue de fuerzas pareciera indicar que se prepara un combate contra un cuerpo armado rebelde o algo similar.'

'Estamos a la caza de un criminal. Un reporterillo que se cree encima de la ley y superior al libertador y caudillo más grande que ha tenido jamás la patria.'

'Disculpe que insista capitán Guerrero ¿A qué se refiere?' Pedro Agustín Severo de la Santísima Trinidad Guerrero Bravo no era un hombre paciente. Entrado en los treinta, hijo de militar, su padre había servido junto a Santa Anna en la guerra contra los Estados Unidos y miraba al dictador no solo como a un héroe, sino como un modelo a seguir. Sin responder a mi pregunta y con una frialdad pasmosa el capitán simplemente desenfundó su arma y la colocó sobre mi sien.

'Tengo órdenes directas de Su Alteza Serenísima, el general Antonio López de Santa Anna, dictador vitalicio del Imperio Republicano de México de capturar, vivo o muerto, al pseudo- periodista que se hace llamar *El Nigromante*. Así que, dime provinciano, ¿tú sabes quién es?'

En el periódico existía una columna, escrita semanalmente por alguien que firmaba con el seudónimo de *El Nigromante*. En ella el escritor criticaba duramente al gobierno de Santa Anna y no solo eso, sino que en más de una ocasión se mofaba de su cojera llamándole "pierna de caño" debido a la prótesis metálica que sustituía su pierna izquierda. Sin embargo los que trabajábamos en el diario desconocíamos la identidad del columnista, únicamente el Director General podía saberla.

'No, señor,' murmuré temblando.

'¡No te escucho, provinciano!' gritó el capitán mientras que con el dedo pulgar echaba el martillo de su arma hacia atrás, preparándose para disparar.

'¡He dicho que no lo sé, señor!'

Juro que pensé que iba a morir, pero en ese preciso momento pude escuchar cómo se rompía la ventana de un cristal. A partir de ese instante todo lo percibí como si estuviera mirando una serie de daguerrotipos. Imagen tras imagen, cuadro por cuadro. Como si el tiempo corriera con mayor lentitud.

De la oficina de Ignacio Ramírez Calzada, Director General de "El Siglo Diez y Nueve" volaron cientos de miles de pequeños cristales cuando una figura voladora los atravesó. Su sombra se dibujó sobre los adoquines que pisábamos el capitán y yo, mostrando la silueta de una gigantesca y esplendorosa águila. Pude verlo cómo desde el cielo estiró el brazo y cerró su puño. Un sonido más se dejó escuchar, como cuando se gira una manivela de alguna fábrica y que deja escapar la presión para que el vapor salga expulsado; entonces vi surgir algo de los brazaletes del caballero águila: dos dardos salieron disparados directamente hacia la mano que sostenía la pistola del capitán Guerrero, clavándose uno en la muñeca y otro en la palma de su mano, justo cuando soltaba el arma. Una verdadera tormenta se desató en ese instante. Truenos y ráfagas eran escupidos por las bocas de los fusiles de los oficiales de la Orden Imperial.

Los aditamentos que lanzaban a presión las municiones — presurizadores especiales de la más alta tecnología, construidos con los impuestos que pagaba la población — eran activados una y otra vez, pero se mostraban totalmente ineficaces en contra del hombre que no solo era capaz de volar, sino que daba giros y acrobacias espectaculares.

'¡Alto el fuego!' gritó la voz que provenía del edificio del periódico.

Todos volteamos a mirar a Ignacio Ramírez Calzada, que salía con las manos en alto.

'No disparen más. Yo entregaré a quien vinieron a buscar.'

'Dinos, Ramírez. ¿Dónde diablos se encuentra quien se hace llamar *El Nigromante*?' preguntó el capitán Guerrero, sujetándose la mano herida.

'Soy yo. Yo soy *El Nigromante*.'

Las palabras de mi padrino me dejaron frío. Recuerdo que me había citado a las 9 de la mañana para que conociera a un tal Juan Bautista Amado Guadalupe Caballero Aguilar, que había llegado de Malinalco para que el periódico realizara un reportaje. Mi padrino me había comunicado además, que el fulano era un arqueólogo que había encontrado —según él— el santuario sagrado en donde se formaban los *cuauhpipiltin*, o guerreros águila de los antiguos aztecas.

La Orden Imperial de Guadalupe se llevó a Ignacio Ramírez, ya no solamente por lo que escribía en la columna del periódico, sino también por asociarse con un peligroso criminal y maleante. Por un momento pensé negociar con el capitán Agustín Guerrero la libertad de mi padrino, a cambio de revelarle la identidad del peligroso criminal que tenía de cabeza a las autoridades.

'¿Y por qué no lo hizo, Justo?' preguntó el hombre, regresándome al presente inmediatamente.

'Bueno, "El Siglo Diez y Nueve" fue clausurado y muchos de los que trabajábamos ahí nos quedamos sin empleo. Fue la historia que escribí respecto de ti la que me dio otro trabajo como redactor de "El Constitucional"; si nunca la hubiese escrito no estaríamos en esta oficina ahora y desde luego no tendría lo que ha sido mi mayor satisfacción.'

'¿Se refiere a eso?' Cuauhtlipoca señaló detrás de una vitrina en donde, además de recortes de varias notas, lucía majestuoso mi premio al reportaje del año.

Me acerqué a la vitrina y a través del reflejo observé al personaje que había acudido a mí, por alguna razón que aún no comprendía. Maltrecho y herido, sin duda con muy poco tiempo de vida si no era atendido pronto. Desde la primera vez que lo conocí le había admirado, se había ganado mi total respeto; además había salvado mi vida aquella mañana cuando tenía el cañón del arma del capitán pegado en mi sien. Había pensado en entregarlo, cierto, pero cuando me senté frente a mi máquina de escribir en casa y comencé a teclear la historia que se convirtió en mi reportaje, me di cuenta de lo que representaba aquel personaje. No era un peligroso criminal tal como el Gobierno lo presentaba, ni tampoco se trataba simplemente de un rebelde con acceso a alta tecnología, como muchos medios habían afirmado.

Aquel hombre vestido como un águila cruzando los grises cielos de la capital representaba la posibilidad de todo un país; era la oportunidad que tenía México para pasar de ser un pueblo oprimido por su dictador a ser un pueblo verdaderamente libre. O al menos mantenía esa esperanza con vida.

'Me refiero a lo que entendí cuando escribí el reportaje. Eres un símbolo Amado y por ello no debes morir, no puedes morirte.'

'Pero solo soy un hombre, Justo, un hombre mortal como cualquier otro. Y suponiendo que no muriera hoy, moriré tarde o temprano.'

'¡No, me niego rotundamente! ¡Tú eres un símbolo! ¡Eres Cuauhtlipoca, el águila humeante! ¡No puedes morir!' grité, al tiempo que golpeaba el escritorio por la desesperación.

Noté cómo me miraba de nuevo detrás de esos cristales color jade, que no solo le protegían cuando volaba sino que junto con el respirador le ayudaban a ocultar su identidad.

'Voy a morir, Justo, eso es irremediable. Sin embargo, el santuario de Malinalco tiene todo lo necesario para que Cuauhtlipoca continúe cruzando los cielos de la ciudad y luchando contra la opresión de Santa Anna.'

'Pero el viaje en tren nos demoraría demasiado y dudo que puedas soportarlo.'

'No viajaremos por tren. La única manera de llegar al santuario es por aire.'

Observé de reojo la pierna de Cuauhtlipoca, gravemente lastimada debido a las quemaduras hechas por las municiones que había recibido. Las heridas del costado de su tronco no lucían mucho mejor, la sangre se veía correr a través de la coraza de cuero y metal que le servía a modo de protección.

'Es muy claro que no puedes volar,' dije con un gesto encogiéndome de hombros.

'Ya lo sé. Por eso lo hará usted, Justo.'

Lo miré fijamente mientras se quitaba el casco, que dejó lentamente sobre el escritorio, justo a un lado de él. Retiró las gafas color jade de su rostro e hizo lo mismo con la mascarilla. Poco a poco el fiero rebelde que había burlado una y otra vez a la Orden Imperial de Guadalupe, el llamado peligroso delincuente por las autoridades, el perseguido, el enemigo acérrimo de Santa Anna y su dictadura opresora fue despojándose de sus vestiduras de héroe. Por primera vez en todo este tiempo pude observarlo mejor. No era aquel gigante que mis ojos habían confundido con un antiguo dios azteca, ni una masa de músculos preparada para dar batalla al más fiero de los infantes de marina. Su negro cabello desordenado y su gesto cansado — no solo por las graves heridas de sus múltiples batallas — lo mostraron tal cual era: un luchador que se encontraba agotado. Frente a mis ojos, el vuelo de Cuauthlipoca se oscurecía ante la espesa bruma de los vapores que diferencian a los hombres de los dioses. La leyenda se convertía en hombre.

*

Salimos por la única ventana no clausurada de la oficina de "El Constitucional" en cuanto las sirenas de las ambulancias se dejaban escuchar por todo el edificio del periódico. También llegaba un grupo de infantes de marina de la Orden Imperial del Jaguar, inconfundibles con los exo-trajes — armaduras con tecnología punta, hechas de la más pura aleación de eritronio y acero — que le daban nombre al grupo.

Pude ver nuevamente impresionaste vista área de la Capital nuevamente. Desde el antiguo Templo Mayor hasta la Catedral; sus calles fluyendo llenas de autos impulsados a vapor y personas que deambulan caminando para después intentar transportarse por medios menos caros; como los trenes, siempre llenos pero siempre a tiempo.

Con débil voz, a veces cortada por el aire, podía escuchar a Amado señalarme algún lugar que, según entendí, debía recordar o tomar en cuenta para la trayectoria.

'Es rumbo camino a Iztapalapa,' decía. '…y ese es el Cerro de la Estrella.'

Otras veces, Amado se dedicaba a hablarme acerca del dispositivo de propulsión, pero el ruido ocasional de los zeppelines volando apenas si me dejaba escuchar algo que me pareciera entendible.

'… en el año dos … Caña …' le escuché. '… y entonces eso activa el gas,' hablaba.

Cuando sobrevolábamos el lago de Xochimilco fue cuando sus palabras fueron más claras para mí:

'En Maninalco encontrarás todas las respuestas a tus preguntas.'

Después de dejar atrás el manto gris con el que se cubría la Ciudad de México, a una velocidad que verdaderamente me sorprendió, continuamos nuestro viaje sin muchos problemas. Aun así, no estaba convencido de cuánto tiempo más soportaría Amado en su condición. La altura, los fríos de Enero y las heladas corrientes nos dieron la bienvenida cuando pasamos por el Ajusco.

'¡Gire la perilla!' gritó Amado, debido a la fuerza del viento.

Cuando se aseguró de que había seguido su instrucción volvió a gritar:

'¡Jale la palanca en cuanto le diga!'

'¿Cuál palanca?' repliqué.

'¡Ahora!' gritó.

Una ráfaga de viento nos golpeó como cuando las olas arremeten contra una pequeña embarcación. Jalé una palanca que apagó de inmediato el propulsor e hizo que las alas mecánicas se movieran un poco. Esa fue la primera vez que en verdad comencé a volar.

La claridad de los despejados cielos me mostró un espectáculo impresionante: desde donde nos encontrábamos sobrevolando podía ver la gaseosa Ciudad de México que contrastaba contra su guardián que, aunque también humeante, se vestía todo de blanco, el glorioso Popocatéptl. Sin embargo, lo que embelesaba a la vista era el volcán Iztaccíhuatl, que a pesar de ser de menor altura semejaba la forma de una mujer recostada, con el cabello extendido opuesto a su cuerpo completamente cubierta con un níveo manto. Más adelante un hermoso valle, que Amado llamó "El Valle de las águilas" y que Alexander Von Humbolt nombrara como "La Ciudad de la eterna primavera".

Todo ese maravilloso conjunto de imágenes logró hacer que solo importara ese instante. Me imaginé a Amado pasando infinidad de veces y fue ahí cuando entendí qué lo motivaba a luchar contra Santa Anna. Mientras que solo los ricos podían darse el lujo de tener más de una ventana en sus edificios y mansiones, el resto de la población apenas podía pagar el precio de tener una sola e incluso algunos ni siquiera eso. Después de contemplar esta vista una y otra vez el imaginar un mundo en donde tu visión se ve reducida a lo que puedes pagarle al Gobierno en impuestos es llanamente imposible.

Para cuando los vientos nos empujaron hasta casi alcanzar Malinalco, Amado me pidió que fuera dando vueltas en círculo y me alertara para encender y apagar el dispositivo de propulsión. No sé cómo no nos estrellamos contra la montaña. Era como si antiguamente ahí se hubiese localizado algún templo a la ladera de la montaña, tallado directamente sobre las rocas. Una entrada que parecía representar la boca de una serpiente se dejaba notar claramente. Sobre piedra labrada diferentes símbolos hacían alusión a que aquella entrada era nada más y nada menos que la puerta hacia el inframundo y que, por si fuera poco, solo los guerreros más fuertes y más nobles podrían regresar al mundo de los vivos, siempre y cuando se realizaran los rituales necesarios.

Crucé el umbral con Amado en brazos. El viaje había sido exhaustivo para él y todavía necesitaba indicarme qué hacer para poder curarle. Bajamos por varias escaleras a tientas, hasta que tosió para después decir:

'La llave, ábrela,' apenas susurraba.

Busqué cerca de la pared hasta que encontré una especie de manivela que giré inmediatamente. Una luz iluminó el lugar, mostrando un enorme salón en el que alrededor se encontraban varias armaduras idénticas a las de Cuauhtlipoca, solo el plumaje de los cascos en forma de águila lucían diferenciándose uno de otro. Una losa de piedra se mostraba al centro, mientras que las paredes tenían diferentes labrados.

'Ahí encontrarás mi historia,' dijo Amado señalando las figuras de las paredes.

Lo coloqué sobre la losa, casi sin poner los ojos hacia el lugar que me señalaba. Con una rápida mirada busqué si alguna señal indicaba que había un equipo médico para atenderle. Ante la ausencia, pregunté:

'¿Qué necesitas que haga?'

'Aprende,' dijo con una sonrisa.

Esa fue la última palabra que dijo. Noté claramente cómo se desvanecía, cómo perdía toda fuerza. Juan Bautista Amado Guadalupe Caballero Aguilar fallecía ahí, frente a mis ojos. Su cuerpo yacía sobre la losa de piedra del santuario de Malinalco. Su espíritu ahora volaba con rumbo al Mictlán.

El hombre que había tomado la decisión de colocarse una armadura, un casco y unas alas para enfrentarse a la opresión de un gobierno que se repetía una y otra vez, sin que nada mejorara más que para la clase privilegiada, había muerto. Pero definitivamente ese hombre era un guerrero noble y fuerte. No era noble porque perteneciera a alguna casa de abolengo, ni siquiera llevaba en sus venas sangre de algún antiguo gobernante azteca. Era fuerte, no por su corpulencia física, que era bastante promedio, sino porque a pesar de todas sus flaquezas había decidido ser parte de algo que quizá lo sobrepasaba en capacidades, pero a pesar de eso no se detuvo.

Definitivamente Amado Guerrero debía regresar al mundo de los vivos. El problema es que desconocía cuáles eran los rituales necesarios de los que hablaba la entrada. Comencé entonces a observar todos y cada uno de los grabados de las paredes, buscando algo que me indicara al respecto. Así fue que aprendí que me encontraba en lo que antiguamente se conocía como "La Casa de las águilas y los tigres". Aquí se formaban los antiguos caballeros águila aztecas, después de que los españoles arribaron el lugar pasó a ser un santuario resguardado por unos pocos que conservaron la tradición oculta, entrenando de vez en vez algún caudillo. Durante más de trescientos años pasando de boca a oído se había mantenido este santuario, hasta hoy que con la muerte del último caballero águila todo terminaba. Al igual que en la cosmogonía azteca, otro sol más se apagaba para siempre.

No sé cuánto tiempo estuve ahí parado cuando descubrí que mi búsqueda por las instrucciones de un ritual para revivir a Cuauhtlipoca eran insulsas. No existía tal ritual, todo era parte simplemente del símbolo

Abril de 1875 Tres meses después

Los frescos vientos primaverales me condujeron con tranquilidad por encima del Valle de las águilas, saludé al Iztaccíhuatl, la mujer dormida que se encontraba despojada de su manto y al siempre humeante Popocatéptl mientras activaba el propulsor en cuanto percibí las grises nubes alrededor la Ciudad de México. Ajusté mis gafas protectoras con cristales en color verde jade y comencé a girar en círculos para descender en cuanto pude apreciar la Provincia de Tlahuac.

Apenas guardé las alas mecánicas pude ver la patrulla de infantes de marina portando el exo- traje que asemejaba un jaguar. Me aseguré de que los brazaletes tuvieran suficientes *atlatl* — los afilados dardos que lanzaban disparados por la presión — ajusté mi mascarilla y me concentré en poder alcanzar el *macuahuitl*. Una vez verificadas mis armas me lancé al ataque. Primero cayeron un par de jaguares que tomé totalmente por sorpresa. Luego varios de ellos comenzaron a disparar con sus armas especiales. Una lluvia de balines ardiendo intentaba impactarme, pero los fui esquivando hábilmente para después contraatacar soltando golpes a diestra y siniestra con el *macuahuitl*.

Llevaban ya tres meses desde que habían perdido la pista del criminal que buscaban, pero los brotes de rebeldía habían comenzado a nacer en Tlahuac, por lo que Su Alteza Serenísima había enviado a la Orden Imperial del Jaguar a acallarlos. Ninguno de ellos esperaba que fueran a tener que enfrentarse a Cuauhtlipoca.

Felipe de Jesús Inocencio Justo Bueno de los Santos había llegado a la Capital del Imperio Republicano Mexicano volando sobre un dirigible, había ganado el premio al reportaje del año y había descendido al inframundo. Tal como le había dicho a Amado Guerrero Aguilar, Cuauhtlipoca no podía morir, era un símbolo y los símbolos son eternos.

Envestido con la coraza, las perneras, brazaletes y un glorioso casco en forma de águila adornado con colorido plumaje me había transformado en el héroe que había defendido la Provincia de Tlahuac de la opresión. Ya no era simplemente Justo Bueno de los Santos, al enfrentar a los infantes de marina de la Orden Imperial del Jaguar y derrotarlos, el hombre se transformaba en leyenda.

Igual que en la cosmogonía azteca, un nuevo sol se asomaba por el horizonte. Cuauhtlipoca, el águila que humea, volaba todavía a través del velo de oscuros nubarrones que se ceñía sobre la Ciudad de México.

www.ingramcontent.com/pod-product-compliance
Lightning Source LLC
Chambersburg PA
CBHW071258190726
48292CB00007B/2587